Also By the Author

The Menmenet Mysteries
The Jackal of Inpu
The Lion of Bastet
The Bull of Mentju

The Founding Fathers Mysteries
Murder at Mount Vernon

The Pirates of Khonoë Series
Hyperkill

THE JACKAL OF INPU

A Menmenet Alternate History Mystery

Robert J. Muller

Poesys Associates

San Francisco

www.poesys.com

The Menmenet Series Number One

ISBN: 978-1-939386-07-6 (paperback)
ISBN: 978-1-939386-08-3 (ebook)

Library of Congress Control Number: 2022903131

Library of Congress Subject Headings
Alternative histories (Fiction)
Detective and mystery stories.
Murder -- Investigation -- Fiction.
Romance fiction.
San Francisco (Calif.) -- Fiction.
Suspense fiction.

Cover Design by Brandi Doane McCann
https://www.ebook-coverdesigns.com
Cover illustration By Jeff Dahl - Own work, CC BY-SA 4.0
https://commons.wikimedia.org/w/index.php?curid=3257647

Manufactured in the United States of America
Published April 15, 2022
First Edition

To M'Linn and Theo

I hold it true, whate'er befall;
I feel it, when I sorrow most;
Tis better to have loved and lost
Than never to have loved at all.
Alfred, Lord Tennyson, In Memoriam A. H. H.

Then spoke his majesty R'a:
Seteh shall not stay in Kemet,
as he has been ordered not to do so.
You rule the desert, O evil one! But he shall not be in Kemet.
Behold, Kemet belongs to Heru eternally,
Kemet is in his hand forever
according to the order which I once issued.
The Rite of Overthrowing Seteh and His Confederates
The Ritual Books of Pawerem

To fall in love is to create a religion that has a fallible god.
Jorge Luis Borges
Other Inquisitions 1937–1952 (1964) 'The Meeting in a Dream'

North America

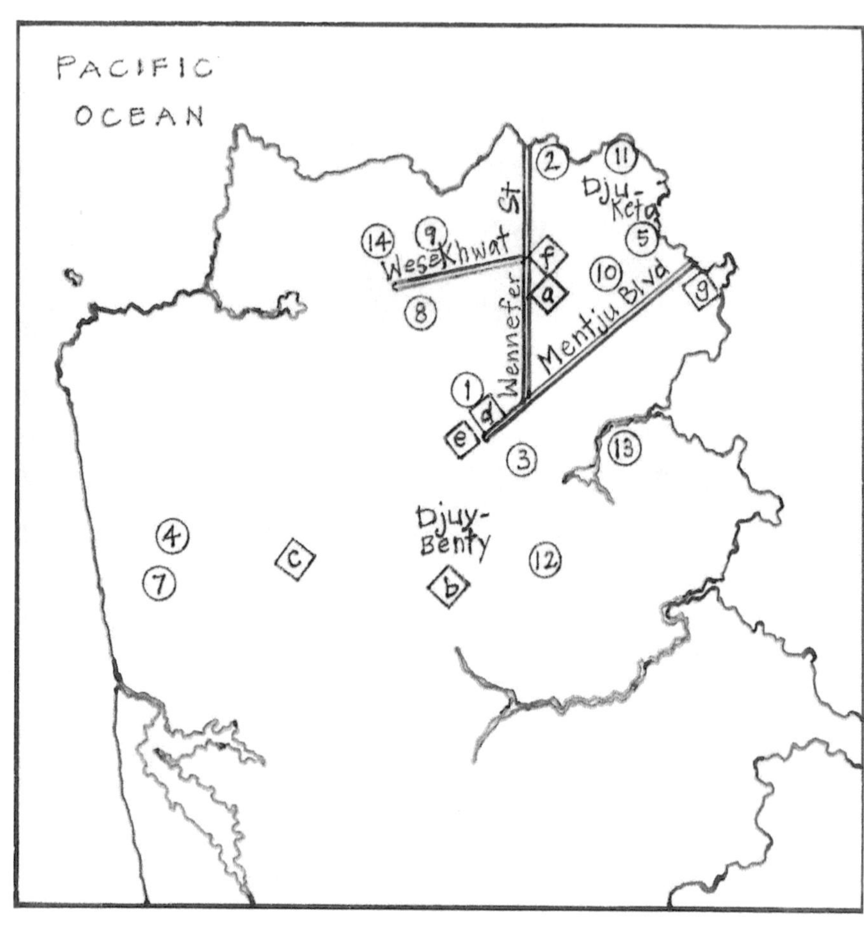

Menmenet

Key

Temples

a	Bastet
b	Imen-R'a
c	Inpu
d	Ma'at
e	Mentju
f	Sekhmet-Hut-Her
g	Seteh

Locations

1	City Palace
2	Ferry Terminal
3	MacIntyre's Apartment
4	Necropolis
5	Neferti Restaurant
6	Nekhen's House
7	Nekhen's Tomb
8	Nesimen's House
9	Palace of the Republic
10	Per'ankh Restaurant
11	Shesmu's House
12	U. S. Embassy
13	Wenmyt Restaurant
14	Yaotl's Palace

CHAPTER ONE
MacIntyre Investigates a Crime Scene

PAPERWORK. HUTYT-ER-SEMETYU CHERYL MacIntyre hated it. She'd been hating it for two solid days. So she rejoiced when her boss tapped her for a murder. Even late in the day, a new body always got the blood moving.

The blood, in this case, was all over the kitchen floor and walls in large spatters. MacIntyre concentrated on the body first. The crime scene photographers had finished and the forensics people had started their search for microclues. She examined the scene from outside the criminalists' perimeter.

Middle-aged, distinguished-looking man. Well-to-do, if this was his enormous mansion on the Tjesut, the prominent Menmenet ridge that favored palaces, mansions, and northern views of the bay and its islands.

No sign of bruising, rigor just setting in, a nearly severed head from a knife cut across the throat, no other wounds she could see. The cut looked deep enough to have partially or fully severed the spine. The man died fast. There were big swatches of blood from the arterial spray, the direction showing he'd twisted as he collapsed. The spatters moved along the wall right up to the kitchen counter. The w'abu from the Temple of Sekhmet-Hut-her would tell them more, and time of death, which wasn't that long ago—rigor not advanced, blood tacky, body still warm. Body sprawled every which way on the floor. No clues there. The killer got him standing up from the height of the spatter.

"Look at this, MacIntyre." Her boss, Idnu-er-Semetyu Djehutymes, held an evidence bag with a knife in it, a large one. Kind of unusual: wooden handle, oldish, well-used, dull gray rather than shiny metal, 25cm of blade, looked damn sharp.

"Where did you find it, Mes?"

He pointed at a spot on the floor marked with tape. Did the murderer toss the knife to the floor after the act? She looked again: lots of blood on the knife and handle.

"Blood?"

"It lay in the pool. There's blood on only one side of the knife. He tossed it next to the body after the killing."

"Murder of passion? Just one cut, solid and deep, through the neck, then threw the knife down? Passion usually means a couple dozen stabs to the body," she said. "Vengeful hate, anger, that's a cut throat. Intent, full intent, but maybe not premeditated."

Her boss eyed her with disfavor, knowing where she was going. "Keep an open mind, MacIntyre. No conclusions. There's one witness to interview."

The Wife. It was always the Wife. She hated interviewing the Wife.

Her boss read her mind. "It's the wife. I'll take this one." Praise be to all the gods of Kemet, she wouldn't have to put herself through another wife interview. He continued, looking at his notebook, "Name of Neferaset. She found the body. Her husband, name of Nekhen. That's what I know so far."

The pair walked into the great room of the mansion. MacIntyre took in the vast picture window looking out onto the bay, a wide vista. She could see the brown mountains across the bay to the west. She could see all the islands in the middle of the bay. The view stretched all the way to Dju-Keta, the hill in the northeast corner of Menmenet. Her attention moved to the Wife, sitting in a chair, dejected. She was one of the most exquisite women MacIntyre had ever seen. MacIntyre's stunning-woman antennae went up, but this was work, so she crushed her feelings and tried for objectivity. This woman was special, though: she looked like that ancient queen, Nefertiti, that became a pera'a. What a scene that must have been, the male nobles bowing to a woman.

"Lady Nekhen, may we speak with you for a few minutes? I'm Idnu Djehutymes." Djehutymes, formal in address, the model of caring officialdom doing its job, showed her his credentials. Was he ever pulled toward the women he interviewed? If so, he disguised it well. Learn from your superior, Cheryl. Mes has been a medja for more years than you've been alive, or so she liked to think.

"Neferaset, please, Idnu. I appreciate your help. I can't..." The woman passed a hand across that delicate brow, and Cheryl MacIntyre knew she was looking at a murderer. Unless she was an actress.

"This is the investigating officer, Hutyt Cheryl MacIntyre."

The woman nodded to MacIntyre, saying nothing. There was nothing to say. Her bottomless black eyes, her flawless hair, her classic square chin....

Definitely a murderer.

"Can you tell us about your husband, Neferaset? Name, occupation?"

This question surprised Neferaset. "Nekhen's a chef, the chef de cuisine of the Per'ankh restaurant in Menmenet, a French restaurant. That's where I met him, I was hostess there for a year before we married. He's quite famous, Idnu…?"

"Djehutymes, ma'am. The knife we found—do you recognize it?"

"Yes, that's his chef's knife, he takes it everywhere. It's from his knife kit—it's on the kitchen counter, lying open." MacIntyre had seen the cloth bundle unrolled. Now she knew what it was. Neferaset had her eyes closed. "I couldn't touch it, pick it up, I just couldn't."

"That's fine, ma'am, you shouldn't touch anything at all. When did you find your husband, Neferaset?" Djehutymes settled back on the sofa.

"I…came home an hour ago. From lunch. A late lunch." She gulped and shook her head. "It was…awful. Blood everywhere. I called 111."

"Yes, and they came a few minutes later. Did you see anyone about the house before you entered?"

"No, no one on the street. I would have noticed. We don't have many people on foot up here, you know?" She gazed at the bay. "No one. I don't know why he was here. He was off to the restaurant early, as usual. He never comes back until late." MacIntyre made a note to check phone records on both their phones.

Djehutymes continued in his sympathetic voice, "Do you have any idea who might have wanted your husband dead?"

"No, I can't imagine who did this. Everyone loves Nekhen." Lying, see her eyes, they're practically spinning with the effort to avoid us. "It must have been a burglar."

MacIntyre stopped listening, she'd read the report later. The lady wasn't…she was cooperating, but she wasn't engaged, and she wasn't telling the truth. Lovely low-pitched, well-modulated voice; you could sense the vibrations warming you up. At least she did; Mes never felt stuff like that. MacIntyre considered whether grief might take up too much of the Wife's bandwidth. The eyes too alert for a grieving widow, no tears either.

MacIntyre looked around. Modern furniture, decor as you'd expect on the Tjesut, books here and there, art objects arranged with exquisite care, thick carpets from the old country. Normal wealthy household, nothing special. MacIntyre got caught up in the view again. She had this thing for vistas.

"Hutyt?"

Her brain snapped to attention: Djehutymes. What had he said? "Questions, Hutyt MacIntyre?"

"Are you an actress, Neferaset?" Why not ask?

The exquisite woman smiled. "No. I'm an artist, and I do a little modeling to keep busy. Why do you ask?"

Was she stupid or just naïve? No; she was smart enough to parry. "We'll be asking quite a few questions to understand what happened, ma'am."

"I don't think…I'm not up to questions right now. Please?" Her lovely voice shook. No, not stupid and not that naïve, either. A damn good murderer and actress. She admired the classic features again. She liked views, and this woman was easy to look at.

"We'll question you later, Neferaset. Tomorrow. Unless…?" Idnu Djehutymes looked at MacIntyre with raised eyebrows.

"No, nothing for me, Idnu. For now."

Nefer-whatsit was guilty. A deep family thing. Couldn't have kids (no toys around, no kid's books). Blamed him, hated him, he hit her (check, no bruises, OK, not hit). He shouted, they shouted at each other, she took the knife and zap, then cleaned herself up and called 111. Late lunch, hmm. Have to ask the criminalists about arm strength. Could they make the Wife cut a pig's throat or something? A resounding "no" to that one. Wouldn't prove anything, anyway. "No assumptions, MacIntyre." Djehutymes's favorite phrase. Gonna be a slog, this one, to prove it. Ma'at wanted proof.

MacIntyre fingered her ostrich feather pin that showed her status as a w'abet of Ma'at. As an American, she'd grown up with a truth about facts and times and simple emotions. She changed her thinking about emotions after years in her adopted country, but not about facts. Facts were facts, and the fact was most murdered husbands died at the hands of their wives. It was even more true when hate, alcohol, or violence filled the marriage. Even with her brief career in homicide, she'd found an amazing burden of hate in marriages. At least it simplified things in her job; you didn't have to search very far for the hate.

Let's get on with it, Mes.

"Thank you, Neferaset, we appreciate your help in sorting out this heinous crime," he said.

"So sorry for your loss," added MacIntyre. She didn't mean it.

"Fuck's sake, Mes, sure she did it."

Djehutymes glanced at MacIntyre, both of his hands firm on the wheel of the big medja cruiser heading back to the Temple of Ma'at. He'd refused to let her turn on the radio to a music station, said he'd wanted to talk about the case. What was there to talk about?

"Assumptions, MacIntyre, assumptions." He kept his eyes on the street.

She rolled her eyes and was silent.

"I expect objectivity on this, MacIntyre."

"Sure thing, Mes." Not a problem. She was always objective. Objectivity was easy when you knew who did it. Simple facts were always the best.

"I'll get right on her alibi. I'm sure that will be the first thing to break."

"Assumptions."

"Right."

Djehutymes asked, "Did you catch her evasion when I asked her about who might have killed him?"

"Sure did. She knows because she did it. I know, I know—assumptions."

"You need to look into the lady's movements, find out who she sees regularly. We'll get details of her day tomorrow and you can check them. Check her alibi. But people—got to be somebody she's got in mind. That's why she evaded answering my question. Right?"

"Right. Watch that bicyclist."

"I'm driving."

"Right." She gave the annoyed cyclist an apologetic wave as they passed by. Community relations. "Why didn't we question her right away? Got to get to it right away on a murder case."

"MacIntyre. Don't things work the same way in America? Where were we?"

MacIntyre considered before answering. The view stuck in her mind.

"Well?"

"The Tjesut?"

"And what is the key, defining feature of the Tjesut?"

"The Palace of the Republic?"

"Aside from the palace."

"A lot of rich people's mansions?"

"Closer."

"Are you saying we need to treat that murderer with kid gloves because she's rich?"

He smiled and slowed for a little old lady crossing the street with a walker. MacIntyre waved at her, too.

"No, I'm saying that we need to treat respectable citizens who are friendly with other respectable citizens as citizens, not as murderers."

"Even if they are murderers?"

"Assumptions, MacIntyre." He flipped the siren on in a brief burst to clear a delivery truck out of the way. It didn't move. He flipped it again, longer, and the driver gave him a two-finger salute before moving on. She didn't wave at the driver, but she didn't give him a return salute either. Road rage can have terrible consequences.

"MacIntyre, you're a good semetyt. The best one we have. That's why you're here, with me, investigating this case. You see things the other semetyu don't. But after that screwup with the w'abu at the Temple of Peteh—"

"Not my fault."

He cleared his throat of whatever expletive he was about to utter and repeated, "*After that screwup,* you're lucky to have a job. I'm giving you a second chance here, MacIntyre. If you don't want it, just say so and I'll sign the papers."

MacIntyre wasn't stupid, and she liked her boss, and she loved her job, so she said, "I'll do my best, Mes, I will. No screwups on this one. She's not guilty until proven innocent. That's the American way." She grinned at him, but he didn't get it. Oh well.

"This isn't America, MacIntyre. I'll take her through it tomorrow. Besides, we have plenty of questions to ask that don't involve Lady Nekhen."

And I'm the woman to do it, she inferred. Well, she was.

"Where should I start?" Put the burden on his judgment.

"When's the last time you ate out at a fancy restaurant?"

She grinned. Now we're talking: a free dinner at the most expensive French restaurant in Menmenet. She could eat in the kitchen while the cooks lined up to serve up answers along with the foie gras.

CHAPTER TWO
Shesmu Gets a Midnight Call

I'D DONE TWO COOKING DEMOS in Niut Shepesu earlier in the day, then spent time in the bar with the other chefs who had performed—there's no other word for it—at the event. Superb wine, good camaraderie, hilarious stories. Back in my room, I wasn't drunk, just relaxed and feeling no pain, drifting off in a very comfortable hotel bed.

My phone buzzed on the nightstand. Grunting, I rubbed my face and reached. Aset. At this time of night? She must miss me.

"Hi there, gorgeous."

"Shes…."

I sat up. Something in her voice…wasn't right.

"What's wrong, princess?"

"Shes…Nekhen is…."

My stomach dropped. Had Nekhen found out? Was he there, listening, forcing her to—

"He's dead, Shes. Murdered."

"What?"

"He's dead, Shes. Somebody cut his throat."

I was in no shape to handle this. I sat up in bed, mouth open, speechless, the phone at my ear, my heart frozen.

"I found him late this afternoon. The medjau have left now."

I clutched the phone tighter. "You found him? Are you OK?"

"I…no, I'm not OK. OK. What does OK mean? Why would I be OK?"

I could hear the grieving anger coming through the ether. I should be there, holding her, loving her.

"Aset, I'm in Niut Shepesu, I want to hold you and be with you but I can't."

"I know, Shes, you told me you were going a few days ago, the last time we… saw each other."

Made love, she meant. My emotions spilled over. "Aset…"

"Shes, I called, I don't—the medjau…. I called to tell you, we shouldn't see each other, OK?"

"But, Aset, I love you, I want to comfort you, help you through this. We love each other."

"Shes, it's, I can't, it's too painful. I think—" She breathed, I waited for it. "I think we need to stop seeing each other, it's not only the medjau, what they think, I can't…I don't want to see you anymore. I don't love you anymore. I can't. It's not right."

"I'll come back to Menmenet tomorrow, Aset, and we'll talk."

"No, Shes. No! It's hard enough." She disconnected. I redialed her number, but it went to voicemail. I left a message asking her to please call me when she recovered and that I'd call her tomorrow when I got back to Menmenet.

I lay awake for an hour, aching for Aset, and for Nekhen. Dead? I'd apprenticed with him at the Per'ankh. He'd given me everything—his friendship, my career, and money for my restaurant. I owed him a lot. My return to him was making love to his wife behind his back. Now he was dead. I had to find a way. Aset.

I got up and made a reservation for the short-hop flight to Menmenet leaving early the next morning. I had to get up there.

Aset didn't love me anymore?

CHAPTER THREE
MacIntyre Eats French

MacIntyre, never having eaten foie gras, looked at her plate in dismay. Liver. It was glistening, soft, a disgusting brown-red color, quivering like brown jello under the grill marks. They expected her to consume raw liver. Almost-raw liver. And people paid a tonne of money for this stuff?

She looked up at Qenna, now chef de cuisine of the Per'ankh. "Can I have this well done or something?"

"Certainly, Hutyt. We can also mash your peas if you like." Qenna smiled with his mouth.

She took his meaning and wasn't sure whether to shrivel up in shame or arrest him for trying to poison her. She carefully wielded her knife and fork to extract a small—a tiny—piece of the goose liver. She inserted it into her mouth, shutting her eyes and hoping that not seeing what she was doing would make it OK with the rest of her body.

If this were a romance novel, her taste buds would awake to the many sensory possibilities of the world at tasting this small bit of heaven. As it was, it was definitely good liver. Superb liver. Even raw. Almost raw.

"Can we get on with it, hutyt?" Qenna was a smallish man, immaculate in his chef's uniform, thin-faced with short, grizzled beard and hair. His lips were thin and very disapproving.

She rolled her tongue around her mouth and swallowed, marveling at the buttery smoothness passing through. "Sure, Qenna, sure." She took a larger piece. "Wow, I could get used to—"

"Hutyt…I have customers, I have cooks, I have waiters, they are puppets on strings waiting for me to make them dance. You are holding up the strings."

"Sorry, sorry. Qenna, we're grateful. I won't take up too much of your time. When did you see Nekhen last?" Another forkful of foie gras. Pay attention, MacIntyre.

"Chef was here this morning, seeing to deliveries and working on the menu for this evening."

"Menu? Don't you just cook the same stuff every night?"

Qenna closed his eyes. "No. No, we do not cook the same *stuff* every night, Hutyt. Chef decides what creations we will cook, based on what we find at the markets, what we have on hand, what inspires him."

MacIntyre was rarely out of her depth. but the level of creativity around necessary provender here plunged her into the deep end. She understood creativity. MacIntyre prided herself at her innovative thinking when finding murderers. But this? She reset her expectations for understanding the milieu of the victim and concentrated on physical movements.

"When did he leave?"

"Just after lunch."

"So around 1:30?"

"We serve lunch until 2, Hutyt. Sorry, I meant he left after the restaurant finished serving lunch, not after his lunch. We do not eat on your, erm, your civilian schedule."

"Right, got it. Why did he leave?"

For the first time, Qenna sounded out of *his* depth. "I do not know."

She gave him an eagle eye. "Why don't you know?"

"It is simply a fact, I do not know why chef left. He almost never leaves until after dinner service is complete." Qenna closed his eyes. "Did not leave."

"Don't worry, everyone has trouble in the first few days. Just tell me."

"Tell you what, Hutyt?"

"Tell me why Nekhen left." She gave him two eagle eyes. He was—well, maybe not lying, just not telling the complete truth.

Qenna's shoulders moved in a shrug. "Very well. The word in the kitchen is that he went home to check on his wife."

"His wife?"

"Neferaset."

"I know who is wife is, what do you mean by 'check on his wife?'"

Qenna rolled his neck and looked away, then back at her. "Must I fill in the blanks for you, Hutyt?"

"You mean he thought his wife was doing something he wouldn't want her to be doing."

"Yes."

"Such as?"

Neck roll, eyes to the ceiling, and he even started wiping his hands on the towel folded neatly across the apron string tying up his white-white apron. He said nothing.

"Qenna. I will get it, if not from you, then from your cooks, or even better, the busboys and dishwashers. They know everything." She had no idea whether that was true, but the logic of a business like this dictated its truth.

"She."

"Yes?"

"She's having an affair."

"Which you know about."

"Yes."

"With whom? You?"

He gave her a look of horror. "Ka of Sekhmet, no! I'm…my husband works in finance, in a bank."

"I see." And she did. "But you've heard something from someone…"

"It is hard to keep any secret in a kitchen like this, connected to the powerful of Menmenet. Everyone here knows anything of importance within minutes. Anything."

MacIntyre noted this remarkable fact for future use. A fast, accurate grapevine could prove useful to a working semetyt.

"Who's the lucky man, Qenna?"

"I don't want to get him into trouble, he's a good man. A friend."

"The only trouble he'll be in is the trouble he brings with him, Qenna."

"He's a chef. A man named Shesmu. He used to be sous chef here, left to set up his own restaurant. Chef was his angel."

"What do you mean?"

"Sorry, our jargon. Nekhen helped finance Shesmu's first restaurant, the Neferti. It's down by the bay, near Dju-Keta. Shesmu was Nekhen's apprentice, then became his sous chef. When he left to start up the Neferti, I became sous chef here; now I am temporary chef de cuisine."

"I see. Neferaset said she worked here?"

"Yes, as hostess, several years ago."

"And she met this Shesmu here?"

"Yes."

"And I suppose now she's the owner?"

"Yes. She made me chef de cuisine. This afternoon."

"How long has this affair been going on?"

"People tell me a few months. I'd heard about the affair, I was watching for signs. I thought this would kill him." Qenna grimaced. "I mean, hurt him, not kill him literally."

"Looks like it might have done both."

During this entire conversation, French delicacies were coming and going in front of MacIntyre. Concentrating on the questions and answers as she forked the remarkable fare into her mouth was hard. OK, Shesmu. Top of the list of possibles. Next to the Wife; she had more to lose. And gain. The Per'ankh. The Neferti. She'd passed by it along the waterfront street that led up to Dju-Keta, handsome place, large, terrific views of the bay. Another superb dinner in store. Shesmu. Have to run his priors.

She thought about what Qenna had said, then asked, "So, Qenna, are you going to be chef, erm, chef de cuisine from now on?" She garbled the French term, but Qenna understood what she meant.

"Yes," he hissed. "But I did not kill him to become chef. Nekhen is one of the greatest chefs that ever lived. A living god. I will pray to him once Inpu entombs his mummy and justifies his ka in the Duat. Chefs do not kill to rise in their profession, they cook. They cook well. His ka will guide me forever, 'ankhu djet." So, Qenna was religious, as only a Remetj can be religious. "And I was right here, supervising the kitchen, all afternoon and evening."

MacIntyre wiped her lips with her napkin. "I can attest to the good-cooking part, Qenna. OK, thank you for your help and for your food. Never had anything like it."

"I can only imagine. Please, Hutyt, if you have any more questions, I will be happy to have someone else answer them."

"And here I thought we were getting along so well."

Shrug, neck roll. "Where do I send the bill?"

Damn. Wasn't Mes going to be happy. She wasn't about to insist on a free meal and start a huge argument on medjau corruption with this punctilious and peeved chef.

"Idnu Djehutymes, Temple of Ma'at. I'll talk to your cooks soon, but I won't take up any more of your time tonight."

"À vote service, Hutyt. Just not at dinner time. Please."

CHAPTER FOUR
Shesmu Returns Home

THE RIDESHARE DROPPED ME AT the front door of the Neferti at the time I would ordinarily arrive there, right after sunrise. I walked down the little driveway to the back loading dock entrance. Two cooks were unloading produce and supplies in the back.

"Chef!"

"Hi, back early. Good to see the hard work!"

They grinned and kept the boxes moving.

Duaneferet, my sous chef, hadn't shown up for work yet for some unknown reason. I called her and left a voicemail, then I worked through the morning prepping for lunch and dinner. My banter level must have been low, I was getting concerned looks from the line cooks by the time Henutsenu showed up mid-morning. I called Aset fifteen times during that period and got nothing but voicemail, but I didn't leave a message. I'd have to go to her house, but I was sure neither of us was ready for that yet.

Henutsenu was the hostess at the Neferti. A gorgeous, dusky-skinned Remetjet, she was perfect for the role, and—no question—my best hire so far in my limited career as a restaurant owner. Today she dressed in a gold-thread sheath dress shimmering with white and red notes. She had braided her black hair with gold beads. Her full lips smiled when she saw me working away in the kitchen.

I set down my knife and went out to the front, wiping my hands on my towel. I noticed Duaneferet—Dua—coming in the back door as I walked out to talk with Henutsenu.

"Henutsenu," I greeted her.

"Chef, I wasn't expecting you back so soon!"

"Yeah. Things happened."

Her face got serious. "Nekhen."

"Yeah."

She hesitated, then grabbed my arm and pulled me into the bar. Nobody was there yet.

"Did she call you?"

"Who?"

She raised her eyes skyward. "Who do you think?"

"Why would she call me?"

"Because you're fucking her. And because she's fucked up in so many ways I can't count them."

"Henut—"

"Shes, please. Everybody knows you're sleeping with her."

Great. Everybody. Nekhen?

Could I ask? No.

"Did she call you?" repeated my hostess. My friend.

"Yes, she called me! OK?" My voice echoed in the empty bar. It sounded angry, and I modulated. "Yes, she did. She did."

"And you came right back."

"I did."

"Like a puppet—"

"Don't go there, Henutsenu."

She compressed her lips and looked me in the eye. "Shes, you're being exceptionally stupid right now. We care about you, I care—"

The front door of the restaurant opened. We both looked over.

"We're closed, ma'am," said Henutsenu. "Lunch is—"

"Medjau, Hutyt-er-Semetyu MacIntyre." She held up credentials. "I have a few questions."

Fine. Just fine. Just…fine.

CHAPTER FIVE
MacIntyre Eats Remetjy

THE PAIR OF THEM STOOD in the bar. The woman was gorgeous, more so than the gorgeous Wife. MacIntyre ran her eyes up and down, her body tightening with lust. Oh my god. What a....

She collected her thoughts. "I'm here about the murder of a chef, Nekhen. He is part owner of this restaurant?"

The gorgeous Remetjet said, "Yes. What do you need, Hutyt?"

The man stepped forward to check her credentials. She saw his name stitched in black glyphs on his uniform. Ah. Shesmu.

He had on a chef's uniform like Qenna's except for a dark red spot on the towel hanging from his waist. Tomato? Not likely to be blood, though you never knew. Handsome enough. Brilliant eyes. Lovely mouth. Nearly a perfect couple, if it weren't for their sour expressions on seeing her credentials.

She bowed and said, "Lord Shesmu, very pleased. Alive, sound, and healthy." Lay it on, why not? Get him in a pleasant mood, then drill down and expose the filth underneath. Being handsome was not a disqualifier for being a vicious murderer.

His eyes turned furious. "Cut the crap, Hutyt. We both know why you're here." The woman grabbed his arm and shook it.

"And you are?" she asked the woman.

"Henutsenu. Hostess here." The Remetjet's eyes moved over MacIntyre, taking measurements and making judgments in a way MacIntyre hadn't seen since she stopped going to lesbian bars. After R'aia. Let's not go there, Cheryl.

"OK. Lord Shesmu—"

"Just Shes." He softened as he took in her attributes. Typical male response, typical Remetj response to blonde hair and blue eyes. Was her superpower her

American looks or the fact that they concealed her true nature, that of a smart semetyt who hated murder?

"Shes. Can we talk for a few minutes? I have questions."

"I'll bet. Sure. Henutsenu, we'll use the chef's table." He looked at her. "Lunch?"

"Only if it's free. No bribe, I just blew my expense budget at the Per'ankh."

He smiled. "Qenna. Only Qenna would bill the medjau."

She smiled. "Yep."

"Yeah, I'll comp you. No obligation, Hutyt." Sure. The American expression about no free lunches darted into her mind. Draw the lines.

"Thanks. Let's eat first, so if I have to arrest you, I can do it on a full stomach."

His wonderful lips quirked. "As bad as that?"

"You tell me."

Henutsenu squeezed the chef's arm and said, "You two have a lot to discuss." She gave Shesmu a direct look, which he acknowledged with a nod. A lot of nonverbal communication going on between those two.

Henutsenu was even more enticing from the back than the front as she led them through the empty restaurant. Unbelievable. Where do they hide? All the bars, all the "social" events. Nobody like this. Except R'aia. What the hell, Shesmu wasn't that bad himself. She was enjoying this investigation. It sure was better than her last case: figuring out which gay, bald w'ab priest of Peteh had it in for the other one.

Before going into the kitchen, she turned to Henutsenu and took her arm as she was turning away. She kept her touch light on the smooth, dusky skin.

"I'd like to speak with you later, if that's all right."

"Of course, Hutyt. I'm here until midnight."

"And after that?"

Henutsenu smiled. "Home. Alone."

MacIntyre smiled back. "Call me Cheryl?"

"Why not? Later, then?"

"Later."

She put aside her lust and turned to the target of her investigation, standing at the little table in the kitchen.

"Now then, Shes…."

"What is this stuff?" queried MacIntyre, looking at the plate.

"Crab tomalley."

"I'm none the wiser. Is it like foie gras?"

He grinned. "You had quite a dinner at the Per'ankh."

"Yeah. Way beyond my usual."

"Crab is the local delicacy. Tomalley is the liver of the crab. So, yes: seafood foie gras."

She took a big forkful and put it in her mouth. Not foie gras. No. Not. Could she spit? No. Swallow, Cheryl, swallow.

"Don't swallow. Let it percolate over your tongue and settle, the flavors will grow."

They did. Disgusting flavors. She was not a crab tomalley kind of girl.

Shesmu, sensitive to body language, asked the server to remove the tomalley salad and bring the lamb confit.

"Spiced lamb confit, the classic dish from Tjenu."

"Where is that?"

"Next country over from Kemet. They like deep, mysterious spicing."

Very nice. Went down warm and inviting. She savored the aftertaste, then returned her focus to the chef.

"Shesmu."

"Call me Shes."

They sat at what Shesmu called the "chef's table," a table in the kitchen reserved for the special guests of the chef interested in watching a master at work. It was Remetjy style, sitting cross-legged on cushions. He was working, sure, but only at not answering her questions. He wanted the food to distract her.

"I'll call you Shes if you'll answer all my questions without reservation."

He looked at his plate, then back at her. "All right, deal."

"Call me Cheryl. Why are you sleeping with Neferaset?"

He gritted his teeth and was silent, then said, "Because I enjoy sleeping with her."

"And?"

"Because she enjoys sleeping with me?"

"Romantic. And?"

"There is no and."

"What about Nekhen?"

"What about him?"

"Did you kill him?"

"No."

"Is he your private god?"

Shesmu smiled. "You've been talking to Qenna."

"Is he?"

"No. A friend."

"Do friends sleep with friend's wives?"

"No."

"Then why?"

A lengthy pause. "Because I loved her, love her, more than him."

"Because you couldn't keep your dick in your shendyt." MacIntyre had heard the "L" word too many times in similar circumstances to be under any illusions.

"You've got a way with words, Hutyt."

"Cheryl, please, if we're going to be friends. Shes." She said this as warmly as she could, just to mislead him. It didn't. "You don't want to talk about her, do you?"

"No."

"You'll have to."

"No, I will not. We broke up. *She* broke up." Shesmu's eyes told her she'd hit a nerve.

The Wife broke up. "When?" she asked.

"Last night."

The server brought the next course, mysterious poultry with a deep brown sauce.

"Duck Mennefer," he said. "You'll love it."

She did, and she lost track of her incisive and deep questioning of the man. Jeez. She didn't get out enough, and her salary wasn't enough to enjoy the authentic food of Menmenet. Get to the point, MacIntyre.

"Did you kill him? You're sleeping with his wife, you owed him money, he could destroy you in a minute. You have every motive in the world. She broke up with you last night. Before or after you slept with her? Did he catch you at it?" She took a mouthful of duck. She felt the familiar thrill in her gut of confronting a murderer. That moment, the one where their eyes filled with knowing that they were at the end of the line. Where she told truth and they had to listen. She looked into Shesmu's eyes and saw nothing but humor. And the duck was calming the thrill in her stomach as well.

"I wasn't here."

"Where were you?"

"Niut Shepesu."

The old capital. How many miles? 120, give or take a few. "Anybody see you there?"

"50 people in my cooking demonstration."

"Names?"

"Here's my publicist, she's got the names." He wrote the name and phone number on his linen napkin and passed it to her.

"And you're here now?"

"Early morning plane." He wrote the flight number on the napkin. A challenging man overall. But alibis need checking. Professionalism obliged her to investigate this man even though she knew the Wife had murdered her husband. Shesmu could be an accessory, you never knew. Niut Shepesu….

The server took her plate and put a tomato, onion, and avocado salad in front of her. A forkful explained to her the contrast between expectation and reality as the subtle spicing kicked in and her mouth acquired a layer of fire and ice.

"Your food—more challenging than the Per'ankh."

He smiled with pleasure. "Yes, well, more Remetjy than the Per'ankh. You're American?"

"Yes, 10 years here."

"But not into food."

She grinned. "Sorry."

Shesmu had such nice lips. He gazed into her eyes. But he didn't mean it. What interesting eyes. Fierce one moment, smiling the next, then searching deep. She'd need her mirror sunglasses if she spent much time questioning him. She smiled. Lots more nice food in this homicide investigation. No more canned ravioli for a while, then. This man was the key to the case; break him wide open and Neferaset would be in jail for the rest of her life, and maybe he would be too. Snap decision time.

She said, "I'll have to arrest you for obstruction of a medjat in the course of her duties."

"Why?"

"No dessert." She pushed her empty plate away with finality.

Shesmu refused to allow staff questioning during lunch, and for now MacIntyre went along with that. She hung around until lunch service was over to talk with Shesmu's sous chef, Duaneferet.

"I wouldn't have a restaurant to run if I let a crazy medjat take my sous chef out of the kitchen right at the service peak." He led her out to the bar. "Have a drink. On the house," he said to the bartender. "I'll send Duaneferet out soon. I have to get back to work now. I won't say it was a pleasure, Cheryl, but it was interesting." He bowed and vanished to his kitchen.

MacIntyre caught sight of Henutsenu coming back from showing a customer to a table, and she beckoned her over. The Remetjet just smiled and shook her head, waving a hand at the line of people waiting.

The bar was long and made of an elegant wood. Barstools lined its length. There were small American-style tables and chairs scattered around, with the big windows looking out onto the bay. MacIntyre looked over the bar selection against the wall and noted just about every brand of alcohol she'd ever heard of and many she hadn't. Like most medjau, she'd put in her time in the dive bars of Menmenet, and the lesbian bars and the pickup bars and the hotel bars....

"What'll it be, Cheryl?" asked the bartender in English. She noted the quick uptake: a single mention of her name by the boss, and he was up with her.

She cocked her head and scanned the bottles. One wouldn't hurt. "What would he give me if he were trying to impress me? A lot?"

The bartender smiled a crooked smile and produced a bottle of red wine from under the counter. He placed it in front of her. "A 1986 Cabernet Sauvignon from a small winery in the Caymus tribal region up north. Best vintage in many years."

"A First Peoples wine?"

"Yep. The Caymus turned out to be great winemakers. This vintage has been drinking well for the last couple of years. Chef has a private deal with the winery."

"OK, pour me a glass. Only one, though, I wouldn't want 'chef' taking advantage of me."

He smiled the professional smile of a man who would never talk trash about his boss. She spent the next hour socializing with one or two interesting but very rich people spending too much money in the bar. That was always a sign of criminal intent of the worst sort. She nursed the wine, which was nowhere near as smooth as she expected; more edgy and complex, though she was not that familiar with the ins and outs of fine wines. She was more of a cocktail person. She thought overall it suited the man she'd interrogated: complicated with hidden depths and many revelations if you knew what to look for. The wine grew on her.

A woman in a white chef's uniform appeared in the bar's doorway, looked around, and came over to her. "You're the medjat?" Her tone was contemptuous, which made MacIntyre bristle, but you never bristled at a witness until you'd dragged everything out of them. She smiled.

"Duaneferet?"

"Yes."

"Hutyt-er-Semetyu Cheryl MacIntyre." She showed her credentials. She looked around and saw a few vacant tables over in a corner. "Shall we sit over there and talk?"

"I'm busy. In the kitchen."

"I won't keep you long."

The woman rolled her eyes and stomped over to a table. MacIntyre followed. No antennae raised on this woman: a square face, squat body, thick legs, muscular arms with tattoos, and no neck. The woman looked like a brick with feet.

MacIntyre asked the basic questions and wrote the woman's name, phone, and position in her notebook, then contemplated her for a minute in silence. This was one of her favorite interrogation techniques. Amazing how people couldn't tolerate a brief silence. It always made them come up with something interesting to say.

"This is about that Nekhen thing, right? Chef wouldn't say what you wanted. Why don't you just leave him alone?" So she was on her boss's side in this battle. And she knew it was all about him, didn't she?

"Should I?"

The sous chef leaned across the table, fierce eyes looking right into MacIntyre's, heavy black eyebrows and sour mouth conveying her displeasure. "Damn right you should. He's got enough problems without stupid medjau coming in—"

"I'll try not to be too stupid, but I need to check on him." MacIntyre interrupted the flow, as she was sure it wouldn't stop on its own.

"Because he's seeing that whore, right?"

"Right."

"Who he fucks is his business."

Duaneferet had a raucous voice. Great for a kitchen, doubtless; the few remaining patrons in the bar looked worried. Nothing she could do about that. Duaneferet was below their pay grade.

"Well, Duaneferet, it's my business if he murdered someone because of it."

"That's ridiculous. Chef wouldn't hurt a fly."

"Where was he yesterday at, say, 3 p.m.?"

"Niut Shepesu. A cooking demo. Two days. I've been in charge of the kitchen."

"And you've met Neferaset, Nekhen's wife?"

"Seen her, the bitch, never talked to her. Here. With chef."

"I sense dislike for the lady."

"That thin-nosed cow has chef twisted around her so tight that the poor bastard doesn't know the which from the other."

"Were you acquainted with Nekhen?"

"Met him. Once."

"What was he like?"

"A big deal, thought he was a pera'a in his own kitchen. He deserved that bitch, but she didn't deserve him or that fancy mansion. Or chef."

"But you haven't met her."

"Heard enough." The sous chef's thin lips clamped in disapproval.

"Anything about her hating her husband enough to cut his throat?"

"She doesn't have the balls, or the brains." Duaneferet placed both palms on the table to emphasize her judgment. "Twisted the pera'a around her finger, took his money, then took chef too. You could see it was breaking him."

"Nekhen?"

"No, you dumb—" Duaneferet stopped before the ultimate insult. "Chef, not Nekhen. Chef thought it was a secret, it was eating him up from inside."

"What did Nekhen think about his wife sleeping with his friend?"

The sous chef smiled a grim smile. "Too wrapped up in himself to see it, the idiot. Nobody wanted to tell him, they just let him be, like the fool he was. That Qenna, he couldn't tell his god—too gay, too stupid. Are we done here, or are you just gossiping for the pure fun of it?"

Customers in the bar averted their looks away from MacIntyre's table. The bartender sent murderous signals in her direction with his eyes. Maybe she'd better get *his* alibi for yesterday too, along with another glass of this wonderful wine. She regarded the sour sous chef. The woman looked of all things worried. Something about the energy of the woman, more than just disapproving. Anxious. What did she have to be anxious about? Have to see. What a mess—a bunch of complicated, messy, screwed-up people.

The afternoon was passing. She had better things to do than to fill her brain with contradictions from this misanthropic brick. "Yeah, we're done. I might have more ques—" She was talking to the back of the sous chef, who stomped out of the bar without another word. MacIntyre held up her glass and gave it the brief wave, and the server hurried over and took it to the bar for a refill. Surely the lovely Henutsenu would have a few spare minutes soon.

MacIntyre was on her third glass of wine. She wondered whether the stuff was staining her teeth red. To fill in the time, she got on her phone. Shesmu's publicist confirmed the cooking demo in Niut Shepesu and gave her names and phone numbers. She called those and got five gushing reviews of Shesmu's cooking demonstrations yesterday. Alibi checked.

The bar emptied as the afternoon wore away, and she moved from her table back to the bar. The bartender was cheerful enough but wasn't interested in talking about anything related to her case. So, they discussed the state of American horse racing, about which MacIntyre knew so little it was embarrassing.

Henutsenu walked into the bar. MacIntyre, whose inhibitions, such as they were, had disappeared along with her second glass of wine, got up and hugged her. She got a nice, smooth, lingering hug back. The bartender turned away and started polishing things, as bartenders do when they don't want to intrude.

Henutsenu steered MacIntyre to a table by the front window overlooking the bay. "Let's sit and talk, Cheryl."

MacIntyre bubbled, "This place reeks of romance and style."

"Yes, Shesmu has great taste."

"You don't call him 'chef' like the other denizens of this place?"

"Not to you, at least." The Remetjet smiled. "You've created quite a stir among the staff. The endless questions."

"They've seen nothing yet," said MacIntyre. "In a murder investigation, the questions are forever until we get the evidence we need to convict. If you have even the slightest connection, you'll get raked over the coals."

"So, I'm here to get raked?"

"I wouldn't do that to you, but I might as well do my job a little. Before."

"Before what?" Henutsenu regarded her.

"Before, well, before whatever develops," said MacIntyre, suddenly shy.

"Whatever," repeated Henutsenu, folding her hands on the table. "Goodness, that sounds exciting."

MacIntyre shook her head in frustration. "You know," she said.

"I do, Cheryl." She reached out with long fingers and stroked MacIntyre's hand. MacIntyre noticed a small, black onyx cat dangled from her bracelet: Bastet. A Bastet worshipper. "Let's see what happens. What are your questions?"

"Um. OK." MacIntyre took a fortifying sip of wine. She said, "The affair between…" She lingered on the pause, unwilling to disturb the air with the names.

"Shesmu and Neferaset? Hot and heavy." Henutsenu's lips formed a disdainful expression, exciting MacIntyre's lust even more.

"You don't approve?"

"No, but it's not my affair. Oh—I suppose I should say, not my *business*." She smiled a gentle smile.

MacIntyre's medjat demon was kicking her in the butt, telling her to ask the same questions she'd asked Duaneferet, but her mouth refused to form the words. They were inappropriate, looking at this woman. But she needed to ask. She'd just ask nicely this time.

"What is Duaneferet's problem?"

Henutsenu raised an eyebrow. "You had a problem with her?"

"Ask the bartender, she could have cleared out the bar."

"Hmm. Well, she's been a little down this week. And…"

"Yes?"

"We had a contretemps in the kitchen yesterday. Just a people problem involving Dua. She's worried about that. Nothing relevant to your problem."

"Where was Shesmu yesterday?" Might as well get confirmation.

"Niut Shepesu, doing his wonderful cooking demonstrations with recipes from the Neferti."

MacIntyre smiled with one corner of her mouth. "Nice marketing, huh?"

Henutsenu nodded, smiling.

"Have you heard anything about Nekhen being upset, or about Shesmu or Neferaset threatening anyone?"

"I don't talk about things I 'hear,' Cheryl. Only about things I'm sure of." The low, smooth voice admonished her, and MacIntyre got mad. How could she do her job if people wouldn't gossip?

"Very loyal, I'm sure. Look, Henutsenu, you can trust me. I need everything about this. Whether Shesmu is a weak, pussy-whipped fool or a strong, clever murderer. Whether Neferaset has knife skills. I need to know—"

"Your need to know is not my problem." The Remetjet's voice was firm and pleasant, her eyes less forgiving.

MacIntyre, finishing her wine, abandoned caution and said, "What has this guy Shesmu got that has you all in thrall? He's sure a smooth talker. If he did nothing, he has nothing to worry about. Jeez, if this keeps up I'll run him in to the temple and put him through it."

Henutsenu put her hands in her lap and regarded MacIntyre with a stony expression. "I think you're on the wrong track, Cheryl. At any rate, I see little thrill or profit in continuing our delightful conversation. Maybe another time?" She got up and walked out of the bar.

So much for a night of ecstasy.

CHAPTER SIX
Shesmu Works the Room

WHEN I GOT BACK TO the kitchen after dropping my new "friend" MacIntyre at the bar, I sensed it right away: something was off. Working in restaurants is like being part of a close family, you can sense when somebody is hiding something.

I sniffed the air; no scorching. I cocked an ear; the chatter was subdued. I looked around, and nobody would look me in the eye. I found Duaneferet and pulled her aside.

"Dua, what's going on? What's wrong?"

"Nothing, chef. Everything's fine." She wasn't looking me in the eye either.

"Dua, don't lie to me."

"We're fine, chef. Let's get on with lunch. I need to get that order out."

I shook my head in frustration, but the lunch orders were pressing, and everybody was working.

"OK. When you get a break, go out to the bar and see this blonde American woman there, she's a medjat, Hutyt MacIntyre. She wants to ask you questions."

"About what, chef?"

"Just answer them."

"OK, chef. When I get a break." She sounded down enough to make me think she would never get a break, but I'd push her out the door at some point. Maybe MacIntyre would get tired and leave. A good-looking woman, but not my type. Aset was my type. Aset. Who had just broken up with me and wouldn't return my calls.

I let Dua go and got to work myself to get my mind off Aset. I checked the stations to make sure the equipment was working and the taste and texture of the cooking were exceptional. All the things that create a world-class cover.

After the third cook told me everything was fine and wouldn't look me in the eye, I took measures; it was ridiculous. I grabbed Khay and took him back to the prep room for a talk. His little round face, pop eyes, and full lips pursed into a frown as he followed me out of the main kitchen.

"What's up, Khay?" Khay was the lead cook, the one with the most experience and the best judgment. I thought we'd developed a good working relationship over the last year at the Neferti.

He blinked up at me, looked down, and looked up again.

"Pabaky."

"What about him?"

"He was here. Last night."

"A visit to Dua?" Pabaky was Dua's unfortunate choice of boyfriend.

"She…Nothing happened real bad, chef."

"What is this, professional courtesy? Bullshit. Tell me."

"She put him on the line."

"What!"

"I know, I know. I tried to tell her but she wouldn't listen."

"Damn it, I've told her to keep that little bastard the hell out of my kitchen!"

"I know, I know, chef. I know."

"I go away for two days and she goes crazy. What's wrong with the woman?"

"She loves him, chef, she…can't help herself."

"What happened?" Anything was possible with that little prick Pabaky.

"A few quail, chef, a little overdone."

"How little?"

"Threw them away." He looked at the floor, then at the meat bins where we put scraps for disposal.

"The organics?"

He looked at the floor and didn't answer. Organic wild quail were a specialty item. They were a separate line item in the food budget. You do not throw them away, and you do not overcook them. Ever. Not in my kitchen.

"Right." I needed to be decisive here. "Did he start any fights?" I'd seen Pabaky in action.

"No, not after last time, we all knew to keep quiet."

"Stupid…." I looked at the kitchen door.

"Dua's good, chef, she's just not all in control of herself."

I shook my head. "OK, get out of here." I waved a hand at the door in disgust. Khay moved fast.

I walked to the door to scout for Dua. Nowhere in sight. She must have taken her break. I hoped the Hutyt would rake her over the coals, then eat her for lunch. I'd have a talk with Dua when she got back, yes I would.

Dua returned from talking with the American medjat very pissed off, which didn't help with what I had to do. I made it quick and emphatic. I sent her off to the dinner work after getting her assurance that Pabaky would never enter my kitchen again.

To shake this off, I worked at a few things myself, switching over to tasting and rearranging at the plating station as business picked up into the early evening. Half way through the dinner service, I did my evening's chef's walk. That's where the "celebrity chef" (me) walks around talking to any VIPs in the house. VIPs were a challenging part of my job. I grew up poor with a healthy disrespect for power and money. I had to unlearn that fast when I got into the business of feeding it.

At night, the enormous windows in the dining room that faced the bay were black to the outside and reflected the warm interior colors. I'd had the walls plastered and painted with modern renditions of ancient hunting and fishing scenes from the River in Kemet to create a heady Remetjy atmosphere. The artist said it made a change from painting tombs. Despite his limitations, he got the right measure of life and action into the murals. The low, Remetjy-style tables with cushions enhanced the Remetjy feel.

My most important VIP that night was the Honorable 'Aapehty, the id-nuhaty'a of Menmenet, who never gave me much trouble. His priorities were first, last, and always keeping his boss the haty'a happy and in office, as that's how he kept himself in office. When he came to the Neferti, it was with somebody he wanted to impress with his connections. His boss could afford Nekhen's Per'ankh; 'Aapehty could afford me, so we encountered each other often. He cultivated me as much as I cultivated him.

'Aapehty's guest looked like an American business executive in town on business from America. Not Boston or New York, somewhere near the border along the Mississippi. He had the smooth look of the very wealthy, who have suits pressed and waiting for them in the cities they visit often. But the dress wasn't the high fashion of the East Coast. He looked out-of-place sitting with his legs crossed under the low table, Remetjy style. His light blue eyes looked up at me, teeth gleaming in a smile through his short, brown beard.

I smiled and said hello. 'Aapehty introduced him as Raphael D. Blackmore ("Call me Rafe"), from Saint Louis. We chatted, and I answered their questions about the food.

Call Me Rafe used impeccable manners to eat his Quail Iunu. These small birds hopped around everywhere in the Ta'an-Imenty. Our suppliers raised them organically, free range, to get the best combination of flavors and qualities. Young birds butterflied and grilled with a dusting of spices like cumin and coriander from the old Remetjy delta city of Iunu made a delicate and unforgettable summer dish.

The eating of the small birds was a challenge best faced by small children who didn't care or by people well trained in the upper echelons of society. Call Me Rafe was one of the latter—he could afford to eat the most expensive item on my menu, and he could do it without messing up his tie.

After finishing his taste of the small bird, Call Me Rafe said, "Wonderful food. Where do you get your inspiration?"

A common question, but there was no proper answer. I answered with my usual brief approximation. "The greatest French chef in Menmenet, Nekhen, took me on as an apprentice. Take that training, add Remetjy flavors and local ingredients, and there you have it." Nekhen was still in my mind from yesterday.

Call Me Rafe smiled and nodded. His icy, dark-blue eyes reminded me of a shark's, frigid and blank. I smiled and turned away to go to the next table, but Call Me Rafe scrambled up from his cushion and touched my arm.

"Er, Shesmu—may I have a word? Two minutes in private?" I looked at 'Aapehty, who made encouraging motions with his hands.

"Sure, Rafe. Let's go to my office." I showed him the way with a hand and we walked back and through to the tiny office where I took care of the bills.

Call Me Rafe was a tall man, lanky but with very smooth movements. Rafe oozed confidence from his expensive haircut to his shiny black shoes.

He said, "I won't take too much of your time, you're a busy man."

"Thanks, I appreciate that. Your Renkemet is very good."

"I learned it from my governess back in St. Louis. She'd immigrated from Waset back before I was born."

"That explains the lovely southern accent. What can I do for you, Rafe?"

"Shes, how much do you know about Remetjy antiquities?"

"Just what I learned in history: the old buildings, the Empire, the gold, the tombs of the pera'au."

"What would you say if I told you there was an opportunity to make a tidy sum for you in the antiquities business?"

"What is this, Rafe, a scam?" I smiled to take the edge off, but I was serious. Americans.

Call Me Rafe laughed, white teeth showing. "No, no, an honest-to-God, legitimate trading opportunity."

"What's your role in the arrangement?"

"I'm a trader. I'm based in St. Louis and have offices in New York and all over the world. I trade in collectibles—art, carpets, furniture, coins, stamps, anything. I'm out here because of this trading opportunity."

"And where do I come in? All I know about antiquities I learned in school. I'm a chef."

"You know more than you think."

"What do you mean?"

"I asked around and wound up in the idnuhaty'a's office, and he told me you were the person I needed to meet."

"'Aapehty is an old customer and a friend. I'm sorry if he misled you."

"He didn't. What I needed was a close friend of Nekhen, the chef with whom you apprenticed."

I kept the shock off my face. I hadn't expected Nekhen to be part of this conversation.

I asked, "Why do you need a friend of Nekhen's?"

"I can't tell you that just yet. I need to know that you're interested, then I need to know you're committed to the project before I fill you in on the details. We need to keep it quiet."

I tried a deprecating smile. "You haven't given me enough information to interest me yet, Rafe."

He considered that, looking at me, then nodded. "True. OK, I'll tell you this much. I think you have knowledge and friendships we can use to get a precious object from a very long time ago. I'm providing the capital and organization, but I need somebody local who knows the people and places. If you can see your way to spending a week or two helping me, I can guarantee you an up-front fee within a month. And after we sell the item, I can guarantee a share of the profit."

"Does this have to do with Nekhen's murder?"

"Only coincidentally. I stumbled on Nekhen's name a month ago in my researches in Kemet and only learned about the murder when I got out here to follow up with him. Local murders here don't make the St. Louis Post Dispatch, I'm afraid. But I was very disappointed."

I wasn't sure how I wanted to respond. More information wouldn't hurt. I probed, "Have you spoken with Nekhen's wife, Neferaset?"

"No. That's one big reason we want you. Your, uh, relationship with—"

I raised a hand, and he stopped before we both became foolish. I just gave him a hint. "That reason may have lost its edge with recent events."

He thought that over. His shark eyes showed he understood my hint.

"I pay well for knowledge and local help. Locals always move things along faster. Even if you're not, er, as close to the source as you were, you have the knowledge."

"I'm busy at present, Rafe." There might be money here, but this business made me uncomfortable. Not all money is worth its cost. And Aset wasn't returning my calls.

Call Me Rafe got earnest, in his American way. "I'm not sure the matter will wait, and the information is time sensitive. If we wait too long, the opportunity will vanish. If you commit yourself, I could double your compensation."

Since he had mentioned no sums, this didn't get my heart racing. Call Me Rafe wanted to close the deal; I could read it in his body language. He radiated sincerity and confidence. But the mists of Call Me Rafe's vagueness filled the little room around me like a dank fog on a dangerous moor. This had something to do with Aset and the murder, and I didn't want to just dismiss it. I said, "I'm sorry. I'll consider it, though. How about if I get in touch tomorrow or the next day? How long is too long?"

"We have only a matter of days. OK, if that's the best I can get." He sounded resigned but positive. "But I can't stress enough that time isn't on our side. There are others involved, competitors, and they may find something first." He gave me his phone number.

The little anxiety lines around his eyes smoothed out as he smiled. I walked him back to 'Aapehty's table and left him conferring with his friend. I had Henutsenu send a bottle of the restaurant's best bubbly to cement a happy evening for them both.

CHAPTER SEVEN
MacIntyre Checks an Alibi

"MACINTYRE? WHERE THE HELL ARE you?" Djehutymes's voice was as irascible as always.

"Uh, a few steps away from the Neferti restaurant, you know, the one below Dju-Keta."

"Perfect. Look, I need to you go up and interview a woman, Sitemhut, lives on the east side of Dju-Keta, she's the alibi for Neferaset. I've talked with her by phone, says she had lunch with Neferaset, a late lunch. Neferaset gave me her name when I interviewed her this morning. The w'abu of Sekhmet-Hut-Her tell me the victim died at about 3 p.m. Sitemhut says she was leaving the restaurant on Mentju at 3, with Neferaset, who says the same."

"Shit. But you're not happy?"

"I'm never happy, MacIntyre."

"True."

"Get your butt up there and talk to the lady, Sitemhut. She lives halfway up the Djedkar'a Steps, number 34. You can walk from where you are. Got that?"

MacIntyre, juggling her phone, had pulled out her notebook and wrote the name and address in it. "Got it."

Mes hung up. Abrupt bastard.

Djedkar'a Steps. She wasn't that familiar with Dju-Keta. Most of her patrol days had been in the southern part of Menmenet. She checked her phone and found that the Djedkar'a Steps were right up the street she was on, two long blocks.

She walked the two blocks. Once she'd found the Djedkar'a Steps, she immediately regretted her decision. Her heart sank as she looked up the wooden stairs that twisted up the hill out of sight. Three glasses of wine had not improved her mood as much as she might have liked, nor had her conversation with Henut-senu. The phone call from Mes had put a dent in her plans to go home and take a nice bath and go to bed early. Alone. A dull pain grew in her head.

Trudge trudge trudge. Half way up, Mes said. He was wrong: three goddamn quarters. Her calves were telling her she needed to up her workouts. Her head was telling her she should have stopped after one glass. Or zero glasses. Trudge trudge trudge.

She came to a little platform and path leading sideways with the number 34. She stopped to catch her breath, then stepped in through the little gate. Several trees obscured the house. When she came to the door, she realized the house extended down, not up. She was at the top floor of a three-level house climbing down the hill.

The door opened to her third ring, and she faced a middle-aged woman trying to appear younger and failing. Nose a little too big, chin a little too big, belly a little too big. Bloodshot, baggy eyes stared at her in dismay, then at her credentials.

"Hutyt MacIntyre? I thought all medjau were men. I thought I'd misheard that gentleman on the phone, what's his name?"

"Djehutymes, Idnu Djehutymes. No, quite a few women on the force now."

"That's right, Djehutymes. A nice man."

"You haven't met him."

"Well, no, I spoke with him on the phone."

Sitemhut didn't get it. Oh well. A sense of humor is as rare as a day in June, at least in MacIntyre's line of work.

"May I come in and ask you a few questions, Lady Sitemhut?"

"Oh, yes, of course, sorry for making you wait." The woman turned and led MacIntyre to a stairwell. "It's the stairs, I had to come up from the great room."

MacIntyre just smiled, her calves aching. More stairs. Shit. Down they went, to emerge into a large room with a picture window at least as big as Neferaset's but looking out to the islands in the bay.

"Nice view."

"Oh, thanks. It's the good part of living on Dju-Keta."

MacIntyre would not ask what the bad part was. She didn't care.

"Can we sit down?"

"Oh, certainly, sorry, I just get so wrapped up in things…. Would you like a drink?"

You bet I'd like a drink. Three or four. But I will not do that to my poor head.

"No, thanks." She settled into a very comfortable chair facing into the room so the view wouldn't distract her. Sitemhut perched on a couch and sipped a cocktail sitting on a small table.

"I was just having my first of the evening. Sure you won't…"

"No, thanks." Nothing like the first drink of the evening, but if this was her first, MacIntyre was a girl scout.

"Lady Sitemhut, I'd like to ask—"

"Oh, sorry, I need to go to the bathroom for a minute, hold that thought." The woman got up and hurried down a hallway. A door closed. Ten minutes later, after MacIntyre had exercised her neck to study the view, a door opened, and Sitemhut came back.

"Sorry, goes through me like water."

"Lady Sitemhut, I'd like to ask—"

"Sure you don't want a drink?"

MacIntyre fell back on her favorite tactic: silence. Talking wasn't getting her anywhere. She stared at the woman with as deadpan an expression as she could muster.

The silence lengthened. Sitemhut coughed and said, "I guess you want to ask about that lunch, with Neferaset, at that restaurant."

"Which restaurant?"

"Oh, sorry, I guess…um, you know, I don't know the name, it's on Mentju right up from that little dress shop, the one with—"

"The receipt will have the name."

Sitemhut's nose crinkled. "Receipt?"

"Piece of paper with your payment details."

Sitemhut sighed. "Oh, sorry, I didn't pay. Aset paid."

Of course she did.

"I'll check with her, then. What did you have?"

"Have?"

"What food did you eat?"

Alarm grew in Sitemhut's eyes. She closed them, opened them, and said in a breathy voice, "Fish. I had fish."

"What did Neferaset have?"

"She had fish too."

"Salmon? Trout? Cod? Halibut?"

"I…just fish. Fish."

Hmm. Maybe, but she didn't think so.

"Well, let's talk time. When did you get there?"

"Oh, sorry, around noon."

"Noon? And you stayed until 3."

"Oh, sorry, that's right, it must have been 2 or so, we were only there for an hour."

"Was it noon, or 2?"

"It, I guess, 2."

"Who waited on you?"

"Oh, sorry, I didn't notice." Dawning horror in the eyes as she realized that if you eat lunch in a restaurant, people see you and can testify to it.

"Man, woman, dog?"

"You don't have to be sarcastic."

Yeah, I do. "Ma'am, are you aware of the penalties for lying to an officer of the Temple of Ma'at? Religious and civil? Do you understand you can go to jail or the temple can flog you if you lie to us?" MacIntyre was lying about the flogging, but what the hell. Throw a scare into the bitch.

"I, I, no, I, sorry..." Words dribbled out of the mouth of the scared woman.

MacIntyre looked around. "You have a nice place here. Who's going to take care of it while you're in prison? Do you have health insurance, just in case, you know?"

"Prison, I don't, sorry, I can't...."

"Come on, Sitemhut. You didn't eat lunch with Neferaset, late or otherwise."

The woman looked at her feet, shaking her head.

"What did she pay you? How much?"

Eyes, terrified, looked at MacIntyre. "Pay? No, no, she just asked me for a favor, we've, she, we've known each other for a long time, she's helped me in so many ways. A small favor, she said."

"Did she tell you why?"

"She said she needed the favor and that it would take the pressure off her, because of the, you know, that young chef...."

"Her affair with Shesmu behind her husband's back?"

"Yes."

"So you lied to us."

"Yes."

"Where were you at 3?"

"Here."

"Anybody else here with you?"

"My cleaning woman was here."

"Great. Give me her name and phone, please."

She wrote the information down in the notebook.

"Now, see how easy telling the truth is? I need to ask a favor of you. Please don't talk to Neferaset at all in the next day or two. I can't make you do that, but we will note it in the Temple of Ma'at in your favor."

"Will I go to prison for this?" Now her entire body was shaking.

"No, I'll put in a word for you. If you stay quiet." A word like stupid idiot dumbass. No, that's three words. Wonderful words, but three of them. Jeez, her head hurt. And what do you think Neferaset was doing instead of eating a late lunch with the dumbass here? MacIntyre was pretty sure she knew.

"Oh, thank you, Idnu! Thank you!"

"Hutyt. Idnu's my boss. Well, I've got everything I need." She looked around. "Is there a back exit down to the Steps?"

"Oh, sorry, certainly. This way."

At least she saved herself another two flights up and two flights down. Trudge trudge trudge.

MacIntyre stood, irresolute, hand on the door of her little red car. She looked at the Neferti, lights ablaze, cheerful people talking at each other in the enormous picture windows.

What she wanted to do was go home and nurse herself back to health, or at least to a point where she resembled the dynamic and successful medjat personality she projected most of the time. What she had to do, despite this want, was to go back into the Neferti, brave Henutsenu's ire once more, and talk to Shesmu. Given the situation, both of them were likely to tell her to go to hell. The only way to do her job was to intimidate them with her badge and with the sheer force of her personality. After the disappointments of the day, and after trudging up and down those damn steps, the force of her personality had leaked away like a punctured tire.

She firmed up her mouth and walked over to the Neferti's front door, swung it open, and strode in as forcefully as possible. She put a pleasant smile on her face as she approached the hostess station. Henutsenu, standing behind the station engaging with a customer, saw her and stared briefly at her without expression. She then returned her attention to a shortish, red-faced, bullish individual. He said, "So how long is it going to be? I wish the owner were here, I'm a close friend, and I'm sure he wouldn't want me to wait very long."

"Sorry, sir, but the restaurant is fully booked. There's nothing I can do for you. I'd be happy to take reservations for a later date." A steel mace in a velvet cover, Henutsenu. She had all the elements essential to a great hostess: a warm personality, a hint of the exotic, a touch of vanity, a body that MacIntyre would die for. Critically, she could say no and keep on saying it.

The hungry almost-guest grimaced, again mentioned how the owner wouldn't like this, and took himself and his party off with only a few more ill-judged comments. Henutsenu turned to MacIntyre. No smile, but at least she didn't call the bouncer over to show her out. Yet.

MacIntyre said, "Sorry to bother you again, but we've had recent information, and I need to talk to Shesmu about it."

"He's busy."

"Now he's busier."

Henutsenu cocked her head. "You're pretty aggressive all of a sudden."

MacIntyre slumped and said, "Look, I've had a rotten day. I screwed up, OK? I drank too much, and I shoved my foot into my throat. I'm sorry. Can we do a reset? I need to talk to Shesmu. I won't beat him up or anything like that. Promise." She held up her right pinky, curled, but Henutsenu had no idea what a pinky promise was.

"You know, Cheryl, you are really quite the character." That assessment might be good or bad news. But the Remetjet picked up the phone on the hostess desk and punched in a number. "Hi, Khay, I need chef." She waited, then said, "Chef, the medjat is back and wants to talk to you. Yeah, OK, but she's insisting, promises not to hit you or anything." She listened, smiled, and hung up.

"He'll be along. Would you care to wait in the—"

"No. No, had enough of the bar today. I don't think the bartender likes me anymore. How about I just lean against the wall here and scare away your customers?"

Henutsenu smiled. "Quite the character. How about that wall over there?" She pointed, and MacIntyre slouched over, leaned against the wall, and shut her eyes. She heard Henutsenu giving the same polite, steel-edged refusal to another party with no reservation.

"Cheryl?"

MacIntyre's eyes snapped open. And there he was. White uniform, dark wavy hair, fierce eyes, charming lips.

"Aren't you supposed to be wearing one of those tall chef's hats? Part of the uniform?"

"Aren't you supposed to wear a gun belt and body armor? Same difference, both costumes make you look stupid."

OK, not in a compliant, helpful mood.

"Sorry, I'm always grumpy when I wake up."

"Must endear you to your bedmates."

OK, bad to worse.

"Let's keep this professional."

"Oh? And how do we keep it professional? Given your rotten attitude and all."

MacIntyre straightened up to her full height, which was about 2 inches under his, and said, "Let's take a walk, chef." She showed the front door to Shesmu with an outstretched arm, inviting him to leave his safe space and enter hers.

The chef glanced at Henutsenu and said, "If I'm not back in 15 minutes, Henutsenu, call 111 and report a kidnapping." Henutsenu smiled and waved them out the front door.

Outside, MacIntyre looked around, then said, "Let's go over to the little park across the street, nobody there."

"Right."

They crossed the street and walked out along the pier sticking into the bay, a park designed for lovers wanting sea air and a magnificent view.

"I've never been to this park before, I missed it despite years in Menmenet," she said, setting the mood.

"Hutyt, I've got 15 cooks burning things in my kitchen. I need to be there. Henutsenu said you have questions. Ask."

"You are one prickly, rude son-of-a-bitch, chef," said MacIntyre.

"Don't call me chef."

"Don't call me hutyt."

"Ask."

"Now we have proof Neferaset killed your friend the master chef, we need your help to confirm it."

"She didn't."

"She did."

His eyes were dark in the evening light. "She didn't kill her husband, she loved him."

"This, from you? Who was seeing her behind his back?"

"She loved me too. Loves."

"I'd watch my back, if I were you. Anyway, I thought you broke up."

"*She* broke up. She loves me, she just has…issues, right now."

"Yeah, the big one being how she's going to rot away in prison for the rest of her life."

"What have you got, MacIntyre?"

"Don't call me that."

"You're reducing me to words you don't want to hear."

"Rude. Anyway, she's guilty. We broke her alibi. She's got nothing between her and a prison cell except a court hearing. Give me one good reason we should think she didn't do it."

"I know her. Intimately. For years. Two years, at least. She's kind, she's gentle, she—"

"Wouldn't hurt a fly, right? Your sous chef says the same thing about you."

He ignored this personal remark and rejoined, "She is not a person who would cut a man's throat. She's passionate, but I've never seen her that angry. And she loved Nekhen. Even if she needed more, she loved him, she needed him. That's why we kept everything secret."

"Not very, according to everyone I've spoken with so far. That's one question: did Nekhen know?"

"Not to my knowledge. I saw him two days ago, right before I left for my demos, and he was unchanged." Shesmu grimaced. "I wasn't aware everybody was gossiping about us behind our backs. I guess that's the fate of most secrets, isn't it?"

MacIntyre repeated, "Did he know?"

Shesmu just shook his head and looked at the islands in the bay. "I hope not."

"But it's possible."

"Any damn thing is possible, hut—Cheryl. Cheryl?"

"Nice. Shes?" She looked at him with a coyness she'd practiced in a mirror.

"You've practiced that in a mirror."

"Shit. Rude."

"Sorry, Cheryl. Ask."

"What did she say when she called you? Last night?"

"Only that Nekhen was dead, his throat cut, and she wasn't OK. She mentioned something about the medjau, then said she needed to break off the relationship." He clamped his lips.

"What else?"

He didn't look at her. "That she didn't love me anymore."

"Now that she had money? Nekhen's money, the house, the restaurant?"

"Aset's not like that!"

"Did you get uglier? Beat her up? Tell her she needs to take more baths? Why did she not love you anymore?"

"I'm not sure. And I want her back." That popped out; Shesmu looked appalled at his own admission and clamped his lips again.

"Is that it? Nothing else?"

"Nothing. I haven't spoken to her since then. She…isn't returning my calls."

"Well, hell, that's sad. Here." MacIntyre handed him one of her cards. "I'll return your calls if you're ready to tell me anything you think I'd like to hear. Or if you need to talk. That's my mobile number, there."

Shesmu didn't seem inclined to take her up on this offer. "We're finished?"

"For now. Thanks for your help, Shes. We appreciate it. *I* appreciate it."

"She didn't do it, Cheryl."

"Sure she did."

CHAPTER EIGHT
Shesmu Pleads His Case

I POUNDED ON ASET'S DOOR with the darkness of the Tjesut all around me. Even if she called the medjau and had me taken away in chains, I had to talk to her. At least I didn't need to worry about the neighbors. They were so far away they wouldn't hear a bomb go off in Nekhen's mansion. I pounded some more.

The light above my head in the papyrus-columned portico went on. I knew Aset was looking at me through the spyhole in the door and I smiled at it. The door opened a crack.

"Shesmu. What are you doing here?"

"Knocking."

"I told you, I don't want to talk to you."

"Let me in, Aset. We need to talk."

"No, we don't. I made it clear—"

"Nothing is clear, Aset. Let me in."

"No!"

I stuck my hand in the crack so that if she closed the door, she'd have at least one or two of my fingers to remember me by. I didn't push my luck by trying to shoulder in the door. She had to want to talk to me, I couldn't force her to do it.

"Take your hand out!"

"No."

Exasperated sigh. "Shesmu, I will call the medjau if you do not remove your hand."

"Aset, you are going to have the medjau all over you, if not tonight, then tomorrow. We need to talk about that."

"What do you mean?"

"I mean they think you killed Nekhen and they're ready to do something about it."

"They can't—"

"Take my word, they can. Let me in, I'll tell you."

Silence for a few seconds, then the door opened, revealing Aset dressed for the evening, illuminated by the light in the portico. She had her long hair down, and she wore an elegant sheath that showed off everything. Framed against her stately mansion, she looked like a goddess, the goddess Aset.

But there was no time.

She stepped back to let me in. We walked about a mile back into the house to the Great Room. The vast picture window was dark and reflected the room rather than the stunning outside view to the north. I'd been here once, at a party that Nekhen gave when he and I opened the Neferti. I had never been here since; Aset and I did not use his house for our trysts.

Aset waved a hand at the couch and sat in an armchair. Her face was grim, as grim as I'd ever seen it. Her eyes were puffy and her expression dejected. It had only been yesterday when she walked into the house to find Nekhen's decapitated corpse. I raised a hand and lowered it again.

She said, "So, talk. Tell me what you need to, then go."

"Aset…why? I love you. I want you, want to be with you forever."

She got up. "This is why I didn't want to talk with you, Shes. It won't do any good. Now you just get out of here."

"Please, please. All right, I'll get to the point. Please sit down and listen."

She lowered herself back into her seat, but her face had anger in it now, not dejection.

"Look, Aset—I was at the Neferti this evening, and a medjat, a blonde American, Cheryl McIntyre, came to question the staff. She came back later and took me off to interrogate me."

"That one. She didn't like me."

"No, I don't think she liked you. She's quick and plays dirty. She moves too fast."

Aset smiled a contemptuous smile. "You like her. Why don't you run after *her* instead of running after me, Shes?"

"Aset, please. Please, please, please. *Listen* to me."

"I'm listening, but you've said nothing of interest so far."

"She said your alibi, they've broken your alibi."

Aset's face took on a look I'd never seen on it. Perhaps fear? Distress?

"I've got to make a call." She got up and left the room. After a minute, I heard her voice rising in distress. "Oh, Sit, no! No. You didn't." I got up and walked toward her voice. I found her in the kitchen holding her phone by her side, her face stricken and pale.

"Aset?" Not able to help myself, I strode up to her and took her in my arms. She froze, melted, then straightened and pushed me away.

"No, Shes! I can't. Not here!"

I looked around and saw a mop and bucket.

"Was this…?"

She looked at a spot on the floor. She pointed. "Right there. I spent most of the day cleaning and polishing and working to get everything perfect again. The blood, it was everywhere, in every crack, telling me I had betrayed Nekhen, over and over and over."

I reached, but she held up her hands and looked aside. "No, Shes. Don't touch me."

I was out of my depth. One thing was obvious: if I wanted anything rational from her, I had to get her out of this kitchen.

"Come on, Aset, let's go back to the Great Room."

She walked over to the little breakfast table near the window and pulled out a chair and sat. I walked over and tried to do the same.

"Not that one, that's—" She stopped and her eyes were large, looking at me, and her face got frantic. If I couldn't touch her, what could I do? Wait. So I waited.

"Sit, sit there. In that one." She had dominated the emotions overwhelming her. She pointed at one of the other places at the table. I sat.

"My alibi…I got a friend to say we were at lunch. She says she told the medjat the truth because she got tangled up in the lies. We didn't think it out."

"Why, Aset? Why do that?"

"The medjau, all the questions, I thought if I had a good alibi they'd leave me alone and wouldn't find out."

"Find what out?"

Aset sat up straight and looked alarmed. "No, I can't tell you, I shouldn't have said that. I, please leave, Shes, I'm a complete mess."

"Aset, they're going to come to arrest you, I'm sure of it."

"I'm so tired, so tired."

"What will they find, Aset?"

"Nothing, Shes. Nothing."

"What will they find?" I insisted.

She shook her head and looked away from me.

"Aset," I said, hating myself with every word, "did you kill him? Please tell me you didn't kill Nekhen."

"You too, Shes?" She looked at me with that contemptuous smile again, her neck straight.

"No, I don't believe it. You couldn't kill Nekhen or anyone else."

"Thanks for that, anyway. And no, I didn't kill my husband."

"Then what, Aset?"

"I can't, can't tell you, Shes. The secret. I can't."

Way, way out of my depth and not breathing too well underwater. I could only abase myself so far, plead just so much. How far would I go for this woman? I'd lie, I'd lie three times to that nice, steely American medjat for her. The trouble was, I had nothing to lie about. I had no idea what was going on.

Aset collected herself and looked at my confusion and distress. It did nothing but set her resolve.

"Come on, Shes, I'll show you out." Aset got up and walked out. I got up and followed with nothing left to say. She took me to the front door.

"I don't want to see you again, Shes."

"Please, Aset. I love you!"

"Goodbye, Shes." She opened the door and waited. I dragged my feet through, and she closed the door behind me. I stood in the foggy Menmenet night. The light in the portico blinked out. I wept in the darkness.

CHAPTER NINE
MacIntyre Closes the Case

MacIntyre got the call from Djehutymes shortly after a skimpy breakfast and three pain pills to ease her hangover.

"Meet me at the Tjesut mansion, MacIntyre. Twenty minutes."

"Mes, give me a break. What's so—"

"We're arresting her, MacIntyre. For murder."

"About time, too."

"Meet me." He disconnected.

MacIntyre pulled up behind the big medja cruiser just as Djehutymes levered himself out of its door. She climbed out of her car and walked over to him.

He said, "I've got the warrant of Ma'at, the hem-netjer signed it last night right after I talked with you about the alibi. We'll go up, knock, I'll give her the bad news, you put on the cuffs and we'll take her."

"OK."

"Oh, and you'll be interested in this." He smiled.

"What?"

"The knife. The one with the wooden handle next to the body?"

"What about it?"

"Crime lab came back and said that they worked with the Sekhmet-Hut-Her folks and it wasn't the one."

"Wasn't the one what?"

"Wasn't the knife that killed him. Something about edge angles and metal particles."

"Jeez."

"Yeah. It turns out to be hard to prove a knife did a job but easier to prove it didn't. Also, the knife had lots of fingerprints, all his."

"He was holding it when he got—"

"I figured that out too, MacIntyre. Well, we don't have a murder weapon, so we need to search the whole damn house. Look at the thing, it must have 100 rooms."

"I'll handcuff her and put her in the car and guard her while you do it, Mes."

"Ha. Ha." He looked at the house. "We're waiting for the criminalists. They'll do it."

The criminalists showed up in their van, and the medjau got to work. Djehutymes and MacIntyre took the Wife into custody with no problem. She seemed to expect them, even to wearing clothes that could stand up to a night in jail. She was as elegant as MacIntyre remembered, just a touch puffier and paler and not quite so queen-like. Maybe the murder had hit home with her. When they got her down to the temple, she'd break.

Djehutymes read the Wings of Ma'at, the set of rights that Ma'at gave every arrested suspect. The Wife phoned a sehy and asked him to meet her at the Temple of Ma'at.

MacIntyre put extra pressure on the cuffs out of frustration. The Wife complained, Mes looked at MacIntyre with a frown, and she eased them up. She took the Wife down to the cruiser, one hand on her right arm. MacIntyre noticed a neighbor looking out a huge window from next door and smiled at them. The neighbor's face disappeared.

"My front door," said the Wife.

"We'll make sure everything is secure, ma'am, after we finish up."

"Finish what up?"

"See those guys?"

The Wife looked at the van.

"Criminalists. They went over the kitchen yesterday. Today they'll take apart the rest of the house."

"Take apart?" The Wife stopped, and MacIntyre pushed her arm to get her going again.

"Figure of speech. Over to the car, ma'am. Back door."

"But—"

"Standard procedure, ma'am. We'll make sure we damage nothing. Beyond what is necessary." MacIntyre had learned early on not to be too reassuring. It turned out upset people concerned about their house and belongings being trawled by the medjau were much more likely to have their defenses down in the interrogation. As true for rich people as for the usual suspects.

"But my sehy—"

"He'll meet you at the temple, ma'am, now just get in the car, please, ma'am." She held open the door and did the head-push thing. The woman looked up at her with fearful eyes as she closed the door. She heard the lock click as the driver locked it. God, the woman was stunning, even at 8 in the morning being arrested for murder after crying herself stupid. Sometimes this job just made you sick with envy.

"MacIntyre, get your butt up here! Now!"

Back to work.

Djehutymes was the best interrogator in Menmenet. He did things by the book and got his confessions easily. MacIntyre, his apprentice, had yet to learn how to be less innovative. Her creativity rarely played well before the hemu-netjer of Ma'at at the trial.

"Listen more, then shut up," was Djehutymes's advice to her before every interrogation.

For this one, he had a request.

"This one, a woman's intuition might help sort the barley, so stay alert and write what you feel, OK?"

"Happy to, Mes."

"Keep your mouth shut. Look threatening. She doesn't like you. Push her toward me, her best friend."

She stuck her tongue out at him when he wasn't looking. Childish but stress reducing.

The tiny, soundproof interrogation room had four chairs and a table. Two of the chairs were normal office chairs; those were for the detectives. The others were folding chairs bent to be wobbly, with seats designed to create intolerable pain in the human butt. Those were for the suspect and her (or his) sehy. The wall color was a sickly, pale yellow, with nothing on them to brighten the place up aside from a mirror that was a one-way glass observation window. The air smelled of disinfectant and vomit. MacIntyre had asked; the janitors smiled and said no one had ever vomited there and something about their secret ingredient. No thermostat inside the room, and the room kept on the hot side. And there was the tea and coffee on offer. Nothing would ever make MacIntyre touch that stuff.

Net result: one desperately uncomfortable murderer. Suspect, that is. Assumptions. Open mind. Mouth shut. MacIntyre repeated this mantra to herself as she waited by the door. The door at the end of the hall swung open, and Djehutymes came through, followed by the Wife, followed by a uniformed medjat. They walked down the hall, the Wife looking straight ahead with a determined expression. A small, bald man, the Wife's sehy, followed this little group. He was expressionless, with a long and gaunt face. Despite his Remetjy name, Nebemhep, the sehy was Persian or Assyrian and wore a large, gray mustache.

After the preliminaries, Djehutymes got down to business fast. Nebemhep said little but kept the questioning corralled. A good sehy, if that wasn't an oxymoron. MacIntyre, in reality just bored, put on a grim and angry face.

Djehutymes was a master of interrogation. He turned on the electronic recording, then started out with basic questions about the Wife's former life in Kemet. He then moved on to how she wound up in Menmenet marrying the celebrity chef Nekhen. This questioning set a baseline for them to help interpret her body language. She started out stiff and unresponsive but thawed out to Djehutymes's avuncular persona. MacIntyre wished he'd use it more often with herself. She kept up a disapproving stare and got narrowed eyes and the occasional nervous glance from the Wife in return. Nebemhep's responses ranged from bland to sharp as Djehutymes got closer to the murder, the Wife truthful and willing to talk. The trouble started when Djehutymes got to the affair.

"When did you meet Shesmu, Neferaset?"

The Wife's eyes moved right, then back. Remembering. "I guess—when I was at the Per'ankh."

"You said you became hostess there two years ago, in November?"

"That's right."

"And you met Shesmu that first night on the job?"

She smiled, remembering. "No, the day I came for an interview. He, well, he dropped a box trying to open the door for me. I flustered him."

"So there was a mutual attraction even then?"

She closed up, realizing where this was going. Pause. Thinking, not remembering. "No—He was just a helpful cook at the restaurant, nothing special."

MacIntyre wrote on her pad, "*Shesmu, helpful cook??*" The wife glanced at her writing with a grimace. She'd lied: Shesmu attracted her right then. So why…. MacIntyre wrote, "*Lie. Wife married the famous chef for the money but wanted Shesmu in bed.*"

This went on for some time. As the questioning probed deeper into the affair between Shesmu and the Wife, each mention of her husband left her more distressed. MacIntyre started a tally-mark count of eye-shifts and mouth twitches, just to be doing something. This unnerved the Wife. More eye glances toward MacIntyre, more distracted and incoherent answers to Djehutymes's questions.

"Had your husband ever asked you about something that made you think he knew about the affair?"

The Wife answered, "I tried—we were very discreet. He—Nekhen—he was very busy with his restaurant and career as a celebrity chef, away from me for days sometimes. It was…one reason for the affair. I guess I got bored roaming around the mansion alone, and girlfriends weren't enough." The ring of truth, there. MacIntyre smiled at that one. Pure heterosexuals were disadvantaged, at least in the love stakes. The Wife looked at her with growing anger. MacIntyre did not write this time, just snorted.

"You don't have to be snarky about it, Hutyt. I made a mistake, I'm paying for it now."

"MacIntyre," warned Djehutymes with semi-wink. "Please stay civil."

"Yes, Idnu." She ducked her head in a pretense of deference and put on an unhappy face, chortling inside.

The Wife talked about her husband with respect and admiration, even love. Djehutymes probed around different areas of their lives together, but nothing showed she was unhappy; the remark about being bored was her only rationale for the affair. Now that MacIntyre had spent time with Shesmu, she had a good idea of his strengths and weaknesses. He was a lover, not a casual partner. Not a boy toy. That wouldn't interest him. And he loved the Wife, he'd said so several times. She wrote, "*Shesmu lover of bored housewives??? Swamp woman? Sex addict? Goddess?*" Something there must have attracted Shesmu, more than the good looks. The Wife tried for him. She didn't fall into bed with him. Maybe he tried for her, seduced her—no. MacIntyre looked at the Wife's elegant, lovely face and body and wrote, "*Seducer, not seduced. Swamp woman.*"

MacIntyre got up to stretch and deliberately walked behind the Wife. You could see the elegant neck twitch as the Wife got more nervous when she couldn't see her. The sehy gave her a flick of the eyes with a bored smile under the mustache. He'd seen it all before. He put a hand on the Wife's arm, patting it to settle her down.

Djehutymes wove the Nekhen-Neferaset-Shesmu triangle love affair story together like a romance novelist, building it up until it mesmerized MacIntyre with the hot-and-heavy action. Nebemhep was immune. Read legal textbooks rather than light romances for leisure, for sure. MacIntyre started another tally as Djehutymes delved into times and places of trysts over the last year. Things had picked up three months ago, but then the Wife pulled back, seeing Shesmu less often. MacIntyre wrote on her pad, "*Guilty guilty guilty. ???*" Was the swamp woman guilty, though? Or had something happened?

It went by so fast she almost missed it; only Djehutymes's eyes told her. The Wife was lying.

"Now, Neferaset, that isn't true." The first confrontation.

"Yes, I, certainly it's true, Idnu," said the flustered woman. It flabbergasted the Wife that Djehutymes didn't believe her.

MacIntyre wrote, "*Female ego the size of a house. A mansion of ego.*"

"Just answer the Idnu's questions, Aset," interjected Nebemhep. He didn't say truthfully, what sehy ever said truth was important? MacIntyre wrote, "*Sehy knows.*"

"Why did you refuse to meet Shesmu for a tryst that Monday? Had he said or done something wrong?"

"No, no, I was, I couldn't face it. That day."

"What was hard about that day?"

Long pause. Eyes everywhere except on Djehutymes, or on MacIntyre. She turned to Nebemhep. "Do I have to answer irrelevant questions?"

"You don't have to answer any questions, Aset."

She turned back to Djehutymes. "I won't answer that one. It's personal and not relevant."

MacIntyre wrote, "*Personal and relevant and way too upset—secret?*"

"And did this irrelevant fact keep you from seeing Shesmu? You pulled back, why?"

"It, no, yes, I—it had to stop, but we were so involved, it was hard. Shesmu—I cared about him, I didn't want to hurt him, but—"

"Why did you have to stop?"

"My husband—" The wife jolted to a stop, her throat wouldn't let the air through.

"Your husband suspected something?"

"No, no—"

"Please, Neferaset, you must listen and tell the truth. Ma'at will weigh your heart against the truth. In the Duat. Everyone at the Per'ankh knew about the affair. Nekhen knew." Laying it on thick, pressing his advantage.

She disregarded this. She was somewhere else. "He, he showed me something I wasn't aware of, something personal. Nothing to do with all this." The Wife's body language got stiff and self-protective. MacIntyre wrote "*Something. Personal.*

Truth, but everything to do with murder. Key key key!!!" The Wife jumped at MacIntyre's sharp movements underlining the words and slashing her exclamation points.

Djehutymes kept right on it. "You need to tell us about that, Neferaset. He's dead now, it can only help his ka go forth by day." Djehutymes's voice enticed her to answer. "Think of Ma'at and tell the truth. All the truth."

The Wife shook her head with gritted teeth.

"Let's move on to the present." Djehutymes moved on; MacIntyre knew they'd be back. "How did your feelings toward Shesmu change after that?"

Eyes left. Not remembering, thinking. MacIntyre wrote, *"Making up feelings. Hasn't got any, narcissistic. Guilty guilty guilty. Shesmu?"* MacIntyre fantasized about what it would be like if Shesmu were in the room. Squirm? Anger? Appalled realization that his lover was an emotional desert waiting for a flash flood? Poor bastard.

The Wife stuttered, "Nekhen, I, I—I had feelings for Shesmu, but my, Nekhen, I realized I loved him and I—could hurt him."

"So you told him about the affair?" At Neferaset's attempt to deny this, Djehutymes held up his hand. "Listen: you told him about the affair, and he started abusing you. You couldn't help yourself. It got worse and worse until yesterday."

"No," she said, with a rise in her voice. "He was wonderful, he loved me, he would never hurt me."

"I understand, ma'am. Sometimes people get to places where they can't control themselves, even wonderful people. It could happen to anyone. Anyone." MacIntyre wrote, *"It happened to you. Out-of-control hate. Then the knife."*

"But—"

"Let's talk about the last couple of weeks, Neferaset. How many times did you meet Shesmu during the last two weeks?"

Rattled, the Wife spent a minute remembering. "Only twice, twice…"

"Did you tell Shesmu you'd told your husband?" Before she answered, Djehutymes said, "How did Shesmu feel about all this?"

"He—"

"Don't answer that, Aset," said Nebemhep. "Idnu, what Shesmu felt only he knows."

"This isn't the Court of Ma'at, Nebemhep. Let me ask it another way, Neferaset: did Shesmu say something about having doubts, anybody talking to him about the affair? Did he tell you there was trouble ahead?"

"Yes—no—he could have mentioned somebody on his staff, I can't remember when he said that, I wasn't paying attention, I was…." The Wife gulped, stopped speaking, and her eyes…. MacIntyre wrote *"Not paying attention, thinking about sex remembering sex."* There was a look in her eye…was Shesmu that good in bed? To screw him even when her husband knew? The points in this love triangle appeared damn sharp to her. As sharp as a knife.

"What were you thinking about, Neferaset? Your husband? What he knew?" Again the start of a shake of the head, and Djehutymes interrupted before she could deny it. "So how did you hurt him? How did you hurt your husband?"

"I—won't answer that." Same self-protective body language.

"Secret again," wrote MacIntyre. *"Thinking about secret, not about screwing Shesmu, secret bigger than dirty sex??? Hurting husband with knife. Husband's secret made her hate him? Knife knife knife."* MacIntyre took a skeptical glance at the Wife, and the Wife appeared as though she was close to tears, shaking, lips pressed tight.

"Idnu, can we take a break?" The sehy patted his client's arm to reassure her.

"Sure, counselor. Interview paused at 1:32 p.m." He turned off the electronic recording. MacIntyre closed her notebook and took it up in her hand. "Come on, MacIntyre, let's give the lady a chance to recover." As though he cared. Djehutymes arose and patted Neferaset on the back. "Take your time, ma'am, take your time. We'll be back soon." MacIntyre rose, threw another nasty, suspicious look at the Wife for good measure, and followed her boss out of the room. As he left, he said to one of the medjau outside, "Bring in some tea, please, for our guests." Oh, God. The coup de grâce.

Djehutymes took a call, his side of which was a series of grunts. Disconnecting, he said, "Crime lab. The only knives they found were in a kitchen drawer, standard kitchen knives. They've sent a couple to the lab, but they're not expecting anything from them."

"Where the hell is the murder weapon, then?" asked MacIntyre. Hard to make a strong case without a murder weapon traceable to the murderer.

"Another question for the lady in there," replied Djehutymes, looking at Neferaset through the one-way window. Neferaset took a sip of tea and made a face. MacIntyre was sure it was the face of a murderer, however beautiful.

"I don't think she likes the tea, Mes," said MacIntyre.

Djehutymes said, "When we go back in I'm going straight to the alibi, take her through it, get her to tell us where she was. With any luck, she'll head straight into confessing to murder, but if not, we'll still have a confession to impeding Ma'at. And I'll get her to tell me what she did with the knife. Let's see your notes."

MacIntyre handed him her notebook. He looked at the English scribble and handed it back.

"Read 'em to me in Renkemet, MacIntyre."

They got through the notes. He had her go back and read a few of them again. "What are your impressions of this guy Shesmu?"

"I like him. He's sweet."

Djehutymes got a funny look on his face, opened his mouth and closed it. He rubbed his brow and said, "What is your professional opinion about Shesmu's testimony, Hutyt?" MacIntyre realized he thought she'd gone soft on Shesmu. Hah—maybe so. Nice lips. But truthful lips? Hum.

"He's as much of a liar as any other man I've met. Seems to love the Wife, though, despite her treating him like shit, I don't think he's lying about that. So he's got to be naïve, or else—"

Djehutymes raised a hand. "Never mind. I don't want to know."

Her boss wasn't interested in her incisive analysis of Shesmu's romantic feelings and general approach toward sex with swamp women. Well, it was all grist for the barley mill. The Wife was guilty as hell, and nothing Shesmu had to contribute, sweet or not, would matter that much unless the Wife implicated him.

"Let's go, MacIntyre." Djehutymes led the way back into the interrogation room. The Wife looked apprehensive, Nebemhep bland. He had not touched his tea, and the Wife had stopped after the first sip. The two medjau took their seats.

Djehutymes asked, "Is the tea all right? I can get you freshly brewed tea, if you like."

Both Nebemhep and his client declined this kind offer, which left the Wife thinking Djehutymes was a nice man. A mistake on her part. Nebemhep just smiled, not fooled.

"Interview resumed at 1:45 pm. Now, Neferaset, let's go through the events of the day of the murder, day before yesterday."

Djehutymes took the Wife through the story of her day: Nekhen's breakfast with her, his departure for his restaurant, a lunch heated in a microwave at home. He moved on to a trip to the local market for a packaged dinner for herself, as her husband wouldn't be home until late.

"So, at 2:00, you're at home, having put your dinner in the refrigerator. Where did you go next?" The Wife looked down without speaking. Djehutymes continued, "You told me yesterday that you were out to a late lunch with a friend. Hutyt MacIntyre discovered that was a lie. Why did you get your friend Sitemhut to lie for you?"

Neferaset opened her mouth, but Nebemhep interrupted. "Let's not talk about that, Aset."

"Why not, counselor?" asked Djehutymes. "We've proved the lie with testimony from Sitemhut."

Nebemhep put his hand on the Wife's arm, and she stayed silent.

Djehutymes came at it from another direction. "Where did you go, Neferaset? Since you weren't with Sitemhut."

"I…can't tell you."

"Neferaset, that's the crucial time. Your husband left his restaurant at 2:15 p.m. to go home, which would have taken him 15 minutes from the Per'ankh restaurant location. Did he have a car?"

"Yes, his own car. It's in the garage, he must have driven it there. I…haven't looked in it."

"We have. There's nothing there to show why he came home. And you were unaware of his coming?"

"Yes—that is, I, I had no idea, I would have stayed…."

"Where did you go after 2? To meet Shesmu?"

"No, he was away…he was giving a cooking demonstration in Niut Shepesu. I had…I went…I can't tell you."

"Were you meeting another lover? Who was it?"

The Wife jumped and said, "No! No, Idnu, I'm not a—I was only seeing Shesmu!" Nebemhep again laid a calming hand on her arm, stopping her from justifying herself more. MacIntyre wrote, "*Sensitive about sleeping around, God knows why. Swamp woman with conscience???*"

"No, I was not seeing another lover."

"You didn't leave the house, did you? You were there when he got there. You argued, and then you killed him."

"No! No. No." The Wife clutched her hands. "I wasn't there. I came back at 5 and…found him." As she remembered the scene, the Wife appeared stricken. Was she remembering the slash of the knife, the spurting blood, her frenzied cleaning of her clothes? MacIntyre wrote, "*Emotions, blood. No tears.*"

"Was there much blood?" Djehutymes's voice was matter of fact.

"It was all over the kitchen."

"How did you feel when you saw it spurting out?"

She looked up. "I found him…on the floor. Blood everywhere. I found him." Remembering. "I called you."

"The dispatch log says you called at 5:30. What were you doing between 5 and 5:30? It doesn't take a half hour to dial 111."

"I…" Thinking, not remembering. "I don't remember. I just remember calling. I must have just stood there for a while." Lying. MacIntyre gave her a grunt of disbelief.

"I don't remember. I found him, I called."

"What did you do with the knife?"

"Knife—that wasn't there, it was—no, I can't talk about that." She paused and said, "What knife?"

MacIntyre wrote, "*Strange reaction to knife. Too much for her???*"

"The knife you killed him with. Where did you hide it?"

"I didn't kill him!"

"Where did you put the knife?"

"There was, er, it was his chef's knife, on the floor. I didn't touch it."

"That's not the knife that killed him and you know it."

"Not?" The Wife looked bewildered, her face a blank. "What do you mean?"

"What did you do with the knife you used to kill him? We didn't find it in your house, so where did you take it and when?"

"I did nothing with it! I found him and called you. It must be there somewhere, or the murderer took it away." Eyes left, thinking furiously, something going on there. MacIntyre wrote, "*She knows where the knife is??? Or not?*"

Nebemhep interjected, "That line of questioning is not productive, Idnu. Let's move on."

"We can't make any progress with your client not telling us where she was at the time of the murder. We can only assume she was there murdering her husband. Because she faked an alibi, her 'late lunch.'"

"I wasn't, I didn't! I couldn't! I was scared you'd find out, that's why I lied—" Nebemhep grabbed her arm strongly, but it was too late, she'd admitted she lied.

"Find out what? Why don't you tell us where you were?"

"It's personal, very personal, very…I promised Nekhen…."

"When did you promise?"

Her eyes shifted, remembering. "Two weeks…"

"When you told him about Shesmu? And slowed down your affair with Shesmu?"

"No, no! He told me—Nekhen—I can't tell you."

"What did you promise Nekhen?"

"I can't tell you."

"Neferaset, he's dead and readying himself for the journey to the Duat. You have only your obligations to his ka, promises aren't important anymore. Tell me what you promised him. Tell me why that made you kill him. Help his journey into the Duat."

Nebemhep again restrained the Wife from answering, and she pressed her lips tightly together, but she still had the bewildered look. MacIntyre wrote, *"Confused, doesn't know which way to look, not confessing—guilty or not??? Evidence????"*

Djehutymes sat back in his chair. He looked at MacIntyre, who shrugged. She had to admit, Neferaset's odd responses and her unwillingness to confess to a perfectly reasonable murder had her wondering. Djehutymes looked done, though.

He was. "Interview concluded at 3:02 p.m." He turned off the recorder. "Neferaset, we are charging you with the religious offense of impeding the path of Ma'at. Sitemhut's confession and your own admitting that you gave false information to a medja justify that. You will be bound over for judgment in the religious Court of Ma'at. We've informed you of your religious and civil rights and your sehy is here. Do you wish to consult with him before we take you to the jail?"

Her eyes wild, the Wife looked at Nebemhep, who nodded with a resigned expression. MacIntyre could tell he was not that pleased with his client.

She said, "Yes, I...please don't do this!"

"I'm afraid it's unavoidable, Neferaset, without your cooperation. We'll speak again once you've thought things through. Come on, MacIntyre."

The two medjau arose and guided Nebemhep and his client to an interview room. MacIntyre knew it wouldn't be long until Nebemhep got her bailed out. People like Neferaset didn't stay in the jail very long for religious offenses. A few debenu in the right palm and the temple would be happy to deal. But the Wife wouldn't be able to leave Menmenet until the court resolved the charge.

It was a puzzle what else they could do. The lack of evidence and a confession were enough to shake her certainty that the Wife was guilty. They couldn't get a conviction on a murder charge with the evidence they had.

As they walked back to the homicide squad office, Djehutymes said, "Well, I couldn't get her to go all the way and confess to murder. The hem-netjer will accept the impedance charge for now with the evidence we have from Sitemhut. We need to get more on the murder, though—be nice to get the knife and evidence that she handled it and was there. I guess we can hope for DNA from something the criminalists gathered, but it's hopeless given it's her house. I don't think there's much more we can do unless something changes her mind and makes her confess or tell us her secret. I'll have to put you on another case for now. Huh. Long day. Why don't you take the rest of the day off, let's talk tomorrow about next steps." He smiled. "I got a nice gang murder case for you."

CHAPTER TEN
Shesmu Grieves for a Friend

I JOINED THE FUNERAL PROCESSION as it descended the necropolis hill through the swirling morning fog. Aset and the Hem-Netjer of Inpu led the procession behind the electric cart with Nekhen's sarcophagus, the gold leaf glistening as it caught the few, feeble glimmers of R'a that broke through the haze.

The professional mourners followed the cart and wailed and tore at their clothes as Aset had paid them to do, and they made a fine job of it. I was in a little group of Nekhen's employees from the Per'ankh, following the mourners. I could only catch glimpses of Aset as she walked down the hill, but even those brief sightings hit me hard. Aset didn't love me anymore.

That refrain played over and over in my heart. Each step down the hill past the enormous array of chapels and tombs of the necropolis played a variation on it.

Rich families could afford to build their chapels and tombs deep into the highest levels on the hill, right below the massive Temple of Inpu at its rocky crest. The elaborate chapels shouted out their wealth and power. Nekhen's chapel and tomb lay part-way down the hill in the precinct for the people with lots of money who worked for a living.

The upshot was that I had a good, long walk to obsess over Aset. She stunned me with her beauty, even in the fog, even mourning for her dead husband. Her red mourning dress sheathed that glorious body that I knew so well, her every move torturing me with the loss of her love. Her long, black hair was down in the current funeral custom, just the way she wore it in bed.

We neared the turn into the street that held Nekhen's chapel. I forced my attention away from my lost love to my lost friend heading to his fate in the Duat. The image on the foot end of the sarcophagus depicted Nebethut, one of the Djerty, the Two Kites. The head end depicted Aset, the other Kite, the goddess-sister of Wesir. These two goddesses guided and protected the ka of the dead person through the trials and tribulations of the journey to the Judgment of Wesir, the god of the underworld. The goddess Aset, the woman Aset a goddess in her own right. I again forced my mind away from the woman to the mummy and its ka.

Each tomb had its own chapel, with varying degrees of ornate architecture and decoration. Nekhen's was little more than a simple stone wall facing the street. It had a door and a wide stairway and two small papyrus-shaped columns. The stairway had two narrow ramps for rolling the sarcophagus up into the chapel. The inside walls told the story of Nekhen's life. There was a hetep altar for offerings and a false-door niche above it which gave entry and exit to the ka. In the back of the chapel, a great door sealed the tomb built into the hill behind the chapel. It was the final destination today for the sarcophagus carrying the mummy of my friend and mentor.

Thinking of the ka made me think of Nekhen. Thinking of the man made me think of my transgressions toward him. I needed to atone; I needed to spend time in the chapel and make my offerings. It was an opportunity to tell the ka why I did what I did, why I regretted it, and why I couldn't leave it alone. Aset was so beautiful.

"Who's that?" said the man next to me, one of the line cooks that had worked under me when I was sous chef at the Per'ankh. He pointed up the hill at the Temple of Inpu.

I craned my neck a little and saw what he was pointing at: the small figure that stood at the observation platform balustrade and looked down at us through binoculars. The tousled, shoulder-length blonde hair and American pant-suit told me who it was: Hutyt MacIntyre, on the job. A tigress, a lioness, a crocodile, waiting for her prey. My heart told me the hutyt would harass Aset into prison, if not into her own tomb. Aset, who didn't love me anymore.

"Must be a tourist," I said to my friend. I didn't want to talk about it.

We arrived at the chapel, and the professional mourners melted away in the fog. Silence descended, only to be broken at once by the hem-netjer and his two w'ab priests as they intoned the rituals for the dead. The hem-netjer performed the Opening-of-the-Mouth ceremony on the mummy and closed the sarcophagus. His w'abu pushed the rolling cart holding the sarcophagus into the chapel and through the great door into the tomb. It trundled out of sight of us all, Nekhen's last journey in our world.

The receiving line formed, and we all drifted into the chapel to leave our offerings to the ka. Aset watched me up the stairs and into the chapel, where I left a leaf-wrapped date-nut bar, the dish Nekhen had helped me invent for my new restaurant. I turned to leave; I would atone later, when I could be by myself with the ka of my friend and mentor.

Aset greeted the woman ahead of me in the receiving line, hugged her, and thanked her for coming. Her eyes turned to me, then twisted away. I understood; she wanted me gone. The forms and rituals forced us to acknowledge each other. But there was no hug for me, no flashing smile, no thanks, just a nod and a turning away of her gaze toward the next in line.

She needed my protection, but she didn't know it.

Aset didn't love me anymore.

Aset and the other mourners walked back up the hill once things wound down at the chapel. I sat on a bench near a chapel across the little street and waited for everyone to leave. I wanted to do my atoning in peace. Seeing Aset walk away did not fill my heart with peace.

MacIntyre no longer watched from the temple above, but I would bet 1,000 debenu that she was up there, waiting to follow or harass Aset. I wanted to help, but I knew Aset wouldn't take help from me, not right now. I walked across the street to the chapel.

Recessed strip lighting and several well-placed spot lights showed off the hetep and the excellent wall art in Nekhen's chapel. In his restaurant, Nekhen always paid attention to details; that's what made it world class. He applied the same attention to detail to his ultimate resting place. The detailing of the tomb itself behind the locked door was likely to be as well designed, though without the expensive lighting. Lighting in the chapel encouraged people like me to come and leave offerings for the ka. The ka itself had little use for light.

All the mourners had gone, and I was alone in the chapel. I knelt on the floor before the hetep altar and sat on crossed legs, scribe-style, to offer my atonement to the ka. The atmosphere was dense with the lingering smoke from the censors used in the funerary rituals. The lemony citrus smells of the sweet myrrh of Wesir filled my heart with sorrow. Sorrow for what I'd done, and sorrow for what I still felt for Aset.

I am not deeply religious. My atonement was a heartfelt meditation asking the ka for forgiveness for my transgression, not mysterious rituals. My only prayer was for Nekhen to intercede with Wesir and Inpu at the Judgment in the Duat when I got there. You couldn't have too many friends helping when the alternative was consumption by a mythical crocodile/lion beast.

I meditated, obsessing about Aset, obsessing about Nekhen, wondering why it had to happen to us, and resolving not to let it happen again. Aset. Aset didn't love me anymore? That angst crept into my meditation, ruining the intention. Put it aside and concentrate, Shes.

I heard a sound from the door. My legs were stiff from sitting too long in the cold chapel. I twisted my head to look to see who had come in, but I was not prepared for the rushing figure that swung something toward me. Before I could see who wielded the bludgeon, it connected with my skull and I fell over. My legs turned to rubber, and my vision focused on the floor as my nose pushed against it. Another blow fell on my head, and I remember nothing more after that.

I wasn't out for very long, but long enough for the intruder to take advantage of my unconsciousness to attack the tomb door. There were stone chips on the floor, and the massive electronic lock on the door showed signs of heavy damage, but the door remained closed. I like to think that my presence kept the robber from succeeding. My heart told me that wasn't true. It told me I had not only failed to protect Aset from the medjau; I had failed to protect her from the pain of a robbed tomb on the very day of the funeral. Only the solidity of the door and the quality of the lock had stopped that robbery.

Given my last experience with Aset, I felt she was on the edge, emotionally. This desecration of Nekhen's tomb might be too much for her. She couldn't afford emotional vulnerability with MacIntyre after her. If I did nothing, the tomb robber might be back with reinforcements, better tools, or explosives, rendering my attempt to protect Aset even more derisory.

I kneeled, then stood up, my head aching. I staggered out of the chapel and leaned against one of the papyrus columns, letting the cool, foggy air clear my head. I looked up at the Temple of Inpu and dialed 111 on my phone to call in the medjau.

Necropolis security showed up after a few minutes, the lights on their car flashing red in the fog still swirling through the narrow streets. I arose from where I sat on the chapel steps. There were two medjau, one big, one small. I showed them the chips and damage and mentioned the recent murder of the tomb's occupant. They decided they needed more authority and called it in to the temple.

The smaller of the two asked whether I needed medical help because of my head. I replied I needed painkillers but declined any other aid. The medja said he couldn't give me any painkillers; the Temple had a rule about it.

"What's next?" I asked. My shendyt was not up to protecting my legs from the increasing fog and chill.

"We wait for the Idnu."

We waited. The idnu showed up after an hour. The medjau waited in their car; I waited on the cold stone bench across the street. Menmenet locals left the formal attire to tourists and high life, as the weather discouraged exposing the knees. Fashion requirements didn't consider waiting for medjau for long periods of time in the fog.

The idnu was a medium-sized, slope-shouldered man with a seamy, nut-brown face. He hadn't shaved in a couple of days, or he was trying unsuccessfully to grow a beard. He identified himself as Idnu Iny of the necropolis security services.

The responding medjau left in their car. Iny wrote a description of what had happened in a small notebook, then looked over the scene.

"Let's see," he said, inspecting the tomb entrance seal. "Everything looks intact here. Hopeless for prints. R'a alone knows how many people have been through here today. Was the robber wearing gloves?"

"I don't know, but whatever he hit me with wasn't soft."

"OK, thanks," he said, closing his notebook and putting it away.

"That's it?"

Iny grinned, showing terrible teeth. "Would have been nice if you'd seen a real live person. I'm sure the mummy didn't do this. That's about all I've got for this investigation." He cocked his head. "Why were you here? By yourself?" His voice was bland and non-accusatory.

"The Opening-of-the-Mouth ceremony. I stayed afterwards to say my good-byes privately." To atone, but I didn't need to burden Iny with my personal life.

"Any idea what the robber might have been after? Did your friend Nekhen have massive gold statues of himself or something? I can check the records, but I'd be interested to learn what the family has said about it." Iny's small, black eyes bored into me. Gold interested him, but stone door chips did not.

"Nothing, not a word. Sorry. He was well-to-do, though."

"Figured that from the quality of the artwork here," he said, looking around at the tasteful representations of restaurant life. "Well, I'll let the widow know about the damage and send her the report for her insurance." He moved toward the chapel door, and I walked with him. This could be an opportunity.

"Iny, could I ask a favor?"

He narrowed his eyes. "Such as what?"

"Let me tell Neferaset about the damage?" We stood on the stone steps outside the chapel.

"And why would I want to do that? She needs official notification." His eyes brightened. Going on my earlier intuition, I thought a small donation to the medjau benevolent fund would help, and it did.

"OK, you tell her. Here's my card. She can call me to get the report." He gave me a card with his name and phone on it. "We done here?"

I hesitated and glanced at the chapel door. "What about Nekhen? What about tomb robbers, intent on breaking open his tomb? What if they come back?"

"We'll send a medja around on patrol, keep an eye out." The standard response.

And if they stumbled over somebody carrying massive amounts of gold out of the chapel, they might look into it. Might.

The Temple of Inpu medjau would not be of much help. I would have to redeem myself to Aset on my own.

CHAPTER ELEVEN
MacIntyre Beats Up a Witness

MacIntyre tracked Shesmu through high-quality binoculars as he walked toward Nekhen's tomb. She stood on the viewing platform at the large Temple of Inpu at the top of the rocky hill that towered over the necropolis. Her view of the procession came and went with the swirls of the oncoming fog from the ocean. She could occasionally see waves crashing on the beach. The Wife stood at the chapel door doing whatever bereaved wives do at funerals.

MacIntyre hated funerals. She dated this to her grandfather's funeral in Boston, when she was small. The service bored the five-year-old MacIntyre, and she wasn't a well-behaved child at the best of times. Her struggles at her mother's hand holding her in place resulted in a quick slap from her mother and a hiss from her father. When they got her home, she spent a day locked in her closet. She'd always associated funerals with death and pain and hurt. The Remetjy funerals looked as though they were much more fun, but still—death was death.

But MacIntyre wasn't watching the funeral, she was watching the Wife. Her lawyer had posted bond within hours of her arrest. The Wife was now free to entomb her husband's mummy and mourn his passing, even though she had killed him. This arrogance toward Ma'at offended MacIntyre enough to make her disobey orders.

MacIntyre should have been hunting down the murderer of a local Ramaytush crime lord, the suspected victim of a vicious gang dispute between rival Ramaytush and Aztec gangs. And she'd handle that case. With luck, her boss need never know she was working the Celebrity Chef case on her own. She needed to do that, even if he found out and got pissed off.

MacIntyre popped the hood of the Wife's car while the Wife grieved over the mummy of her victim and installed a nifty little box attached to the car's computer. There were remarkable tools available now for surveillance. Once installed in the car, this small box sent everything but the brand of corn chips being consumed in the back seat to the semetyt's phone. Illegal, of course, couldn't go before Ma'at as evidence. Sometimes the gods and their priests created rules that cried out for breaking.

She could find something that cleared the Wife; much more likely, the Wife would do something stupid because she was guilty. To encourage this, MacIntyre had in mind an open tail, letting the murderer know she was under surveillance. The pressure would build on the Wife until she popped.

MacIntyre walked back to the viewing platform with her binoculars. On the steps of the chapel, Shesmu spoke to the Wife, both bowed, and the Wife turned her head away. Shesmu's face showed all the pain of rejected love. The woman had no heart.

The Wife walked up the steps to her car in the parking lot a half hour later. By that time, MacIntyre was in her little red convertible, waiting in plain sight. The Wife stood at her car's open door gazing with narrowed eyes and compressed lips at the little red car and its occupant. She got into her car, slammed the door, and drove away. MacIntyre followed at a sedate pace. Up and down, around and around, and up into the Tjesut and into her garage. As the garage door closed behind the car, MacIntyre stopped across the driveway just to be noticeable. The Wife appeared at a front window and looked at the little car and its occupant; MacIntyre raised her binoculars to get her expression, but the face disappeared. MacIntyre checked her phone and saw the little box was doing its job of locating the car. She waited for a half hour, but nothing more happened. The Tjesut was not a hive of urban action. She made sure her tires squealed as she executed a U turn and drove away.

MacIntyre's observation of Shesmu at the funeral got her thinking. Her following the Wife would push her into something stupid, but attacking from another angle would generate heat. The face she had seen through her binoculars was a face that could offer another wedge into the woman's guilt.

The next day, MacIntyre searched the web. She discovered Shesmu was not only a celebrity chef but was the winner of several local tournaments in 'ahamedu —Remetjy stick fighting. She grinned; this was one Remetjy thing she was good at. MacIntyre had adopted stick fighting because the Tae Kwon Do dojang in Menmenet only existed when a master passed through on the way to somewhere else.

She had made little impression on Shesmu at his restaurant, not being a food person. Perhaps beating the hell out of him with a stick would give her the wedge she needed.

Shesmu's stick-fighting club was in North Shore. The 'Ahamedu Imenhetep Club had an open sparring policy once a week according to its website. Anyone could suit up and spar for a low fee. She noticed two medjau acquaintances in the member pictures and called them. One of the two told her that Shesmu usually worked out at the gym every day, midmorning. MacIntyre stopped off at her gym, collected her equipment, and headed north.

She was early, so she warmed up with a bout with a big Remetj with brawn but not much brain and trounced him. This demonstration scared away the rest of the members, and she sat for a short time on a bench, waiting. Shesmu came in, took in her blonde hair, and did a double take. When he reached her bench, he bowed and said, "Cheryl, nice to see you." His gaze took in the small, gold fork-tailed swallow on her sleeve, the wer-glyph showing her werkhet master's status. "Hmm. Unless you borrowed that uniform, you're an excellent match for me. Where do you work out?"

MacIntyre looked up at him, smiling. "Harry's Stick Gym, down in the American district. There are a few of us now."

"I have no idea what they teach down there. Werkhet?" He looked skeptical.

"I'm sure I'll learn a lot here." She looked around. "Not much happening, though, at least after my first match."

"How did you find out where I would be? Are you following me?"

She smiled again. "Should I be? I detect things, remember? Got time for a match?" A minor mystery helped any relationship, especially when you wanted something.

"Sure, let me suit up." He smiled, lips curling attractively, and disappeared toward the men's locker room. Ten minutes later, he emerged, suited up, the little bird on his own sleeve confirming his equivalent status.

One fighting circle was still free. They put on their masks and faced each other in the circle, sticks in the on-guard position, both right-handed. Shesmu took a passive stance, waiting for her. They circled. She didn't try to prove anything. They circled. Hisses from the watching noncombatants showed they were getting bored. MacIntyre ignored the hisses and waited Shesmu out.

Shesmu shifted up on the balls of his feet and moved his stick a centimeter toward his body. MacIntyre moved with him into a mid-point defensive posture, waiting for the swing. He started the swing as a straight over, then flicked into a fast side swing under her blocking stick coming up. But not fast enough; she got the stick over, sweeping aside his stick and moving up for the counterattack to his head. His stick was already there, meeting it. They held the pose, then withdrew back into guard. She wasn't breathing hard yet, she'd anticipated the classic moves, and her footwork felt good, supple and solid.

Suddenly, he shifted the stick to his left hand, rolled around her stick to his left, and sidestepped past her before she could turn. Wham, right to her side. Breath whooshed out of her while her reflexive counterstrike swung around to meet only his stick. Damn, he was fast! She had twisted away, raising her stick in guard again, breathing hard this time.

"Tricky one. Where did you learn that?" she asked. Control the anger, Cheryl. Anger is your enemy. Anger, anger, anger, breathe, breathe, breathe, yes. Damn, that was a fine hit. The man had something, something more than most of the men she fought.

"A southern friend, they're unconventional."

"I'll say. Two out of three?" She was already breathing normally. She hoped it would fool him into thinking she didn't realize he was better than she was at finding vulnerable points.

"Sure."

His mask waggled, the eyes and intentions hidden. The mask and suit distanced them in a formal dance. With no masks and no suits, it would be just the raw emotions and the sticks. Kind of like a love affair, but with bruises.

They faced off again. This time there was no waiting; she mounted a direct attack at his left knee, swinging down as soon as she'd come to full guard. He made the classic response and shifted back, but she was already moving forward with the stick swinging up toward his arm, then his head. He blocked both with sharp cracks, then countered toward her arm. She saw he'd moved too close and opened himself to an attack. She swung around, stepping back to the edge of the circle. She feigned a block, then flipped the stick over and slammed it up against his head.

Shesmu stepped out of the circle and shook his head to clear it. MacIntyre knew he heard bells ringing. They were even, one strike each. One tricky move on his part, one forceful move on hers. He stepped back into the circle. His mask hid his eyes, forcing her to imagine what he would do next.

There are two ways to beat someone at your own level: use something new or wear them down until you get an opportunity. Shesmu tried to create a weak spot. They blocked and circled with neither connecting and both taking care.

MacIntyre made a mistake. On the low parries, her counterattacks didn't come as fast or as hard. Shesmu aimed lower each time; she saw but couldn't respond. After a few more blocks, instead of blocking her counterattack, he dodged back and, before falling out of the circle, swung back and got her arm as it swung by. She dropped the stick. Shesmu picked himself up from the ring perimeter where he'd fallen, and they unmasked and nodded to each other. MacIntyre leaned over and picked up her stick. She bowed, loser respecting winner.

She said, "Great match, I learned a lot. May I have a word with you after you dress?"

She noticed he wasn't even breathing hard. In good shape, she judged. He looked good. He'd won, and he knew it. She could see it in his eyes. She'd shown him a side of herself that impressed him, but he was still skeptical. Maybe more willing to cooperate, though. Now that he knew she wasn't all female fluff and mouth.

"More questions? All right, I'll change and meet you in the lounge."

MacIntyre, while waiting at the juice bar that labeled itself as a "lounge," promoted Shesmu through the stages of suspect to witness to potential friend. Anybody with stick-fighting instincts like that was not ordinary. Nowhere near ordinary.

What did he see in the Wife? How far did she want to delve into him to understand the why? He wasn't a killer, no instinct for it, and a cast-iron alibi. Good with a knife, sure, but pffft—didn't matter. He could cook, run a business, inspire the people working for him. All loyal to him, to a fault. Stick fighting was one thing, but this was her game, not his: finding murderers. She had the advantage.

She didn't need to figure out the why. What she needed to do was to get him to see that loving the Wife to distraction wasn't working for him. She needed to get him to help her put the woman in jail, where she belonged.

Shesmu emerged from the men's locker room and walked into the lounge, self-possessed, walking with an assured step and looking her straight in the eye as he sat. He had all the attributes of a St. George, looking for the dragon to slay to save his princess. MacIntyre liked the image of herself as the dragon, and she knew the dragon would win this one. She lit the fire that would toast him to a crisp, this culinary St. George.

"So, Shes," she said, "Why were you sleeping with Neferaset?" The burst of flame should have crisped him, but he grinned.

"Sorry, Cheryl. Not playing that game. I won, if you hadn't noticed."

"Well, shit. The dominant male in the troop." She contemplated taking the stick out of her bag and knocking him unconscious, but it wouldn't be helpful to her task. Dragons didn't do sticks. And her superiors at the Temple of Ma'at might just consider it a transgression of her oath as a w'abet. She was mixing her religions again.

She cocked her head and said, "Winning buys you something, but just answer the question."

He shook his head. "I don't know what to say. I love her."

"Say I accept that. Say you're just blind stupid in love. She sure doesn't act like she's in love with you. What makes you think, in a rational version of yourself, that she didn't kill your friend Nekhen?"

"She wouldn't."

"Now, Shes, that is not a rational argument."

"I know her down to the bottom of her ba. She's not a killer. Not somebody who would wield a knife and cut her husband's throat. Especially her husband. She loved him."

"But she loved you too."

He said nothing.

"Once the medjau showed up, she panicked and broke off the affair with you. She didn't want us to find out about it. Shes, she loves herself a lot more that she loves you."

Shesmu ignored this conclusion. "You found out anyway. It's all nonsense. She wouldn't kill him."

"Prove it to me."

"I don't have to. You need to prove it to Ma'at."

Damn, a religious lawyer as well as a chef and werkhet. An exasperating man.

"Look, Shes, I've got an open mind. I'll try to find evidence she didn't do it, but in the end it's about what I can prove, either way." Hold out a sliver of hope to get him going, then slam the cage door shut.

He shook his head again. "I've got a closed mind. I love her. It's all nonsense."

Her first approach to St. George had gone about as far as possible, so she changed tactics. Lancelot, think Lancelot—a different kind of knight entirely. She could force him to see the error of his ways, sleeping with his king's wife.

She moved her pawn forward. "It was a nice funeral."

"Nekhen? I noticed you in the parking lot."

"Seemed like many people loved the man enough to mourn him."

"He was...yes, he was important. Loved and respected. Worth mourning."

"And yet—"

"Yes, I was sleeping with his wife."

"I wouldn't be so crude, but yes. Did you—"

Shesmu got up and bowed. "Hutyt. A veritable pleasure exploring our relative stick-fighting levels. I hope we can have a rematch under better circumstances for us all. For now, I'm done. Please excuse me."

He walked out, leaving her to finish her juice alone. Exasperating man.

CHAPTER TWELVE
Shesmu Gets Back in the Game

ANGRY AND FRUSTRATED BY MY battle with MacIntyre, I worried about Aset. What could I do to help her if she wouldn't even talk to me? I drove up the hill from the waterfront with only a vague idea of what to do.

Nekhen's mansion was on the north side of the Tjesut. The back of the house faced north with a wide view of the bay and the rolling, brown hills to the north. He'd bought it years ago when even mansions were cheap. Now it was Aset's, her home and refuge. I parked right in front and sat and watched. I didn't even know what I was watching for or why I was there, but the house was a magnet for me. Aset was a magnet for me. But she wouldn't talk to me. I'd called four or five times to let her know about the tomb, and she didn't return my calls. But MacIntyre was hot on her trail, and a tomb robber was after her husband's treasures.

My phone rang. The caller id said it was Aset.

"Shes. What are you doing?"

"I—"

"Why are you lurking outside my house?"

I looked across at the house and saw her standing in the window, staring out at me.

"I love you." This hoarse declaration leaked out without my knowing what I was saying.

"Shes, I told you—"

"Yes, but you need to tell *them*."

"Them who?"

"The medjau."

"That semetyu trapped me into saying things. They wanted to put me in jail. That awful woman, that hutyt, she hates me. She's been following me. Now you are too. I'm—I can't stand much more of this."

"Aset, they're serious. Let me help you."

"Shes…it wouldn't work."

"They're questioning me, questioning people that work for me, about you. I tried talking again to MacIntyre but she won't listen, she's—"

"She hates me. Look, Shes—I can't stand this. I, I get that you care, but I can't, I just can't handle any more."

Encouraged by the emotion I heard in her voice, I said, "Listen to me, Aset. I've got things, things about Nekhen, things about the tomb, that I need to tell you. All the time we've spent together, you owe me. Let's have dinner. At the Neferti. Neutral ground."

Silence for a full minute. "The Neferti is not neutral ground. It's your restaurant."

But she didn't say no. "It's yours too. At least it will be once all the dust settles. Nekhen's share."

"Nekhen, I miss him so much. I miss him."

"I do too, Aset, I do. It's hard, but we have to talk. Please!"

I saw her turn away from the window and walk back into the room. Long pause. She said, "Oh, all right. I suppose…all right. I'll drive down there and meet you tonight at 8, all right? For dinner. At 'our' restaurant. Neutral ground. Just this once. Now go away." She disconnected.

The call came at 8:15 from Henutsenu: Aset had arrived. I doffed my apron, washed up, and walked out through the dining room saying my hellos to the usual patrons. I didn't linger. This was not a celebrity chef walk, this was personal. I had to convince Aset to let me help.

Aset waited by the hostess's station. Uncomfortable, she twisted and untwisted her necklace. That necklace was a wedding gift from Nekhen, an exquisite thing of gold and turquoise. She wore it with a long, white dress with gold edgings and nearly invisible purple threads that transformed her into a goddess. The other goddess in the room, Henutsenu, looked at me with a neutral expression.

"I've reserved the private dining room for us, Aset," I said. Henutsenu shot me a scornful look, then turned to answer the phone.

I guided Aset to the back of the restaurant. We'd built in a small, private room in the back as an enclave for private dining. I'd spent a lot of money soundproofing the walls, both to keep noise out and to keep conversations in the room private. The mural painter had outdone himself; you could imagine yourself sitting in a red stone pavilion overlooking the Great River in old Mennefer. You could almost smell the water and hear the birds in the marsh. The low table was in the Late Empire style, surrounded by cushions rather than chairs.

Aset folded herself onto her cushion. I sat on mine, scribe-like, with legs crossed. The server appeared and took our orders, then left, closing the door. We looked at each other, both unable to be the first to break the silence.

Finally, Aset spoke. "That medjat…she showed up at the house again late this afternoon. Parked across my driveway again in her stupid little red car, staring at the house." Aset looked at me with lips pressed tight and a look in her eyes I had never seen. Fear.

"Aset, she's trying to scare you."

"It's working." She twisted her necklace. "After we talked, after I saw the medjat, I…it scares me, Shes. I have no one else to turn to. I have lots of friends, but none for this. Who can I trust? I trust *you*. Nekhen told me once that you're the most trustworthy person he knew."

Nekhen told her to trust me. Now that, that was ironic.

I had to make things clear. "Aset, Nekhen was a great man, even though you and I both know he couldn't trust me. How far *you* trust me is up to you." I was all in. "We could get married. Will you marry me, Aset?"

"Let's eat our dinner, Shes."

I loved looking at Aset's face because of her infinite range of elegant, earthy, and lusty expressions. What I called her Hut-Her smile—the Remetjy goddess of love and sex—was a full-wattage invitation to love that overwhelmed me. Tonight, she flashed a low-power version of that smile, acknowledging her trust in my loyalty. That smile gave me hope, though she didn't answer my question.

The server entered with the starters and drinks, arranging them on the table along with our plates so we could share everything. Corn fritters with Tjeny ham, dates wrapped with thin slices of spiced lamb, roasted mild green chiles on a bed of roasted red barley, fresh-baked whole-wheat flatbread. Heavenly aromas. I'd chosen a medium-bodied red Behedet Mautet vintage to complement the food.

After we'd sampled the dishes, I said, "Aset, you can trust me. I can help you. You're in a bad fix, Aset."

She nodded and said, "I don't have an alibi, and I have a lot of money now that he's dead. That medjat follows me everywhere. She thinks I did it for the money and won't stop until she has me in jail."

"You should talk to your sehy. He likes money and knows things about the law and the medjau that I don't."

"I have. He's told me not to say or do anything at all. Stay at home and keep quiet. Lock my windows and doors and not answer the phone. Ignore the medjat. But how can I do that? I can't ignore it all, or they'll never catch the actual murderer. They'll keep chasing me. I want them to catch the murderer. Not just because they're after me, but because…." She twisted her necklace without finishing the thought. "And I don't want that woman to put me in jail. Just being in that room with her was too much for me."

"Can you tell me where you were that afternoon?"

"I can't, Shes. I won't. It's too private."

I let it go and suggested, "What about a private inquiry agent? It will take money, but you have it."

"I considered that, but I need somebody I can trust, not somebody who's working for money. I need to find Nekhen's murderer. I can't ask people things because I'm a suspect and because I'm a woman. I need help." Her eyes stared at the image of the river. Her voice was full of questions, questions to herself about whether she could trust me to help her.

"I'll help you any way I can, Aset. I can find things out and track down the murderer. But I'll need information from you."

"What do you want to know?" Aset asked this oddly. Her voice had a hopeless, guarded tone, fearing me more than the medjau. She still didn't trust me.

"First, I have something to tell you about the tomb, Aset."

"The tomb?"

"Nekhen's tomb."

She stared at me in surprise. "What about it?"

"They…someone broke into—tried to break into it."

"But it's only the day after the funeral," she said, bewildered.

"It was right after you left. The day of the funeral." I didn't tell her about the robber knocking me out, no need to make it clear I had been little help so far.

Aset shut her eyes again, her mouth down-turned in despair. "Awful. How could they? The same day as the funeral? Awful." Something moved in her face. "Did they—get in?"

"No, chips and dents here and there." I followed up with Idnu Iny's question. "Do you think they had something in mind? What's in the tomb?"

"There was a small, gold-plated statue of Nekhen and me." She smiled. "Nekhen had it done right after we married, when we couldn't afford solid gold. He said it was never too soon to prepare for the afterlife."

"That doesn't sound like a huge thing that would attract a robber."

"No, I guess not."

"Anything else?"

"No. Nothing."

I pressed her. There had to be something. "Are you sure?"

A little exasperated, she said, "I sat the vigil in the tomb, the night before, I arranged all the tomb goods myself. There was nothing that valuable."

I knew her too well, and my intuition was telling me she wasn't telling me the whole truth. "What are you hiding, Aset?"

"What? Nothing, it's…nothing."

"It's something about the tomb, the things you put there."

"Shes, stop."

"Why not tell me?"

"I can't." She compressed her lips. "I won't. It's nothing."

"Can you list the items for me?"

"I'd rather not. In fact, no, I won't—it's too private. I'm religious enough to want to protect my husband's privacy in the afterlife."

"Religious?"

"Do you want to start an argument? Let's talk about something else. What else do you want to know?" Back to the fear, this time colored with a light red blush of anger. She took a sip of wine, and the blush faded.

I asked, "Any reason anyone would want to kill Nekhen?"

"He had competitors, not enemies. He didn't make enemies."

"Have the medjau asked about anyone else?"

"Other than you, you mean?"

I smiled. "Other than me."

She thought about it. "They asked about Qenna, but I told them he worshipped Nekhen."

"How about your alibi? What happened there?"

"I'm so embarrassed by that. I'm so mad at Sit, she told that medjat everything."

"But why did you do it?"

"I was just afraid, afraid they'd put me in jail."

"Where were you at the time of the murder?"

"I was shopping, looking for a present for a friend's birthday. I found nothing I liked, didn't see anyone I knew." She was lying. I could tell she was lying.

"You're lying, Aset. Don't lie to me."

"I…I'm not…" She wouldn't look at me.

"You are. Why?"

"Shes, stop."

"Do you want my help or not? Then don't lie to me. I can't use lies."

"I can't tell you where I was."

"You don't remember?"

"I can't tell you." She set her jaw.

The server delivered our mains and poured us more wine, then left. Unsettled and avoiding my eye, Aset took a bite of the dish she'd ordered: lamb with leek sauce, an old Delta favorite brought up to date with baby valley leeks. Aset winced and took a drink of water.

"Wow, and ouch. Is it supposed to be this hot?"

I reached and took a small piece of lamb with sauce, tasted, then spat it onto a side plate. Very hot indeed.

After taking care of my problem with a drink of water, I said, "Sorry about that. Something slipped in the kitchen." Fine. Very nice. A hot date with Aset.

I picked up her plate and walked through the big swinging doors into the kitchen. Dua was there, supervising a cook plating quail. She looked at me and froze at my expression and the plate I held. I pointed at the prep room. She nodded and followed me in.

"Taste this," I said, pushing the plate toward her. She did, then she grimaced and took a drink from the prep sink to clear her mouth of the sudden fire.

"Well?" I asked. My face must have been grim; she laughed. Her laugh was not a merry laugh. It had sharp edges to it that cut.

She shook her head. "Sorry, chef. You look…."

"Huh. How do you think that went? Blasting hot lamb for the woman I love?"

Dua smiled, unworried. "I plated that myself, both plates. They were on the service counter. Somebody must have added red pepper powder to the sauce on that plate. Probably meant for you. Stupid. A joke on you, chef. Did it screw up your sex life?" Adventurous for a sous chef under warning. But I had to grin.

"Nothing to screw up. OK, I won't call the medjau in on this one. Still, you might keep a closer eye on things."

"Do my best, chef."

"All right. Things are looking good in the dining room. Keep it up, Dua. Can I get this replaced?"

"Right away, chef. Couple of minutes."

I had to get Aset to trust me, despite every damn thing working against that. I walked back to the private dining room. Aset sipped her wine with a contemplative look on her face. She looked up at me as I came in, and her full-wattage Hut-Her smile appeared. That smile always made me forget whatever I was thinking and doing.

She said, "Sit here, Shes." She patted the cushions next to her. I sat.

"Shes, you're right. I was too hard on you, I need to trust you. I want—I need your help." She caressed my cheek. I kissed her, and she responded. But the server was on his way with her plate. I pulled back.

"Aset, you know what I want."

"I do, Shes. I want it too. Can we go to your place, after? My house…Nekhen is still there—his ba."

"Yes," I croaked, aching for her. The server came in, and we ate, loving each other.

CHAPTER THIRTEEN
MacIntyre Tries to Impeach a Witness

MACINTYRE SAT AT HER BREAKFAST table and checked her phone while she ate.

Ah, movement! Where was the Wife this fine morning? Somewhere other than her house. She flipped through the history. The Wife traveled to the Neferti the night before, then drove up the hill somewhere. Her car was on a street on Dju-Keta, let's see. Zoom in, Meryimen Street. Why was that name familiar?

On a hunch, MacIntyre queried Shesmu's police file and checked his home address. Yep, Meryimen Street. Now there was an interesting development. Why did he lie to her? Why say that the Wife had broken off their affair? There was the scene at the funeral where she hurt him. But now they were together. All night. There was more to Shesmu than met the eye. A strong alibi, but good detectives can break strong alibis like the rotten eggs they are. And she was a good detective.

Instead of heading into the temple, she drove over to the waterfront. "Chef" would not be in early today, but others would. Such as Duaneferet. An excellent opportunity.

She parked in a loading zone in front of the restaurant and walked around to the back kitchen door. She stepped inside and saw Duaneferet and two chefs working at stations. Duaneferet looked up and saw her.

"Shit. What the hell are you doing in my kitchen? Out!"

"I need to ask more questions. I warned you...."

"Out! I'm busy." She pointed her massive chef's knife at the kitchen door.

A cook came over. MacIntyre thought she recognized him from her earlier visit. "What is it, Dua?" the cook asked.

"This bitch is a medjat ballbreaker, Khay, wants to screw over chef and wants me to do it for her."

Khay asked MacIntyre, "Can I help you? I'm Khay, the grill chef." A peacemaker.

She showed him her credentials. "Hutyt-er-Semetyu Cheryl MacIntyre. I need to ask more questions. I'll start with Duaneferet there, since she's been so helpful."

More obscenities from the cooking station. Khay turned and said, "Dua, talk to her, OK? We don't want any trouble. We can take care of things here." He turned back to MacIntyre. "It would be better to wait until chef gets here, he's running late this morning."

"I'll bet." MacIntyre had a brief vision of "chef" and the Wife running late together and dismissed it from her consciousness. "No, I'll get it done now, thanks."

Khay said, "Go into the dining room, you can talk there." Duaneferet put down her knife and followed MacIntyre through the big, swinging doors.

"This place sure has class," said MacIntyre, sitting down at a table.

"Unlike you."

"Now, now, Duaneferet, let's not get off on the wrong foot."

Duaneferet glared at MacIntyre and pressed her lips together. MacIntyre judged that not only were they off on the wrong foot, she'd be lucky if Duaneferet didn't chew her head off. She'd seen rabid attack dogs with better looks and manners. MacIntyre tried to disarm the woman with a pleasant smile, but Dua wasn't having any of it.

MacIntyre stated, "I want to ask again about Shesmu's whereabouts."

"I told you, Niut Shepesu, a cooking demo."

"And you were in charge of the kitchen, you said."

"I was. I'm sous chef." She sounded defensive. Why?

"Why so defensive?"

Duaneferet looked down. She forced it out. "I got a warning. From chef."

"Why?"

"None of your business."

"Why?"

"It's nothing to do with the great Nekhen, that's why."

"But it is to do with Shesmu. When did he warn you?"

"The night you were here."

"Why did he warn you?"

"Go to hell."

"I can ask him, and I'd be sure to tell him how cooperative you've been. I'm sure that will do your career even more good."

"Go to hell." The cook gritted her teeth, then said, "I brought my boyfriend in, against orders, and let him cook."

"He's a cook?"

"He would be if chef gave him a chance, get the experience, work with the tools. You learn by doing."

"So the cat went away and did cooking demos and you brought in the rats. And the cat found out and plugged the rat-hole."

"Go to hell." MacIntyre said this along with Duaneferet, further enraging her.

MacIntyre smiled and said, "OK, now we're all up to speed on career developments and Shesmu's management style. Why are you lying about Shesmu being away?"

"I'm not! He was down south. Ask anybody! Why would I lie? I was here, I screwed up, I got warned about it, and that's it."

"When was the last time you saw Nekhen?"

"Why?"

"Curiosity."

"Go to hell." Duaneferet did not have an extensive range of expletives available.

"Was he ever here, visiting? He was a part owner, no? Why not tell me?"

"Yes, he's been by."

"Was he here within the last week or two?"

"No."

"Sure about that?"

"I didn't see him, if he came by."

"How well did you know him?"

"I didn't. I'd seen him, met him, we all had. Big deal."

"You didn't like Nekhen?"

"No I didn't, I don't like that kind of big-deal, puffed-up performer. He had it coming."

"A lot of judgment for not knowing him all that well."

"It was obvious, him standing there patronizing us all."

"Even Shesmu?"

"What do you mean?"

"How did he treat Shesmu?"

The cook hesitated. "He treated chef OK. Like he thought chef was ready to run his own restaurant."

"Not like somebody who was sleeping with his wife."

"No!" Duaneferet shouted in exasperation. "He didn't know it was going on!"

"But you all did."

"She came here a few times…it was obvious." Duaneferet shook her head. "Chef followed her around like a lap dog."

And vice versa. At least that car tracker log suggested she was following him to his house for the night. Nekhen knew. Why didn't he show it to his staff or Shesmu? But his wife? No way he didn't confront her. No way. Then she killed him.

Duaneferet continued, "She has it coming. I don't think she killed him. But she deserves whatever you can make stick to her. That will get chef back to business, back to everything he's doing here."

"Where is he, this morning?"

Duaneferet's eyes were down again. "I don't know."

"Sure you do. She was here last night."

The cook's eyes were glaring right at MacIntyre. "So you already know. Yes, she damn well was! They ate together in the private dining room, and they left together, all right? Where do you think he is? Bitch. She's ruining his life, over and over."

MacIntyre would like to ruin Shesmu's life herself now that he was lying to her. But he didn't murder his mentor. Should she push further with Duaneferet or abandon this line and get on with pressuring the Wife? Or should she stay and pressure Shesmu when he showed up?

The man himself burst through the kitchen doors in his bright-white chef's uniform. Problem solved.

"What are you doing here?" he asked, stamping over to their table.

"I'm asking questions."

"Get out."

"Make me."

Angry, his hands clenched into fists. Duaneferet got up, grinned, and said, "Beat the crap out of her, chef. She needs a good slap or two. Try cuffing her first! She'll love that. I could help." MacIntyre smiled. He'd already tried that with a stick.

Shesmu unclenched his hands. "You get back in the kitchen, Dua. You've got work to do."

Duaneferet flipped some insulting sign language to MacIntyre as she turned and brick-walked back into the kitchen.

"Now, you. Out." He stood glaring at her, arms crossed.

"Touchy, aren't we? Bad night?"

Shesmu took a deep breath. "It's none of your business."

"Let's see: tampering with a suspect, lying to a medjat, suborning a witness. That sums up to a hefty jail term for impeding Ma'at. I'm using the verb 'tampering' as a euphemism."

He put a hand on the table and leaned toward her. "You're impeding *me* and I want it to stop. Don't disrupt my work team! And stop following Neferaset! Out!"

She grinned and shook her head. "My, my, what's she been doing, washing the invisible blood off her hands? She did it. *You* didn't do it, but—"

"Hutyt, please. Leave. Now."

MacIntyre, sure she'd got the needle in, stood up. "All right—for now. But I'm not going to stop prying, Shes. And sleeping with her will not make things better for you. If you help her cover up her guilt, you're an accessory. I'll tag you for it for sure. Help me, and I'll help you."

He said nothing but glared at her with a clenched jaw. It didn't improve his looks any, she decided. Too bad. He'd allied himself with the opposition. She moved toward the front.

He walked with her to unlock the door. "Don't come back," he said, then closed the door and locked it behind her.

CHAPTER FOURTEEN
Shesmu Attacks the Problem

THE LIGHTS IN THE BAR came on. Henutsenu said, "Shesmu? Why aren't you in the kitchen?"

I flapped a hand at her to tell her to go away. Instead, like any good friend, she came over and sat down at the bar table where I had retreated after kicking MacIntyre out of my restaurant.

Henutsenu said, "You look like shit. You took her home with you, didn't you? You spent the entire night with her, didn't you?" Her tone was accusatory.

I dredged up a smile from somewhere, despite the fog of lust, love, and lack of sleep that had me sitting in a dark room rather than working in my kitchen.

"Are you asking as a friend or as a concerned employee, Henutsenu?"

She didn't see the funny side. "That woman is making you into a complete fool, Shesmu!"

"What?" Outraged, I looked her in the eye. "What are you talking about?"

"Shesmu. I've tried before, I'll try again. It's absurd. Sleeping with her was dumb enough when her husband—your friend—was alive. Sleeping with her now when she's playing you—that's idiotic."

"She's not—Henutsenu, that's outrageous. We love—"

"No, no, no. Get a grip, Shesmu. She doesn't love you. She never has."

"I can't—" My chest hurt and my brain was on fire.

"You can. You must."

"She loves me, last night was amazing, it was—"

"All you know about women would fit on the tip of a tiny pyramid." Henutsenu shook her head in wonder, a smile of disdain on her lovely lips.

I rallied. "Henutsenu, let's pretend, just for now, that she loves me. Let's do that. Otherwise, I'll take a dive into the bay. It's all I have." I waved a hand at the vista before us.

"Get a grip, Shesmu." She leaned toward me, held my head with both hands, and forced me to look her in the eye. "You have the restaurant. You have us, your friends. You've got your life. I understand you're feeling terrible. I hear that. You can't go on this way. You've got to get past this." She let go of my head and sat back in her chair.

"How?" I challenged her. "How can I get past it? I can barely get out of this chair."

"*Do* something about it."

"What? How can I help her, show her I love her more than—"

"Stop it. You're whining."

I made a face, mostly at myself. She was right; I was whining. I'm not a whiner.

She suggested, "What about Hutyt MacIntyre? Why not let her help you find the truth?"

"Because I kicked her out of the place fifteen minutes ago."

"What?"

"She was here when I came in, questioning Dua. I closed that down and threw her out."

"Shesmu, you didn't!"

"Yes, I damn well did. She had no business—"

"She's a medjat! That's her business!" She sat back in her chair, lips tight, and leaned forward, arms on the table. "Look, Shesmu. She's doing her job. And I've seen another side of her."

"You mean she has a side that isn't a wolf with bared teeth?"

"All that energy covers up a sweet person underneath, Shesmu. She can help, if you'll let her."

"You're attracted to her!" Henutsenu had taken on as many girlfriends as boyfriends in the time I'd known her, but she'd never fallen for someone as tough as MacIntyre.

"I may be. We'll see. That's not the point, is it?"

"She's convinced herself that Aset murdered Nekhen. She won't stop until Aset is in jail. I can't work with that. I need to trust Aset and fight MacIntyre and her stubborn insistence on Aset's guilt. And I've burned that bridge, I threw her out."

"Shes, in this state, you're useless in the kitchen. Go home. Go stick fighting. Take a break, do something else. Investigate."

"I can't do that, the restaurant—"

"Dua can handle things."

"Dua can't even handle herself."

Henutsenu's lips curved in a satisfied smile. "There, you're judging like a chef again. See how easy?"

Easy. Great gods.

"Investigate it yourself, find things out, clear her name. Do what you have to do, just do it."

"I can't leave the restaurant. Henutsenu, Dua is…she's not ready. Her judgment is terrible."

"Rough edges. Rough middle, too. All right, hire somebody. A temporary chef."

"Who?"

Henutsenu smiled a cat-like smile. "Nekhetsebek."

Nekhetsebek was Henutsenu's current boyfriend. I'd known Henutsenu for several years. Her girlfriends and boyfriends came and went with regularity. She was an optimist, but a fastidious one. She would take somebody on, have fun, then discover their hidden flaws. Then she'd kick out the offender and move on.

Nekhetsebek had lasted the longest of her lovers. No flaws? The hint about her attraction to MacIntyre suggested a change, which could create a problem if she and her ex-lover had to work together. He was a nice guy, tall and slender, with smiling eyes and messy black hair. Nothing like his namesake, Sebek, the crocodile fertility god who takes women from their husbands. He had a good rep around town among the top chefs, though he hadn't yet broken into the big time.

The biggest problem with this idea was that I was abandoning the hierarchy by bringing in an outsider over my sous chef. A real insult. But I couldn't help it; Dua wasn't ready.

"I'll consider the idea. Is he available?" I asked.

The smile widened. "Very. Sebek hates his current place, the Cape Cod Café. He'll tell you about it. But he's ready to move on. He'd be perfect for a temporary position here."

"And what about MacIntyre? Are you going to create a melodrama by leaving him for a medjat?"

"No." My confronting her potential infidelity didn't offend Henutsenu, who smiled an indulgent smile. "I like her, but I never create melodrama."

She gave me Sebek's number, and I called right then. I described the situation to him in a few words. He invited me to lunch at the Cape Cod Café. Henutsenu expressed her satisfaction with a hug, then told me to go home and get some rest.

Instead of going home, I rested by walking down the waterfront to my lunch engagement. It was a pleasant morning, and I needed air. From the base of Dju-Keta, the bay curved in, forming a tight north-to-south arc.

The Cape Cod Café billed itself as an American-style restaurant that catered to the American hotels to the south. I knew about it in the way any chef knows about all the restaurants in his area. I'd never eaten there: not my kind of food, and so not my competitor. Was Sebek up for innovative Remetjy cuisine, or did his skills end with flipping burgers and deep frying potatoes?

The café was in a six-story building that housed a small boutique hotel. From the outside, it looked like any no-fuss, storefront American restaurant. I went in, and they directed me to the back, where I found Sebek supervising the unloading of what looked like Asian vegetables from a truck.

Spotting me, Sebek waved his arms around in frustration and said, "It's unbelievable. He ordered a week's worth of this crap without asking me. I ought to tell them to turn around and truck it all back to the valley."

"My sympathies." I wondered who "he" was, and why he was into Asian vegetables. I sensed an opportunity.

Sebek said, "Let me finish up here, I'll meet you in the bar in five minutes."

I walked in through a door propped open with a captain's chair and sat at the bar. I poured myself a chilled sake. I looked around. The décor in the bar was very American, with a television over the bar showing a ball game from St. Louis. They didn't even turn it off when the place was closed.

Sebek came in, saw what I was drinking, and smiled. He reached behind the bar and brought out menus. "Order whatever you like."

A quick glance showed me the story. I opted for the boneless buffalo chicken with ginger juice and a pickled konbu side and a sour ale to wash it down. I wanted the full experience, and I got it. Sebek, knowing his cuisine, ordered steamers and a light beer. He gave the order to the kitchen over the bar phone, then sat and turned to me.

"So, how can I help you out?"

"Are you sure you don't need to be in the kitchen supervising the konbu?"

He grinned. "The konbu can take care of itself, it doesn't need my help."

"I need someone to take over in my kitchen for a week or two. You seem like a suitable candidate, given your reputed skills. Henutsenu recommends you without reservation." I grinned. "My guess is that she doesn't eat here that often."

"No, she does not. Nor do I, though I do like the fresh seafood."

"What's your availability?"

"Oh, I'm available. What time is it?" He looked at his watch. "Ten? How about starting at lunch? But I'd like to know what I'm getting into, and why."

The lunch mains came, and it looked about as appetizing as it had appeared on the menu. I took a deep breath (a mistake) and ingested a chicken nugget with sauce. I swallowed and washed the hot sauce, vinegar, and ginger juice away with a swig of ale, then a swallow of water. It was like diving into a freezing river and realizing you couldn't swim. I cleared my throat. Sebek laughed.

I got specific. "Well. We've got menus worked out for about a month. I rotate most dishes through once every few months with seasonal variations. The chief thing is, I have a couple of problems in the kitchen."

"Such as?"

"The wrong spice, the human kind. Duaneferet, my sous chef."

"I've worked with her." His face was a mix of glee and expectation.

"She has terrible taste in friends."

"Oh, yeah. I've seen her in the bars after work. Ouch."

"Her current mistake could cost her the job. He's the second problem. He persuaded Dua to let him work in the kitchen when I wasn't there."

"Not good."

"So I warned her. She may work out, but I can't put her in charge. So I'm bringing somebody—you—in over her."

"So, I come in and she's pissed. I can deal. OK, what else?"

"Henutsenu."

"What about her?"

I grinned. "She's plotting something, and you're the linchpin for the plot."

"Henutsenu doesn't plot." He grinned. "She eases you into things, and then you wonder what hit you."

"True, so true. Is she easing me into something? Is that going to create problems for the restaurant down the road?"

"Not from me. The kitchen is separate from the front of the house in my world. Still, it's good for both sides to have confidence in the other. So, I don't see a problem."

I needed somebody in the kitchen I could trust—but so did Henutsenu. Right. "Then neither do I, as long as you keep on her good side," I said. I thought again about MacIntyre and Henutsenu. Sweet? Or spicy? I eyed the chicken. Risk it? Sure. I was hungry. Another nugget, another gulp of beer, another swallow of water. I let the konbu alone. Should have had the chowder.

My phone rang. I didn't recognize the number, but in my business you take calls no matter what. I apologized to Sebek and answered.

"Shesmu."

"Hello, there, Mr., uh. Shesmu."

It was Call Me Rafe. I'd forgotten about him. I switched to English. "Hey, Rafe. Sorry, I can't talk. Can I call you back? I haven't had time to think about your proposal." Blackmore agreed on a time the next day, and we disconnected.

"What was that about?" asked Sebek. "An American?" He asked in English.

I diagnosed a concern with my interest in American doings; he might be afraid I'd be switching to that kind of food on him. I switched back to Renkemet. "Nothing to do with cooking. A guy named Blackmore wants me to vet an antiquity. I—"

"*Rafe* Blackmore?"

I put the Eye on him. Was he involved in that stuff? "Yes, what about him?"

"I was at university with him. In St. Louis. Washington University." His mouth quirked. "Hold on to your wallet."

"What do you mean?"

"He was our frat boss. Money had an interesting habit of collecting around him in unsavory ways. He was never around when the university wanted to know how and why."

"Fraud?"

"And theft and everything between, yeah. Hold on to your wallet." He made a brief gesture of apology. "Sorry, not my business, I'll shut up now."

"Next question. Do you think you can handle my Remetjy cuisine? This stuff…." I gestured to the dish in front of me.

"Oh, I can handle it. The guy who owns this restaurant is a rich investor with no taste buds. He started out catering to Americans, and now the Japanese tourists from Hawai'i have taken over, so he's shifting to Asian one dish at a time. Insisting on it. It makes me itch. It's time to move on."

"But can you handle the complex stuff?"

"Fully trained, no worries. Even French."

"Where did you train?"

"Apprenticed at L'Orangerie and the Per'ankh."

The Per'ankh. "Under Nekhen?" He must have apprenticed before I started.

"Yes, though I didn't last long. Why do you need somebody to take over?"

"Have you followed the news on Nekhen's murder?"

Sebek looked startled for a moment. "The murder? A little. Nekhen and I were never close."

"Why is that?"

"Oil and water. I was young and brash, and you know what French cuisine is like."

"Nekhen wasn't hard to get along with."

"I was, but I've grown up since then. So, what about the murder?"

"Neferaset. They think she did it."

"Nekhen's wife?" His eyes betrayed him; he had heard about the affair. I was suddenly sure that the entire restaurant world in Menmenet knew about the affair.

"Yes." I stared him down.

"OK, I've heard the rumors. Your business, not mine."

"It's gotten to where I need to help her. I need to investigate the murder. The medjau think she did it, and they're hounding her."

"So, it's personal."

"Very. But I can't cook and investigate, and I need somebody I can trust."

"That's me."

I considered his pluses and minuses, which didn't take very long, as there weren't many minuses that mattered. And I needed help now. The alternative was to look for somebody else, and that might take weeks. I didn't have weeks. I asked the only remaining question I had.

"When can you start?"

We haggled for a while over the price, and I settled for a salary I'd like to get myself, wincing over the lost profits. Trust is expensive. Sebek said he'd be there for dinner, as he would quit as soon as I left. And he grinned with all his teeth. At least I'd made somebody happy in my world.

I walked back to the Neferti. Henutsenu, hearing my decision, gave me a heartfelt hug. I took Dua aside in the kitchen to give her a heads-up.

"For how long?" Her expression was grim.

"I'm not sure; for as long as I take to deal with the murder. Any problem with it?"

Her grim expression didn't change, but I got the impression she thought I should let sleeping mummies lie. But she didn't object. We gathered everyone together and told them what to expect. There was surprise and concern at my jumping ship for a while, but everybody accepted the situation. Lunch orders came in, so we broke it up and got to work. I forced myself to focus on getting the orders out. It was a busy day, and the time passed quickly.

I stuck around until Sebek appeared. I showed him the ropes, then turned him over to Dua and vice versa. I walked home up the hill, ready to start my new detective career.

Dju-Keta was a warren of tiny streets that dead-ended in crumbling, red-rock cliffs or meandered around in circles around the hill. Where the hill was too steep for streets, several long stairways to heaven served instead. The most famous were the Djedkar'a Steps. You had to know where you were going to make your way from one side of the hill to the other. Tourists wandered for hours. They either got lost as the fog rolled in over them or wound up where they started rather than where they wanted to be.

I lived on Dju-Keta because it satisfied my urge for complexity. Navigating the mysterious, twisting streets energized me. I wouldn't last a week living on the Tjesut. The hill and ridge provided exercise and a view, but the lines were straight, and the only mystery was how anybody could afford the palaces there. On Dju-Keta, I had complexity and a big view as well—ma'at.

That evening, the walk home from work calmed me down. I let my mind roam, letting go of the evening's stresses and disappointments and upsets. I headed up the west side of the hill rather than along the steep cliffs on the east side. I needed more twists and turns to give myself time to think. My ambling took me in and out of little alleys and streets curling up the side of the hill. I was halfway home when I felt I was not alone. I sensed someone behind me, making the same turns I'd just made. Paranoia? Or had my resolve to be a detective made me think like one?

I needed an edge. I looked around through two more turns, then I found my edge, the perfect find for a werkhet stick fighter. An old push broom leaned up against a basement door. Not the best stick in the world, but it would do. I picked up the broom, unscrewed the handle, and hefted it. The metal that covered the end of the handle provided a nice grip. The stick itself was smooth wood, showing its age with raised grain here and there. It was longer than a regulation stick and had no guard, but it was solid and sound. I found the balance point, then gripped the stick and waited.

R'a sailed toward his rest in the west, throwing long shadows across the little streets. A shadow moved toward the corner, telling me that my follower was there, and that whoever it was, it wasn't an expert at surveillance. I waited, pressed against the stucco of the house as the shadow grew past the corner. The shadow's movement stopped. I withdrew into the basement door and held my breath. It was silent in the street.

A head poked around the corner, eyes searching for my trail. Then he saw me in the doorway and jumped back, his eyes big. It was Pabaky, Duaneferet's boyfriend.

I moved fast around the corner and saw Pabaky stepping backwards along the street, fumbling at his midriff. I strode toward him, holding the broomstick in guard, getting ready. The dim light of the sunset glinted off the steel of the knife in his right hand.

It was a short sword, a long, wide chef's knife with a point and a lethal edge honed to perfection. I recognized the make: a thousand uses, its maker advertised. This wasn't one of them.

"Put it down. You don't want to get in more trouble than you already are," I said. Concern for others was always the mark of a good manager, I thought to myself, and smiled. I've seen kitchens where the chef should have doled out spoons instead of knives as an occupational safety measure. I have always thought that being a jerk in a roomful of knives held by people who don't make very much money is purely bad judgment.

Pabaky, unimpressed by my management style, judged badly. The knife showed no tendency to leave his hand, which looked small gripping the big knife. His rage and humiliation brimmed over, and he raised the knife and charged me. I slid sideways to the left before he reached me. I slipped by him and used the stick on his back to push him off balance. He was quick; the knife grazed my coat as I went by. I turned as he staggered, recovered, and moved toward me again.

He was not a trained fighter, that much was obvious from his feet. His balance was off. He was stumbling around, not working toward a power stance from which he would launch the knife at a vulnerable spot. I stepped back a half step to position myself, took the length of the broomstick into account, and swung.

The stick connected with his rising wrist at the point of the greatest force of the swing. I had swung wide to get momentum, and I applied all the strength my shoulder could give. There came a crunch as the stick connected with his wrist.

The broomstick survived the blow; well made. It's a joy to work with good equipment. Pabaky dropped the knife and staggered again, crying out with the sudden pain. I stepped forward and kicked the knife away from him down the street. It disappeared into the gathering gloom.

I looked around. There were few windows on the street in this old-style part of the city. No neighbors had emerged to investigate the noise. No tourists were on hand to enjoy the spectacle. Nobody was out walking their cat. Pabaky, swearing in a loud voice, was rushing at me to tear me apart with his bare hands. I warded him off for a while with the stick, telling him, "Leave it, it won't do you any good, and you'll just get hurt more." He ignored me, but not the stick.

But somebody had noticed. Blue lights flashed as a patrol car edged into the small street. Pabaky ignored the emerging medjau, who ordered him to stop. They grabbed him, one of them grabbing his wrist. With a howl of pain, his knees buckled, and the two medjau held him.

I looked over the stick; not a scratch on it, despite the damage to Pabaky. I described the scene to the medja who held Pabaky. The other medja radioed for paramedics. I told them about the knife, showing where I'd kicked it. The long slit in my coat let me know how lucky I was not to be bleeding to death on the street. I showed the medjau that too. Pabaky said nothing through it all, groaning and shooting evil looks in my direction as the medjau guided him into their cruiser.

I restored the broom to its place and walked home. I was now a seasoned detective and had the fabric damage to prove it, but no clue about Pabaky's motive. Tomorrow, I'd have to talk to Dua about her choice of boyfriends.

CHAPTER FIFTEEN
MacIntyre Harbors Doubts

"I'M JUST A SIMPLE BUSINESSMAN, Hutyt. I know nothing of these matters."

Yaotl, the Aztec crime lord, had a smooth, low voice and a way of hooding his eyes that suggested that he knew many things you did not. MacIntyre knew that was indeed the case, but that it was her job to learn about those things.

"So, you have no idea why your late competitor died in traffic on Mentju Boulevard in broad daylight in a hail of bullets from a car that has since been identified as belonging to an associate of yours?" MacIntyre felt this jargon-filled summary was not her best effort. Too long, too complicated, and too vague. The man ordered his minions to execute a local rival. Right in the middle of the busiest street in Menmenet. In broad daylight. With no witnesses. Sure.

Yaotl was a small man, about sixty years old, with gray hair and piercing black eyes under hooded lids. His high cheekbones, grim-set mouth, and strong nose gave him an austere, powerful presence despite his size and relaxed manner.

Yaotl had agreed to meet with MacIntyre in his mansion on the Tjesut. His mansion was two blocks along the ridge from Nekhen's mansion, but a world away in style. An Aztec architect from the Modernist school had produced a wonder of technology. The mansion was a pyramidal building that joined glass and concrete into layers, a bold statement among the staid, white palaces of his neighbors. She would bet they loved the mansion no more than the man, an interloper in their midst. MacIntyre sat in a room facing the bay through a wall of glass. Her host sat in a large, modern chair facing the bay; she sat in a smaller chair at right angles to him. The walls displayed all kinds of Aztec antiquities: textiles, feathered costumes, weapons, and the occasional idol gazing on in astonishment at the riches. Gold glinted in many places, the ancient Aztecs sharing the Remetjy obsession with the metal.

"As I recall, Hutyt, my butler Eztli reported that car stolen well before this incident. I'm sure that if you check with your fellow enforcers of Menmenet law, you will find—"

"I've seen the report, Yaotl, and I don't believe it for a minute."

"But, Hutyt, the report is a fact. I must proceed based on facts in my business. Is that not true of yours?"

MacIntyre preferred intuition to facts. When she needed facts, she used pressure, as on the Wife. This wily old Aztec would not respond to pressure or intuition, and he had firm control of the facts, true or not. It was a primary reason for his not being in jail for life, considering what he had done in his career. His default argument in a dispute was the machete, or rather the Aztec version of that weapon, the macuahuitl, a nasty, flat wooden club with embedded razor blades. Modern Aztecs had rebuilt their country on modern principles and eschewed the macuahuitl. Yaotl was not a modern Aztec. While the macuahuitl resolved issues quickly, it often brought Yaotl unwelcome attention from the medjau. So far, that attention had not resulted in serious prison time. MacIntyre's job was to change that, and she could tell that it was going to be an uphill climb.

Her mind wasn't on Yaotl and his evasions. Her intuition told her he would evade responsibility despite her best efforts. Instead, her mind roved over the actions and behavior of her two biggest problems: the Wife and Shesmu.

The Wife had gone home from Shesmu's house and stayed there for two days. MacIntyre had parked her car near the mansion on the Tjesut and had watched the woman gardening. The sight of a goddess digging in the dirt was startling. Goddesses didn't do dirt. What the Wife *wasn't* doing was making mistakes and incriminating herself.

MacIntyre's intuition frayed. Doubt gnawed at it. If the Wife was washing invisible blood off her hands, MacIntyre hadn't seen it. Time would tell.

But Shesmu, now. A rock-solid alibi removed him from consideration as a murderer. His tight relationship with the Wife made him MacIntyre's best bet for evidence. Since he'd thrown her out of his restaurant, she'd considered various ways and means to get at him but had failed. She tried once to follow him in her car, but he walked everywhere and took pedestrian shortcuts. Mes wouldn't have approved the personnel for a proper tailing job. Not her case anymore, he'd say.

She had heard about the knife attack on Shesmu through the medja grapevine. She'd considered questioning him about it, but there was no way in hell Mes would approve of that. He'd fire her for sure. She downloaded the patrol report on the incident and laughed out loud at his defense. Who would attack a werkhet with a knife? Only a brain-dead loser like Duaneferet's boyfriend, Pabaky; she'd seen his record of encounters with the medjau in the past. Would Duaneferet give him the toss now? The sous chef was enough of a loser herself that MacIntyre doubted she'd have the wit to get rid of Pabaky. Pabaky's interrogation report would come along in due course. That would give her more to go on, and a way to turn Shesmu toward Ma'at, and even to turn Duaneferet.

So, all she had was Shesmu's certainty of the Wife's innocence. MacIntyre believed the Wife was the least innocent woman in Menmenet. She couldn't *prove* anything more than fashion sense and sexual excess. Her intuition about Shesmu, though—an honest man under the spell of a swamp woman. Had he seen any sign of guilt, she felt sure he would not cover for his lover. A knight errant. Doubt, doubt, doubt. But who else could have done it? The Wife fit the murder like a sheath dress.

Proof. What about Yaotl? What could she prove there? Nothing. Mes put her on this one on purpose to keep her busy. Yaotl would not go to jail. She switched tactics.

"Look, Yaotl. Facts are facts, yes. We should stick to them. Your business will not go well if you have to shoot up your rivals. They're just going to retaliate. We don't want a major gang war. I'm not worried about one less Ramaytush crime lord, I'm worried about civilians getting in the way, right? So far, you've been lucky."

"Luck is in the beholder's eye, Hutyt. Hard work and acumen have made my business successful. I know little of your 'crime lords' and 'gang wars.' I sell things to people that want to buy them. As you say, violence is a frightful thing. What would you suggest?"

"Say, Yaotl, that I was in the business. I would find subtle and peaceful ways to outmaneuver forays into my businesses. Medjau such as myself are all about ma'at. From time to time, you may learn facts that will bring more ma'at to the world—if the right people know those facts. A rival's misstep, a word in my ear, and the rival may prove less competitive. Facts speak volumes, as you might say."

Yaotl smiled and shifted to a more comfortable position in his expensive chair. "That is a much more reasonable approach to business, Hutyt. I feared on your fierce sally earlier that I faced an unreasoning personal attack, but I see now I was mistaken. I am often mistaken. I am prepared to advance ma'at as you suggest. Such missteps among my competitors occur often. I sometimes think they know more about Menmenet authority and procedure than do I. That may be because they devote more monetary resources to that side of their businesses. But with an ear such as yours available, we could do much. And business should be a two way boulevard, don't you think? If you wish compensation—"

MacIntyre smiled. "Oh, no, I want information. Ma'at is free for all." She extracted a card and placed it on the little table next to her chair. "Here's my phone number, Yaotl. It's private, my ear only. Take advantage of it. We want no more unfortunate deaths among either your associates or your rivals. Such events might even force a close examination of various business affairs. Affairs that we all would prefer to ignore. Don't you agree?"

"I do agree, Hutyt. Good business people handle business affairs in businesslike ways. We may do much business together, with time."

"May I call you if I find myself in need of business advice?"

"My private secretary will give you a number to call that will find me should such a rare occasion arise." He nodded his dismissal, and she rose to leave. She'd prefer to leave with a murderer in cuffs. Leaving with a compromise that might produce ma'at was at least something, queasy-making as it might be. As the butler guided her out, it occurred to her she might have to compromise on the Wife as well.

CHAPTER SIXTEEN
Shesmu Meets an Outlaw God

The day after my encounter with Pabaky, I sat kitchen table looking out at the foggy bay morning, drinking my morning cup of tea. Where to start? I thought over the day before and decided I might as well start with Rafe Blackmore. With Sebek's stellar reference, he was a logical candidate for thief and villain. His interest in Nekhen and his association with the most corrupt bureaucrat I knew, 'Aapehty, suggested he could be of real interest in the hunt for Nekhen's murderer. I also wondered whether the attempt at tomb robbery at Nekhen's tomb had anything to do with Blackmore's urgency.

I checked the time; he ought to be thinking about business by now. I picked up my phone and called him.

"Rafe Blackmore, how can I help?"

He spoke in Remetjy; I replied in English. "Hey Rafe, Shesmu here, returning your call. Sorry I was so busy, things have been hectic at my restaurant. I've freed up time now."

His voice sounding more confident in English, Blackmore said, "Fine, Shesmu. We're OK on timing now, but we shouldn't delay."

"Why the urgency?"

"Are you on board?"

"Depends on what you need me to do. Explain, please."

"Not on the phone. Can you come down to my office? I'm at 134 Liberty Street, in the American financial district."

"Sure. In an hour?"

"Great, see you then."

It was a little too far to walk, so I drove. As I navigated the twists and turns across the city to I'ahmes Creek and Liberty Street, my heart navigated the twists and turns of Blackmore's interests, and how Aset might respond to them. Blackmore's caginess made me nervous.

The office building at 134 Liberty Street was modest and modern. I saw from the directory in the lobby that it housed many small businesses. I took the elevator to the third floor, walked down a dim hallway, and found Blackmore's suite toward the end. I entered and found myself in another world, a world of elegant furniture and artwork from long ago. Blackmore emerged from the inner office and welcomed me, shaking my hand as Americans do, with both hands gripping mine in an effort to show how much he valued my presence. He drew me into his inner office and sat me down in an opulent armchair, then took the other chair. He leaned forward, arms resting on his legs and hands clasped, blue eyes looking straight into mine. His neat, curly brown hair and beard were cut short, and his whole face radiated sincerity. I instantly recognized the attributes of an excellent con man. You see so many in the restaurant business.

He was earnest. "I've got to have your assurance what I say will stay with you, and only with you. A lot of money is involved."

"Short of major crimes, sure."

Blackmore laughed. "No major crimes, Shesmu. Only a lot of money. Very well. There's an object, an ancient object, your friend Nekhen had in his possession. The urgency was we heard the object was going into his tomb with him. Unfortunate."

"And did that happen?"

"No. We have excellent information that Mrs. Nekhen—sorry, Lady Nekhen —I'll never get used to these Remetjy titles. We have excellent information she has the object. Which brings you in."

Excellent information from whom? My adventure in the tomb on Nekhen's funeral day came into my heart. I would need to speak again with Idnu Iny.

I said, "You think I can get Neferaset to sell you this object."

"Yes."

"What is it?"

"A knife."

I opened my mouth and closed it again. "Rafe—you must know—"

"Yes, yes. Killed with a knife. Not this one." His smile was a bit grim.

"How do you know?"

"It's an art object, an antiquity. No one would use that particular knife to kill someone." There was something in his voice that bubbled below the surface like suppressed laughter.

"You sure?"

"Very. Especially not Nekhen."

"Why?"

"Let's just focus on the deal." His eyes locked on mine to keep me centered on his needs, not mine.

"What do you want?"

"I'd like to make Lady Nekhen an offer that will persuade her to part with the object. I'd like you to talk to her, find out what kind of arrangement would be welcome, get her to call me."

"What is this knife? Why so valuable?"

"I can't go into that." He smiled.

"Why not?"

"No trader reveals everything he knows. We find out what the other party knows first." He leaned back in his chair, relaxed. Nothing unusual in all this, his body said.

"Rafe, I'm in love with the lady. If the antiquity is truly valuable, and she wants to sell, I'm on her side in the negotiation."

"An even better reason not to tell you what I know, Shesmu," Blackmore replied in his smoothest tones. "No offense."

"I'll push for the best deal she can get."

"Fair enough." He nodded and smiled again.

Did I want to go through with this? Talking to Aset about a knife? Would I get more understanding of what Blackmore was doing? Maybe. Would it hurt her too much? Would she think I was betraying her in some way? I'd tell her it was part of my helping with the murder to take the sting away. Now that we were speaking again, she'd assume the best, not the worst.

I said, "How should I describe the knife to her? So she'll understand what knife I'm talking about."

"Huh. Well, let's see. The knife is about a foot and a half long, curved, with a wood handle." He used his hands to show the size he meant. "The handle has carved hieroglyphs. The blade has writing too."

"OK." I asked, "What if she gets the knife appraised?"

"I'd recommend against, Shesmu. If word gets out, it could be…well, dangerous." His voice dropped a little on the last word.

"What do you mean?"

"There's quite a lot of money involved. Not everyone in the business here in Menmenet is as scrupulous as I am."

That didn't fill me with confidence.

"And somebody might try to rob her?"

"Or worse. You don't know with these things. It'd be different in the States, but here…." He shook his head and looked down, unwilling to offend me by trash-talking my town. Flawless.

"This isn't a lawless backwater, Rafe. This is Menmenet."

"No offense. Things I've seen, people…and the diversity of types. Well, for example, you don't want the Aztecs involved. And they will be if you get the knife appraised. All the appraisers in Menmenet are Aztecs. And…there may be other parties, truly unsavory ones…."

"Hm. OK. Interesting. Another question—why didn't you approach Nekhen on this?"

"I learned about the knife a few days before his death, didn't get the chance. Then, after, 'Aapehty gave me your name. I couldn't call up Mrs.—Lady Nekhen, not so soon after the funeral, but with you having such a close relationship…." Earnest again, eyes on mine again.

"Yeah, OK. I see." I did see; I just didn't believe a word. He could easily have killed Nekhen for the knife. But why get 'Aapehty involved? It would raise questions. It did that right now in me. Only one way to find out.

"OK, Rafe. Fifteen percent."

"Your fee?"

"That's right."

"Eight."

"Twelve."

"Ten."

"Done." I'd give the money to Aset, to show her how much I loved her now that she was speaking to me again.

I appreciate knives. I can whittle a complicated flower out of a carrot in a minute flat. But an ancient knife with hieroglyphs was not something I had encountered in any kitchen I'd trained in. I needed help to find a connection. That meant Ruty.

Ruty was a man I'd met at the Imenhetep Club. I'd never seen him stick fighting. He was always in the locker room talking to someone. In some underground way that I didn't understand, Ruty made his money helping people through the planning and construction bureaucracy in Menmenet. There were rumors that he had too much influence, but then there are always rumors like that about people who get things done. Ruty wasn't shady; but if you needed shady, he could refer you.

When I walked into the locker room the morning after I talked to Blackmore, I could hear Ruty, who had a clear, deep voice that never tired. I walked up through the two rows of lockers. His subject was carpets, the expensive kind. He ran down a long list of things to look at in carpets from Persia, China, India, and a dozen other places. Then he started in on thread counts and dyes and how to tell whether a carpet was real or fake, aged or new.

I cut into Ruty's monolog and greeted him as a long-lost pal. The other guy finished dressing and escaped with an air of gratitude and a last recommendation from Ruty to check out a shop that Ruty told him would give him a good deal. Ruty could then turn his attention to me.

"Still cooking up a storm at that restaurant, Shes?" he asked. His grizzled beard and mustache framed his grin of welcome, the smile lines crinkling all over his middle-aged face.

"Yes, it's going well. How come I never see you there, Ruty?"

"Your stuff is too rarefied for me, Shes. Why don't you open up a café with normal food? With your talent, you'd pull them in like flies." He said this so inoffensively that I couldn't take offense, even at the flies.

I said, "Your friend there didn't seem interested in carpets."

He snickered. "Yeah. He pissed me off early in the conversation, so I made sure he'd be late for his next appointment. Too bad you interrupted so early. I was about to get into how indigenous tribes in Asia make the things."

"How much do you really know about carpets?"

"I read an article in the newspaper a couple of weeks ago. That's about it."

"And the shop?"

"Rip-off artists from the old country. They'll take care of him." I'd have to be careful about Ruty, I thought.

I sat down on the bench that stretched down the middle of the locker bay and prepared for talk. I spent a half hour working my way through restaurants to government to the antiquities trade. Then I got to business.

"Do you know any good antiquities dealers here?"

"Good... Do you mean good for you, good for them, or good for the legal trade?"

"A fair price and not too many questions."

He mentioned several names, Blackmore's not among them, and started talking about the economics of antiquities trading. I learned the tradeoff between dealers who understood what they were doing and dealers who would give you a fair price. Trading in Remetjy artifacts was practically nonexistent in Menmenet, where trade focused on Chinese and Japanese artifacts. Remetjy government control was too tight on Empire relics. Ruty, too, suggested avoiding the Aztec assessors for one's health. I learned many irrelevant things, too. Many.

Finally, I got specific. "Well, I've got this old Remetjy knife, and I'd like to see if it's worth anything. I'll take it to the dealers you mentioned and see what they say."

Ruty smiled and said, "Knife, eh? Look, you ought to show it to Hernefer, the collector. He knows a lot about Remetjy antiquities, and he's a knife guy. He's a little eccentric, but he loves those knives. Let me call him." He grabbed his mobile phone from his locker, looked up a number in his contacts, and called. He spoke briefly, then handed me the phone, saying, "Hernefer; he'll help you."

I said, "Hello; this is Shesmu, a friend of Ruty's. He thinks you could help me."

The voice on the other end was gruff and cautious. "What can I do for you?"

"Well, I have this old Remetjy knife. I want to find out what it's worth."

"Describe it."

I gave him Blackmore's description. The voice sounded even more cautious. "Who are you fronting for?"

"Excuse me?"

"You heard me."

This must be the eccentric part. I gave the phone back to Ruty, and said, "Tell him who I am. He has doubts."

Ruty did his thing, extolling my cuisine, praising my honesty, and vouching for my very ka, none of which he'd ever seen. He handed the phone back just as I was thinking he'd run the phone out of battery.

Hernefer said, "OK, so you're a superb chef and you're really real. So what are you after?"

"It will take time to explain, and I don't want to do it over the phone. I don't have the knife, but I know where it is. I just don't know enough about it. Can we get together so I can explain?"

"Come now." He gave me brief directions and hung up.

Eccentric? I looked at Ruty. I said, "Iu-Sedeg? The big island in the bay? Just how rich is this guy?"

He smiled. "Billions. A magnate." Not eccentric. Rich. Very rich. The very rich differ from you and me; they are never eccentric.

I pulled my car up in line on the lower deck of the North Bay ferry and found a seat forward on the viewing deck. As the ferry pulled out into the bay, I had a magnificent view of the north bay and the islands. Iu-Qedju, to the east, was just a smallish rock with a military installation. Nobody knew what the army did there. It was top secret.

Beyond Iu-Qedju loomed the much larger Iu-Sedeg, home to billionaires. Millionaires and lesser gods had their places on the next island over, just a bump out of the mainland. But Iu-Sedeg was where the true elite lived in the Bay Area. Everybody called it The Island. It had stunning views of the entire bay. And it was very private.

When somebody needed to go to the Island, or somebody on the Island needed to be picked up, the big ferry veered north, off the direct line from the city. You paid double the fare. The Island ferry dock was on the north side of the Island, near a tiny village of shops that had grown up to serve the needs of the Island residents. Billionaires divided the rest of the Island into a very few estates with large, palatial houses built into the hillsides. Double fares kept it private along with the lack of anything useful to do besides looking at the water and counting your money.

The road rambled around the perimeter of the Island. This afforded the driver the simultaneous joy of seeing forever and the fear of diving into the bay by missing one of the tight turns. It was one lane, and the residents had large, fast cars with drivers that didn't care whether anyone else was on the road. Car size controlled the local right-of-way rules. When two cars faced off, the smaller one backed up until it could pull off the road and let its superior by. After some harrowing adventures, I got to the turn that led to the winding road that became Hernefer's driveway. The last part of the driveway followed alongside a tall stone wall and ended at a gate framed by large, red stone pillars. The two gates were an ornate twirling of metal upon metal, but I saw when I pulled up to it that the metal was heavy enough to resist a tank.

A guardhouse bristling with electronics stood at the right side of the gate. As I pulled up to the gate, a guard approached my car. He had the slow assured step of a military man, and his guard's uniform was crisp, down to the pleated shendyt and new dress sandals. As I opened my window, the guard smiled frostily. "Shesmu, from Menmenet?" I nodded. "Park in the guest lot, up the hill, first turn on your right. A guard will meet you and take you to the house." Before I even had the chance to nod, the guard turned and sauntered back to the guardhouse, about three points short of total rudeness. The gate swung open to admit me.

I drove up the hill and turned into the parking lot cut into the side of the hill. I've shopped at superstores with smaller lots. At the top of the hill was the house.

It was ridiculous even to call this thing a house. It made the mansions and palaces of the Tjesut, where Aset lived, look like suburban boxes. Built on a hill, it spread up at least four stories, with setbacks and ornate balconies. The house was the same color as the surrounding hill. I'd never spotted it while admiring the view from my house on Dju-Keta. The guard met me and took me in through the servant's entrance.

The guard took me through lots of doors and halls, finally reaching Hernefer's inner sanctum. It was a library and display area for antique artifacts from all over the world. In a house with tremendous views, there were no windows. The room smelled faintly of old leather books and temples. Shelves stretched from floor to ceiling, interspersed with display cases and stands holding statues, books, pottery, scrolls, jewelry, and things I couldn't name. Half were Remetjy. The rest were native artifacts from this hemisphere, plus a motley assortment of items from the Wadjwer and surrounding areas. There were several security cameras; I assumed that there were other, less visible security arrangements. The collective worth of the items in the room staggered me.

The door swung open again, and a short, rotund individual entered and dismissed the guard. He dressed in expensive clothes, high-quality linen that he hadn't cleaned in some time. He hadn't pressed his shendyt in a while. His sandals were as old as the other antiques in the room but hadn't been cared for of anywhere nearly as well.

No greeting. "What have you got?"

"A story."

He shook his head. "No time. Business waiting. Get to it. Keep it short." He waved at a chair, and we sat.

"A friend just inherited a knife from her murdered husband. A trader expressed an interest to me, wants me to talk to her about it and make a deal. I need to learn more about it."

"Are you getting anything out of it?"

"10%, which I'll give to her. I have other motives."

A phone buzzed. It was an ornate European thing on a table to the side of our chairs. Hernefer reached for the handset and listened. He stared at me while somebody talked, and said to the phone, "Nothing else?" There wasn't, and he hung up.

"You may be interested in knowing that you check out according to my sehy. He says your food is good."

"My food is terrific. Is this relevant?"

"It is to me. I don't like dealing with people I know nothing about, and I don't, or didn't, know anything about you. Or your lover. Now I do. A romantic." He grinned. His teeth were perfect; that must be where he put his money. So he, too, had learned about Aset and me.

I tried on a confident smile. "Sure. So where does that take us?"

He leaned back in his chair and stared at me with unblinking eyes. He got out of his chair and waddled over to a set of drawers built into the wall between two bookcases. I got up and followed. He manipulated a digital lock on one drawer and pulled it open. I saw, nestled in form-fitting inserts, a series of knives. They varied in size and shape, but all looked like Blackmore's description. They all had the curve to them, all had glyphs on their handles and blades. The handles were all different; this wasn't a matched set. Ivory, different woods, and one that looked like gold.

"What am I looking at?" I asked.

"These are Remetjy ritual sacrifice knives from the Middle Empire period. How much do you know about animal cults?"

"I cook them; I don't spend much time in temples worshipping them."

"I buy and sell them—cattle, sheep, that kind of thing. Animals are at the center of temple worship in Kemet, and these knives are how the hemu-netjer of the temples sacrifice them."

"Are they valuable?"

"Value comes from rarity. Knives passed from father to son or mother to daughter among the hemu-netjer; they still are. Only occasionally did a knife get mislaid." His voice emphasized the last word.

"You mean stolen."

"Yes, we don't like to use the word. It can prejudice negotiations."

"I'll bet."

"Also, if a hem-netjer died without passing on his duties to a family member, often they entombed his knife with him. During the Old and Middle Empire, tomb robberies were common. These knives probably, but not provably, come from such robberies. They have little scientific or historical value as they have no provenance or context. But these two other knives have provenances."

Hernefer pointed out two smaller knives that didn't seem any different from the others in quality. "They belonged to a family of hemu-netjer of a cult that worshipped some kind of large Amazonian monkey. When the people down there wiped out the monkey habitat, the monkeys disappeared and so did the cult. Foolish." I wasn't sure whether he meant the people that wiped out the monkeys or the hemu-netjer. "These knives were no longer sacred, so they came on the market and here they are."

"How rare are these knives? How many of them are out there?"

"Old ones like these—you're looking at them. I've got them all. Except for the one your lover has." He gave me a sharp glance. "Have you seen it?"

"No, the trader told me about it."

"And she's never mentioned it?"

"No."

"And your lover's husband never mentioned it?"

"Never."

"How sure are you she has it?"

"Not absolutely."

"What did the trader say it was worth?"

"A lot. He wouldn't be specific, part of his negotiating strategy."

"Huh." Hernefer rubbed his mouth, eyes on his toes. He looked up. "What is your lover's husband's name?"

"Nekhen, he was a celebrity chef in Menmenet, owner of the Per'ankh restaurant."

He locked the knife drawer and waddled back to his chair, and I followed. He reached and punched a number into the phone. "Hernefer. A man named Nekhen, chef, owned the Per'ankh restaurant in Menmenet until last week, murdered. Genealogy back to forever, anything interesting. Now." He disconnected. He stared at me in silence. I debated: should I make small talk? Ask about his collection? Ask for tips on becoming a billionaire? The phone rang, and he picked it up and listened. A gleam came into his eye, and he hung up.

"I want in."

"Sorry?"

"I want into the deal. You want information, I want the knife. We can cut the trader out if you like. Not good business though. Not ethical."

This deal was getting complicated. "Why do you want in?"

"I'll save that for later. Deal?"

"Blackmore, that's the trader, may not agree."

"He will. Blackmore? Crook."

I smiled. "You know your business."

"Damn right. Deal?"

"OK, deal."

"Seteh."

I waited for the rest of it, but that was all. "Excuse me?"

"The god. Seteh, Lord of Chaos and the Desert. Your friend Nekhen descends from the last hem-netjer-tepy of Seteh."

"But Seteh—isn't he outlawed? No temples. Not for centuries."

"Right."

"So the knife would be a ritual knife of Seteh, is that your big revelation?"

"There's more. I'll save that for later too." But the gleam in his eye grew brighter. "I'll say that your trader is right, there's a lot of money involved. But I have a lot, and I don't have that knife, and I want it."

"Does Seteh being illegal mean the knife has legal issues?"

"What do you care?"

"It wouldn't be ethical."

He gave me a disbelieving stare. "Can you use 100,000 debenu?"

The quick answer was yes, but I don't like quick answers. "That much? 10%?"

"Yes. At the absolute least."

"You're saying that money drowns ethics."

"I am saying exactly that." His round face looked at me with a serious leer.

"I won't do that, I won't get involved in illegal trading."

He smiled. "Good for you. But there's still the knife. Who has it?" He waited.

I thought it through. Aset had the knife; the knife was illegal as hell; therefore....

"She's in danger, isn't she? While she holds this illegal knife?"

"Huh. There are two kinds of law: civil and religious. You can't inherit an illegal good, and you can't sell an illegal good, and you can't own an illegal good. Both civil and religious laws apply. The Knife of Seteh might get people in various powerful temples very excited, Shesmu, excited enough to consider human sacrifice."

"I hope you're joking."

"Well, yes. Even Imen-R'a doesn't go in for executions anymore. Only the Americans still do that. Blackmore can worry about that. I doubt anyone would miss him if sacrificed. But look, Shesmu—the point is, you've got to keep this quiet until we know what's what. Messy, but we can get there. Illegalities have a way of fading away when faced with lots of money. But let's avoid juggling too many illegal knives at once. Do we have a deal?"

"Deal," I said. Hernefer gave me his personal mobile phone number and told me to call when I had something for him.

"She's out there," said Aset. I'd showed up at her house the morning after my session with Hernefer, and she was glad to see me, but then she noticed another, unwanted, guest.

"Who?" I asked.

"That semetyt. MacIntyre. She's parked in my driveway again."

I walked over to the front windows. Yes, there was the little red car with the blonde American sitting in it in bright morning sun. With binoculars. She waved at me. I gave her the two-finger salute. I walked back into the great room. MacIntyre hadn't been there when I'd arrived. Aset had greeted me with love and a passionate kiss as soon as I'd come in the door.

"I'm sorry, Aset, she's a pain. She has nothing, that's why she's still there."

We went into the great room. I told her, "Nekhen left you an old knife that's related to Seteh, and his family has a history with the god. It's illegal. Just having this knife is risky, Aset. You've got to sell it."

"Seteh." As I'd spoken, Aset's face darkened and grew angrier and angrier. "Shes, I asked you to help me stay out of jail for murder. Now you're talking to me about Seteh. What are you doing? What are you doing to me?"

I pointed out the palace on Iu-Sedeg as I told Aset about what I'd discovered from Hernefer the day before. I told her about Blackmore and his offer and about Hernefer, his collection, and his lust for the knife. I told her about Seteh and how dangerous the knife was. Her stormy face just grew more clouded. Those lips I'd just kissed with passionate abandon, now pressed tight with anger. Concentrate, Shes.

"If you sell the knife, Aset—"

"Get out."

"Aset, I can't—"

"Get out of my house."

"Aset—"

She got up and pulled me up and turned me toward the door and pushed. She was crying. "Out. Now."

"But, Aset—"

"You don't know what you're getting yourself into, Shesmu. Seteh. Get out. I never want to see you again."

The door slammed behind me. I stood again on the portico, looking at a little red car.

CHAPTER SEVENTEEN
MacIntyre Overdoes It

AND THERE HE CAME. MACINTYRE had waved at Shesmu when he appeared in the window to make sure he knew she knew he knew she was there. Or something like that. And he'd flipped her off. And now, here he came to confront her, to tell her to leave, to yell at her. She braced herself. But he just scowled and walked away down the sidewalk. She levered herself out of her car seat and trotted after him, touching him on the arm. He turned.

"Hutyt."

"Hi, Shes. It's Cheryl, remember?" He wasn't yelling yet.

"Yeah. Look. I'm—tired. No more questions."

Surprised, she examined his face. Not angry, weary. Body language was weary, too. Maybe she could help him. Maybe….

"What's up, Shes?"

He said nothing, staring at the house. MacIntyre re-ran the scene: was the Wife pushing him out of the house to have him confront her, or was it something else?

"What happened?" she asked.

"She threw me out of the house. Never wants to see me again. She said."

"OK. Tell me all."

"No."

"Oh, come on. You can't just stand there looking like a wet rag and tell me she's hung you out to dry and that's it. Why?"

"You'll just use it against her."

Exasperated, MacIntyre agreed with him. "Damn right I will." She turned and marched up to the house and pounded on the door with her fist. She kept pounding until the door opened.

The Wife appeared as though she'd gone through a wringer, much like Shes. "Go away," she said.

MacIntyre pushed inside, and the Wife retreated backwards in alarm. MacIntyre hadn't thought through her tactics, hadn't thought much at all. She had formed a nebulous intent to force a confession. Intuition told her that the woman was distraught. She'd just broken up with Shes again. There was no better time to get a confession than when the subject's emotions had exploded in a cataclysm of nerves.

"Why did you do it?" she demanded.

"What?" The Wife's eyes were enormous as fright took hold of her.

MacIntyre clarified her question. "Why did you kill your husband? Cut his throat? All that blood? Why?"

The tears were flowing, a good sign, but MacIntyre didn't care. She wanted this done and this woman in jail. Shes deserved better than what the Wife had done to him.

The Wife said in a high-pitched voice, "I didn't. I did not kill him. I couldn't kill him. Why are you doing this to me? Why did Shesmu send you in here? Does he hate me that much?"

MacIntyre backed off, cooling down. Tactics. Try again. Persuasive. "I'm here to get you to confess. Shes has nothing to do with this. Tell me. Get it off your chest. Believe me, you'll feel better. Tell me what you did with the knife."

"Get out of my house!" The Wife, hysterical, pointed at the door. "Leave me alone! I did not kill my husband!"

MacIntyre backed away, worrying that she might have overdone it. The rational part of her brain engaged. She had broken about every rule in the medjau book under the assumption that the Wife was ready to crack. She wasn't. That put MacIntyre in an awkward position. She'd acted rashly out of anger, and it hadn't worked out. More doubt about the woman's guilt clouded her intuition. Best to leave without making things worse.

She turned on her heel and walked out. Shesmu stood at the base of the stairs to the portico.

"What did you do?" he shouted. He'd heard the screaming; MacIntyre was sure all the neighbors had too, distant as they were from the enormous mansion.

"Can I give you a ride somewhere?" she asked, her voice hoarse. She cleared her throat. Shes could tell her—

"No! Get out of here! Leave us alone. Leave us alone!" He started up the stairs to the door, pushing past MacIntyre, but the Wife had slammed it shut with a finality that stopped him cold, shoulders sagging.

MacIntyre, without saying a word and with a face like a thundercloud, walked down the path, got into her car, and drove away.

"That's it. You're done. Gimme." Djehutymes held out his hand, palm up.

"Give you what?" MacIntyre gripped the arms of her chair.

"Badge and gun. You're suspended without pay. Until we figure out what to do with you." He continued to hold out his hand.

"Look, Mes, I'm sorry. I got hot and overdid it, OK? I know you'll have to take me off the case, but—"

"Badge and gun, MacIntyre. And you were already off the case! That just makes it worse. Badge and gun."

"What about the Aztec—"

"Badge and gun, MacIntyre. Now!" He curled his fingers twice for emphasis. She'd never seen his eyes so furious. The Wife had every right to complain, and she had. Or her sehy had. MacIntyre sat, frozen, her sense of ma'at violated by the injustice of Mes's suspending her for this.

"Do I have to arrest you?" Mes curled his fingers again, staring at her with his fiercest expression.

MacIntyre could sense the anger making her face burn. Another reason she'd never be a champion poker player—her face. She stood up, dug out her credentials and her gun, and handed them to her superior. She turned and walked out before she said something she'd regret. Why add to the pile?

She wiped a lone tear of frustration away. Elevator. Down. Going down. She pushed the button.

CHAPTER EIGHTEEN
Shesmu Tangles with Inpu

I WOKE UP THE NEXT morning feeling like a 5,000-year-old mummy with clinical depression.

A walk across the waterfront and three good stick bouts at the Imenhetep Club cleared away the cobwebs and the despair. It got me thinking about next steps. I sat in the club lounge drinking Remetjy tea and considering the events of the day before.

Aset's emotions made little sense to me. Her reaction was excessive, given the facts. I don't believe the bullshit that all women are irrational. I couldn't reconcile the beautiful, loving Aset I adored with the angry and hysterical woman that threw me out and screamed at MacIntyre. Well, the screaming at MacIntyre part, OK. But Aset had told me I didn't know what I was getting myself into. I turned that around in my mind until it came out the other side. I didn't know what Aset had gotten herself into, but everything she'd reacted to centered on the knife. The knife was in the tomb, and the tomb was the realm of Inpu, god of the necropolis.

The Temple of Inpu was at the crest of the hill, above the rows of chapels and tombs. The building was low and massive, with sloping pylon walls and thick papyrus columns. There was a security station in the lobby with a w'ab on duty. I asked to see Idnu Iny. After a wait of a few minutes, Iny came out, greeted me with informal bows, and took me back into the warren of offices.

"Is there anything new you can tell me about the tomb?" I asked.

"Not much. We picked up prints from the tomb door, but so far they match nothing on file. We're sending digital prints to the international agencies to check as a matter of routine."

"What's your next step?"

"The logical one." He smiled.

"Which is?" I asked.

Iny smiled again and looked at me. He said nothing, rocking his chair back and forth behind his desk. He wouldn't tell me anything, at least not without persuasion. Instead, he deflected the conversation back to me.

"Why are you here?"

"Nekhen was my friend."

"So was his wife, as I understand it."

I smiled. "Off and on."

"Is she pressuring you on this nothing robbery?"

"No, I'm here on my own. Come on, Iny, I can't help you if you won't help me. I'm sure Inpu won't mind." I waved a hand at the picture of the necropolis jackal god on the wall, which snarled down at me.

"What do you want me to do?"

"Take me into the tomb so I can see what goods are there."

Iny looked at me with a blank face. "You don't have a clue, do you?"

"I like to think I do."

"'Take me into the tomb,' he says." He shut his eyes, then glared at me. "Do you know what the penalty is for opening a tomb? Without very special permission from the Hem-Netjer-Tepy of Inpu?"

"No."

"Ten years hard labor on the temple's tomb-building gang. And that would be me. For you, twenty years and entombment proscription—no mummy, tomb, or chapel, ever." He tapped a finger on his desk. "These guys are serious, Shesmu. Tombs stay closed."

"And if you took something?"

"You do know that the temples don't come under the civil laws about torture, right?"

"No, I wasn't aware of that. I'm not religious."

"You would be, after a few weeks of it."

"When I talked to you before, you said something about records. Do you have a list of tomb items?"

"Sure, but it's private. Only family can see it."

"I'm family."

"Sleeping with the guy's wife does not make you family, Shesmu."

"Harsh, Iny."

"True, though."

I tried for persuasive again. "I could help a lot, Iny, but I need that list. Make me a copy."

"I can't let the list out of this building."

That sounded as close to a yes as anything I'd ever heard, so I pressed on.

"How much?"

He sat back in his chair. "Are you offering me a bribe?"

"I'm trying to, yes." I fished out my wallet and checked; 237 debenu. I extracted 200 and waved it at Iny.

"That's not enough."

"It's all I have with me. How about 200 now, 200 later?"

"How much later?"

"Tomorrow or the next day?"

"All right. Fine." He took the money and put it away. He stared hard at me for a minute, then leaned over to his computer, pressed a few keys, and motioned toward the screen. I walked around his desk and glanced over his shoulder. He'd opened an insurance document that listed out the contents of the tomb. It wasn't a long list.

"Is this the usual stuff you find in tombs?" I asked.

"About average. Most people have one or two required religious items, a few favorite items, and funeral gifts, maybe a dozen things. People are passing more on to their families and surviving with the bare minimum in the Duat."

Nekhen and Aset had rich friends and relations. There were few items, but they were expensive. A golden statue of Nekhen with Aset, a custom copy of the Book of Going Forth by Day, and two cookbooks, one French, one Remetjy. You never know who's coming to dinner in the afterlife. There was a knife and a silver cow with a huge udder; even in the Duat, a French chef will need a knife and butter.

Total value appraised at 9,000 deben, about $30,000 American at current exchange rates. The insurance company was Greater Menmenet Property and Life, the biggest tomb insurer in the sepat. The family had insured the tomb items for replacement value with a discount for an electronic security system built into the tomb and a second discount for 100-year renewal.

"Does this office check the security system?"

"Not in this case. That's a private firm with offices down the road. They call us if there's a problem."

"Do you have any pictures of these things? I want to see that knife."

"Why?"

"It's come up once or twice in conversations."

He turned to his computer, scrolled and clicked.

"That's the knife in the tomb. I got to tell you, it doesn't seem like much to me. I've seen a lot of tomb robberies, and none of them were for items like this. Robbers like gold and silver and jewels, not keepsakes. Unless we're dealing with an obsessive, barking-mad archaeologist?"

I ignored the heavy-handed humor and asked, "Can I get a print-out of this?"

"No, you can't. I shouldn't even show it to you. You have nothing to bargain with."

"I guess not."

I scrutinized the picture—two pictures, one from each side. There was a rule next to the object showing that it was a touch less than 47 centimeters long. A handle made of wood, smooth, with small animal decorations at the top. The picture wasn't any too clear, but at least one animal looked like a Seteh beast—a jackal with big, square ears. The iron blade was wide and curved like the ones I'd seen in Hernefer's drawer.

Solid and heavy, designed to chop through things that resist cutting, the blade had a worn and wavy edge and the brightness you get from frequent stone sharpening. No rust. But this was no chef's knife, wrong shape. This was a sacrifice ritual knife that looked just like the ones Hernefer collected.

I asked, "Where and when were these pictures taken?"

"The necropolis bureaucracy keeps excellent records. Everything that goes through the purification rituals gets imaged and stored in the confidential scribal archives. The w'abu of Inpu took these pictures as part of the purification process."

"So unless there was a major screw-up, or a w'ab stole it, the knife is in the tomb."

"That's pretty much it. For what it's worth, the chances of either of those things happening is nil, at least in my experience."

"And there's no chance of opening the tomb to make sure. How about another 200 debenu?"

"Don't even ask. Believe me—not a chance. I can't do it myself, and the w'abu of Inpu aren't anywhere near as corrupt as I am."

"And there's no surveillance equipment in the tomb itself?"

"Like a web-cam, you mean? No. There's not much going on for people to watch, you know? And the religious court of Inpu has ruled that putting a camera in the tomb can happen only with proper ritual blessings to propitiate the ka. Kau don't like people watching. Unless you pay for it. A lot." There was a gleam in Iny's eye. "The widow didn't pay for it. Why are you so interested in this knife?"

I explained about Blackmore and Hernefer. The gleam grew brighter.

"So that might be a reason for the attempted robbery?"

"I'd bet on it."

"I'll look into this guy Blackmore. Throw a scare into him."

"You do that. Let's keep that knife safely in the hands of Nekhen's ka."

But with the knife in the tomb and things arranged just as they should be, I was back to square one on the senet board. I couldn't understand why Aset had thrown me out of her house.

"You don't look happy about it all, Shesmu," commented Iny, getting up.

I got up and bowed. "I'm not, but that's not your worry, Iny. Thanks for the help, and I'll get the 200 debenu to you. I'm sure Inpu approves." The god still snarled down at me from his picture, but Iny seemed pleased as he showed me out.

CHAPTER NINETEEN
MacIntyre Finds a Soft Spot

MacIntyre's chin wore out the skin on her palm as she leaned on her elbow at her kitchen table. She stared into space, trying to make sense of it all. Much of the day had gone by, and she had made little progress other than taking care of basic bodily needs. By late afternoon, she was ready to go back to bed.

Her phone buzzed and showed a number she didn't recognize. On the third ring, she picked up. There was no other entertainment on tap for the evening.

"Cheryl?"

After listening to the nuances of the Remetjy female voice, she smiled.

"Henutsenu. How nice to hear from you."

"I'm sorry, I should have called before, but I waited until my day off." That sounded promising. "Shesmu told me about his throwing you out. I'm sorry about that. He made a mistake."

"Did he tell you about yelling at me to go to hell last night?"

A long pause. "No, I haven't seen him today. Look, are you all right?"

"No."

"Let's meet."

MacIntyre sat up. Now things were moving. "Sure, where?"

"Nebu's?"

Nebu's Place was a popular lesbian bar near the harbor. MacIntyre had gone there twice with R'aia. The bar was great but a bit too high-toned for her late lover, who ran more to tattoos and dancing than to businesswomen and polite drinking. It was exactly the sort of watering hole to find followers of Bastet.

"Sure. When?"

"An hour? We can have dinner after." Sounded promising.

"I'll be there."

A pause. "Have you been before?"

"Oh, yes. Don't worry, I have good clothes."

"I never worry, Cheryl. Except about Shesmu."

"Well, join the club. OK, see you there."

MacIntyre spent some time on her choice of clothes. She wore full Remetjy style rather than her usual mixed Remetjy-American melange. It wasn't up to Henutsenu's fashion level, but the white dress with gold edges and red highlights was her best. She put on the bead necklace R'aia had made for her, the turquoise picking up the blue of her eyes, but she wore no makeup.

Nebu's calm, warm atmosphere greeted MacIntyre like an old friend. She spotted her new friend Henutsenu right away at a little table in the back. A glass of white wine stood before her, untouched. Her smile told MacIntyre she hadn't been waiting long. She got up to greet MacIntyre with a sinuous, cat-like motion ending in a cheek kiss. MacIntyre saw she was wearing another gold dress that put her own to shame. A subtle onyx cat with ruby eyes curled around one wrist as a bracelet, showing her devotion to the goddess Bastet. MacIntyre pretended all this style didn't intimidate her. She sat and asked the server to get her a glass of the wine her friend had in front of her.

Henutsenu said, taking a sip of wine, "I thought Nebu's would be good because you can hear yourself talk in here, and we need to talk, Cheryl."

"What about, Henutsenu?" She loved the way the name sounded; it translated to "package of kisses," which summed up her feelings about the woman. Or did it? How well did she understand this elegant Remetjy woman? There was the Bastet business, which was a mystery to her. There was the strong steel hand in a velvet glove that she had felt herself when she had criticized Shesmu. And there was that devotion to Shesmu and his restaurant. A very different woman from R'aia, much more reserved and fashion conscious. Just as sexy, though. Cats. Her family had run to dogs, not cats, and she'd always wondered about them. Now she could find out what it was all about.

Henutsenu dashed her hopes. "Shesmu."

Oh well. "Right. Bring me to a lesbian bar to talk about a man."

Henutsenu smiled. "It felt right."

MacIntyre winced. "Yeah, well. You're the first thing that's gone right with me today."

"Have we gone right?"

"Not yet, but I have hopes."

"Do you? I like you, Cheryl. We could have a delightful time. But."

"There's that word. But?"

"I'm in a committed relationship with a man. I don't want to break out of that."

"May I ask about him?"

"A chef named Sebek, Nekhetsebek. He's taking over for Shesmu at the Neferti, while Shesmu works through his current problems."

"Oh, a long-term position then."

Henutsenu smiled, but it was clear she didn't see the humor in it.

MacIntyre said, "Sorry, I realize you care about Shesmu. I'll try to be serious. About him, anyway. Commitment aside—a little fun, for a little while?"

"I'd like that. It's been too long. Too many men."

"And Sebek won't mind?"

"No. He doesn't like the idea of other men, but women don't bother him."

"I've always been more of a one-person woman."

"Is there someone in your life now, Cheryl?"

"No, I..." MacIntyre's throat closed on the words. "There was. R'aia. She's dead."

"I'm sorry," said Henutsenu, compassion in her eyes. "It sounds like it still hurts."

"She was raped and murdered. It's why I became a homicide semetyt."

"Oh, I'm so sorry."

"It's been years now, I haven't...you know...been with a woman since then. Some men, nothing permanent."

"Are you ready now?" Henutsenu's voice was warm and inviting.

MacIntyre hadn't thought about it until now. R'aia. The pain was still there, wasn't it? Would she ever get over the loss? She closed her eyes and fantasized about what was underneath Henutsenu's dress. She discovered she was not ready. Then what was she feeling? Her anger as she departed the Tjesut, scorning Shesmu's defeated back, popped into her mind. Her anger as she marched up to the Wife's door to make a fool of herself.

"It's Shesmu," she said.

"What about him?"

"I didn't see it until now. He's...I like him. A lot. Even though he hates me."

"He doesn't hate you. But that's in the way of our having a good time?"

"I guess, for now. I'm sorry I didn't understand myself better." A thought occurred to her. "Oh no—you're not in love with Shesmu, are you?"

"There was a time," smiled Henutsenu. "But sanity prevailed. That's not to say he's not lovable, but he's my boss and he's not my type. I like men with less intensity, more carefree. Like Sebek. No, it's loyalty, for me. But it sounds like *you've* fallen for him."

"If Shes doesn't hate me, he's putting up a good front."

"He does that. But look, the real problem is that woman."

"The Wife."

Henutsenu grinned. "Is that what you call her? Neferaset?"

"Force of habit. Medjau categories of guilty people. The wife is the murderer, most of the time."

"And in this case?"

MacIntyre sipped wine. "If you'd asked me two days ago, I'd have said yes, she's the murderer. Now, I have doubts. I put pressure on her, and instead of confessing, she got hysterical in her denials."

"Oh, she can control her emotions." Henutsenu put contempt into her voice.

"Not always. The usual sex stuff, sure, she's good at that. But there's something deeper going on with her. Yesterday she was out of control, hysterical. I would have known why if she confessed, but she didn't."

"Are you going to arrest her?" Henutsenu sounded hopeful.

"I can't arrest anybody. I'm suspended without pay. This is my day off too, not by my choice."

"I'm sorry, I hadn't heard about that."

"I stepped over the line with her yesterday. I deserve what I got. And Shesmu told me so too, just before he told me to stay the hell away from him."

"Shesmu, always intense. And he thinks he's in love with that woman." Henutsenu sipped her wine, thinking. "Shesmu needs help. He doesn't grasp that simple fact. And, Cheryl, I got you here today as much to convince you to help him as to explore other things. But if you've got feelings for him...."

"I'll do what I can, short of convicting the Wife of a murder she didn't commit. What can you tell me about what's going on with Shes right now?"

"He's hurting. She's got her hooks in deep, she started up the affair again."

MacIntyre smiled. "You're out of date. As of yesterday, he's on the outs again. She tossed him out of her house. That's when I stepped over the line."

Henutsenu's eyes got big. "Oh, I see." She considered. "That will make him hurt more."

"What do you think he'll do next?"

"Shesmu doesn't give up, Cheryl. As long as that woman is around, he'll keep trying."

"So it's put her in prison or kill her?"

"Oh, ha. Shesmu needs to understand down deep that she's not emotionally there for him. Your experience with her suggests you might find something… something dark in her. Find it and convince him. I've tried the direct approach, didn't work."

"Gives me an idea. If I can't get it done with a badge, I'll make do without, but I'll keep trying. OK, enough about men. How about that dinner? Just friends?"

"Just friends." The two women finished their wine and left the bar, arm in arm.

CHAPTER TWENTY
Shesmu Gets Whipsawed

"Shes!"

I rolled over on my back, holding my phone to my ear in the early morning blackness of my bedroom.

I cleared my throat. "Aset?"

"Shes, you've got to help me!"

I sat up, gripping the phone. "What's wrong, Aset?"

"My house, they broke in, they…."

"Take a deep breath, Aset. Take your time." I switched my phone to my other hand and reached for the light. My heart started functioning, and coherent thought started. The silence lengthened. I reconsidered my automatic responses. Burglars?

"Are you safe, Aset? Are the people who broke in gone?"

"Yes, they're gone, but—"

I said, "Aset, why call *me?* You threw me out, told me you never wanted to see me again. Call the medjau."

"Oh, Shes. Can you help me?"

"Did you mean what you said, Aset?"

"No, Shes, no. I didn't." Her voice filled with tears. "I need you, Shes. I… panicked." Why?

I asked, "What happened, Aset?"

"Something downstairs, a noise, woke me, I—"

"No, Aset. What made you panic? Yesterday. Why throw me out?"

"Can't we—"

"Tell me, Aset."

"Oh, Shes, that's—it was the knife, and Seteh, and that woman forcing her way in, accusing me of murdering my poor Nekhen."

"Tell me. Please, Aset. Tell me. What about the knife?"

She screamed, "You're not letting me *tell* you! The knife's gone. Burglars took the knife."

"The Knife of Seteh is in the tomb, Aset."

Silence. "How—"

"I saw the pictures, Aset. At the Temple of Inpu. Yesterday."

"How…you didn't go into the tomb!"

"No, I'm not a tomb robber. Pictures, Aset. In the temple records."

"It's not there, Shes." Her voice had a distinct quality I'd never heard in Aset's voice before. Fear.

"Sure it is, Aset, you put the knife there."

More silence.

"Aset?"

"I…took it. Shes, I took the knife." Her voice quavered, then firmed up.

"What do you mean, you took the knife? When?"

"During the vigil."

"The vigil the night before the funeral? At the Temple of Inpu? You sat up with Nekhen's ka all night? What did you do?"

"I switched them."

"Switched what?"

"Knives. I switched the knives."

My heart lurched. "What knife did you leave in the tomb?"

"The…it was the one that killed him, my poor Nekhen. I brought that knife to the vigil inside my mourning dress. You know how those dresses hide everything. I switched the knives when no one else was around, late in the night. Took the big knife, left the smaller one in the box. That one. With his blood. His ka, the ka didn't care, not about that." She was on the edge of hysteria.

I rubbed my mouth. Was taking a tomb item before they closed the tomb a religious crime? A civil one? But I was sure that hiding the murder weapon in a closed tomb for all time was a crime, a big one.

"Why, Aset? For the money?"

"No, Shes, no!" She hesitated. "I can't tell you any more, I can't."

"Why can't you tell me, Aset? Don't you want my help?" I was getting mad.

"Don't make me, Shes! Please help me."

Something was wrong here. Knives and blood and lies, that wasn't my Aset. The one I'd made love to, over and over, while my friend Nekhen slept. I had to admit, I didn't know this deceitful Aset well at all. I wasn't sure anymore that 'my' Aset even existed.

"Will you help me, Shes?"

"What happened tonight?"

"Oh, thank you, Shes! I don't have anyone else."

"Aset…." I let my exasperation creep into my voice. I wanted to reassure her, love her…but things had moved on.

"Sorry, Shes, sorry." She gathered her thoughts, settled her panic, then said, "I crept downstairs, found my back door open, broken open. I closed the door, then I ran to the…." She stopped. "Oh, gods. That's how. That's how."

"Tell me, Aset."

"A secret panel, Shes. In the library. A section of books. I swung it open, and the knife was there. I closed the panel and went back upstairs. Then I heard a bang and ran back down…the panel was open and the knife wasn't there and the back door was wide open again. Shes, I showed them!"

"Deep breath, Aset. Calm down."

"But the knife, it's gone. And I showed them where it was."

"It's just a thing, Aset. Call the medjau."

"Will you come, Shes? I—I can't call the medjau, not…for this."

"I'll come in the morning, Aset. We need to go to the Temple of Inpu, we need to talk to a man there. During business hours."

"What?"

"Try to rest. I'll come by and pick you up, OK? Sleep."

"But, Shes—"

"Get some rest, Aset. I'll be at your place in the morning." My voice was hoarse. I wanted more than anything to go to her right then and console her. But I knew it wouldn't make anything easier for me or her.

"No, Shes. I need you, I'm afraid, you're the only person I can trust…please!"

What I knew and what I felt no longer jibed. As usual, I went with what I felt.

I'd never seen Nekhen's house in the dark. I parked my car and walked up the path to the house, the very path of pain I'd walked down two days before. Aset had turned on the light over her front door and the lights along the path, welcoming me before I even saw her.

I held her close after she closed the door behind me. I suppose I made sooth-
ing noises and professed the usual things; I can't remember. I can only remember
the feel of her body close to mine and the kisses, the taste of the long kisses. I
don't know how long we simply stood and held each other. Finally, Aset broke
away and led the way into the great room, huge windows showing only the lights
of the city below. I suggested the bedroom, but she just shook her head and
turned her red, tired eyes toward the window and the lights. I went to her and
wrapped my arms around her from behind and just held her, my chin on her
shoulder, smelling her, saying nothing.

She said, "I know…I know who it was, Shes," in a quavering voice.

"I do too, Aset. Blackmore."

She pulled away from me and looked me in the face. "Who?"

I'd told her about Blackmore the day before, before she threw me out. "Don't
you remember, Aset? What I explained to you yesterday?"

The confusion on her face eased into shocked acceptance, and she said, "I'm
sorry, Shes, I don't…I wasn't listening, not after you started talking about…Lord
Seteh. I got so angry, Shes. I'm sorry. Tell me again, I'll listen this time."

"Aset, get some sleep. I'll make some calls, but it will have to be in business
hours, tomorrow morning. Let's go to the bedroom, Aset."

"No, Shes, I can't sleep."

"We could make love."

She shook her head, her face tired. "No, Shes, I need…to think, to be alone,
to be free." She reached and hugged me. "I'll try to get some sleep. Wake me up if
you learn something I need to know, all right?"

We kissed, and she walked off to her bedroom.

I called Blackmore early, but not too early. I needed to get a response from
him, but I needed him to think I was on the level. That meant not calling him
frantically at six in the morning. I waited until nine. Aset slept on; she must have
been exhausted.

Blackmore answered right away, in English. "Shesmu, how are you?"

"Just fine, Rafe. There's bad news."

"How bad is it?" I would swear he smiled when he said it, something in his
inflection.

"Bad enough. The knife is gone. Stolen. I nearly convinced Neferaset to sell it
to you, and then she got burgled."

"Well, that's unfortunate, Shesmu." Definitely a smile this time.

"I might have a lead or two about it, and I want to make sure our deal is still on," I said.

"Well, I don't know. I don't want to get involved in anything illegal," he said. I choked a little on that one, given how illegal the whole thing was from the start. And that was assuming he wasn't Nekhen's murderer. He continued, "We'll call it a day on that one, Shesmu. Thanks for your efforts, but I'll pass on this."

I pretended to put up a losing fight. "Look, Rafe—I'm sure my contacts in the medjau can track this down. Neferaset is really eager to make the sale—"

"No, Shesmu, I don't think so. Medjau? No, not in my business. Again, thanks, but I'm no longer interested. Call me if you find out anything, but I need to move on. Look, I gotta go. Some people just walked in. Bye," and he disconnected.

I concluded that Blackmore had the knife. His interest in it had been too firm, too resolute. He wasn't a quitter, and he didn't care about the medjau. He had the knife, and my job was to get it back.

I had to talk to Hernefer before I could talk to Aset. I had to understand more about the situation from Hernefer's point of view. He might be able to come up with an angle that would help.

"Hernefer."

"Shesmu here. I'm afraid there's bad news."

"I heard."

Startled, I asked, "Heard what?"

"About the burglary."

Unless Aset had connections I wasn't aware of, the only way Hernefer could have heard about the burglary was from the burglars. He disabused me of the notion.

I asked, "How?"

"Contacts. In the medjau."

"She didn't report—"

"Not those medjau, Temple of Inpu. How do you think Blackmore learned the knife wasn't in the tomb?"

"Idnu Iny?" An educated guess on my part, given Iny's knowledge about the tomb and its contents.

"Sharp, Shesmu. I've had a long-term relationship with Iny. He tells me things I need to know. What's in various tombs, who's willing to sell things, like that. And who's willing to keep me informed about things like burglaries that he comes across."

"He's working both sides of the street. Blackmore told him, and he told you."

"This is a warren of streets, Shesmu. You're out of your depth. Iny told me he figured out that your girlfriend had the knife because of your interest in seeing the pictures of it."

"And he told Blackmore."

"I want that knife. Blackmore's got it. You need to get it back. That's our deal."

"There's more to it."

"Such as?"

"Such as Aset doesn't want to sell the knife."

"That's on you, too. You need to get her to sell it. To me. Or steal it back and sell it to me yourself."

"With all your resources, why don't you do it?"

"I can't get involved in this mess. I can't engage with Blackmore. My reputation would never recover. A lot of the people I deal with regard me as perfectly legitimate."

"They're wrong."

"Sure, but they don't know that. I deal with people like Blackmore, and they'll think I've gone bad on them. They'll know it."

"But I can do it, that's what you're saying. My reputation doesn't matter."

"Not in this. And I don't know if you can, Shesmu. Blackmore seems to be more than a few steps ahead of you. Your reputation isn't an issue with this and mine is, so all I can do is help you where I can. You go to work and let me know what I can do to help. Anything else?"

"I can't—"

"Get to it." He disconnected. Pretty damn abrupt, but his billions let him do or say whatever he wanted. And what he wanted was the knife.

I gently put the phone down and suppressed an impulse to throw it across the room.

"I don't know what to do, Shes," said Aset. "I don't know...I can't think."

"And that's even without my making love to you," I replied, trying to lighten the mood. She wasn't having any of it. No smile, only a dark look. I had awakened her as gently as I could. I needed to talk about things. I sat on the side of her bed, looking at her sleepy eyes, still red from crying the night before. I rubbed a round bump through the covers and said, "Let me hold you, Aset. Comfort you."

"No, no, Shes, I'm not ready, I can't. I have to…I want to find my knife." Blinking the sleep from her eyes, she kicked me and I got up, and she threw off the covers and got up. She pressed her lips tight in annoyance. She wore the same dress, she'd just gone right to bed without taking it off. She stalked out of the bedroom and went to the great room, and I followed, aching for her. Her bare feet caressed the carpet as she walked, making me ache more.

I cleared my throat. "Aset, I made some calls. I know who stole the knife. I have someone who can help me get it back. And I will. You can be sure of that."

She turned and stared at me, hope entering her eyes. "Who was it?"

"Blackmore."

I told her what I'd learned from Hernefer. I told her about the offer from Blackmore and how his taking it back convinced me he had the knife. I told her about Hernefer's collection and his obsession with ritual knives and his offer to buy the Seteh knife. I told her about Idnu Iny's duplicitous ways.

"I don't understand, Shes," Aset said, bewildered. "How…what's his name? The medja?"

"Iny. I got him to show me pictures of the knife, I told you, Aset. But you switched the knives. According to my source, he takes advantage of his position to look for valuable artifacts that Blackmore or other shady dealers might want to buy."

"So he learned the knife in the tomb wasn't the Knife of Seteh." Her eyes bored through me.

"When I had him show me the pictures, I think he put two and two together, though he might have already done that. Hernefer told me he figured out that you had it, and he sold that information to Blackmore."

"It's your fault, Shes. He broke into Nekhen's tomb! How could you deal with that man? He's nothing but a tomb robber. And your billionaire isn't any better!"

I tried to bring her back to the main point. "It doesn't matter, Aset. That knife is trouble. Whatever you want it for, it's not worth it. If anyone finds out about it, you'll go to jail, or worse. Seteh is illegal. Proscribed."

"I'm aware of that, Shes. That doesn't matter. Lord Seteh…it doesn't matter. I need to get the knife back. It was Nekhen's. Now it's mine, and I need it. I need it, Shes."

"Why, Aset?"

She got up and walked to the window. Her voice vehement, she said, "I can't tell you. You shouldn't ask. You should just help me get it back. Don't you love me enough to do that for me, Shes?"

I couldn't speak. Did I love her enough? Yesterday, I would have said yes without hesitation. Today…today I saw an Aset that I didn't recognize at all.

"Stop staring at me and say something!" Now there was anger in her voice.

I got up and went to her. She crossed her arms and glared, red eyes accusing me.

"Aset," I said, "I don't know what to say. Nekhen had that knife his whole life. He kept it secret. He kept his family associations with it secret. He wanted it entombed with him, he wanted to carry it into the afterlife. He didn't want you to take on its burdens. It's illegal. I can get it back, but we need to get rid of it. If you don't want to sell it…we'll have to get it back into the tomb. Somehow."

"Shes, you do not understand what you're getting into."

"You said that before, Aset. Why not tell me?"

"I can't."

I may have loved her enough to do her bidding, but she wouldn't let me into her life, she wouldn't tell me what was going on. She wouldn't explain the feelings that made her obsess over a knife that could get her chopped into pieces, or whatever the temples did to people who worshipped proscribed gods. Her refusal put a distance between us greater than the short space that separated me from her crossed arms. Those arms, and the feelings that made her cross them, were a barrier that kept me from embracing her and her desires. She didn't love me enough to let me embrace her, comfort her. My mind jumped to Henutsenu angrily telling me about puppets on strings, just before I met Hutyt MacIntyre.

Aset said, "Just get me the knife, Shes. Then we'll talk."

She turned back to the window, arms crossed, her stiff back dismissing me. I left without another word. I'd get the knife back for her, but I wasn't that happy about it.

CHAPTER TWENTY-ONE
MacIntyre Dates Shesmu

CHERYL MACINTYRE WAS NOT IN the habit of chasing after men—aside from murderers and gang lords, that is. Mostly, men came to her. But she'd thought it through. If she called Shes up and invited herself over, he'd tell her to go to hell, which wouldn't help things any.

So, she'd arranged a trap with the lovely Henutsenu, over dinner in a very nice Amazigh restaurant. MacIntyre's traps involved lots of medjau descending on the suspect at once with guns drawn. She felt that might not work in this case, and Henutsenu agreed. Henutsenu suggested getting Shesmu to come into the restaurant. Henutsenu would arrange a nice dinner with Sebek, then they would surprise Shesmu with a blind date setup. What could go wrong?

MacIntyre walked into the Neferti at dinnertime. A server recognized her; how many blonde, blue-eyed Americans were there in Menmenet? The serving staff were all in on the plot. The woman showed her past the bar and restrooms and down the little hall to the office. MacIntyre checked her dress for stains and proper arrangement of details—all good—and opened the door.

Her eyes met Shesmu's as they lifted from the paper he was holding. His eyes caught fire, but it wasn't the fire she wanted to see. Or was it?

Henutsenu said, "Chef, just settle down and listen, all right?"

He looked from the Remetjet to the American and back. "It's a plot, isn't it? You're in it together." On the good side, his tone did not drip with hate.

"There, see? He isn't stupid, and he doesn't hate you, Cheryl."

"What's this all about?" he asked.

"I'll leave you two to get acquainted," said Henutsenu, and she walked out and closed the door.

"Am I under arrest?" he asked.

"For what?"

"Given it's you, for murder."

"Who'd you murder?"

"What are you doing here, MacIntyre?"

"Cheryl. It's Cheryl, Shes. Remember?"

He shook his head. "That was before I knew you."

"Low, really low, Shes. I'm here to get you to buy me dinner. I'm suspended without pay, so I can't arrest anyone. That's your fault, so you owe me. I need consolation. I need solace. I need *food*."

"If you're going to grill me, I have to tell you I already have a better grill chef than you'll ever be."

"I don't grill boyfriends."

"I'm not your boyfriend."

"Not yet."

This idea started nudging its way into his eyes. Some of the fire left. His lips tugged into a doubtful smile.

"What *is* this all about?" he repeated.

"Dinner. Pleasant conversation. Getting to know each other. Chef's table? Henutsenu has set it up with Sebek."

"It's a plot," he mused to himself. "They're all in it. Together."

"What have you got to lose?" asked MacIntyre. "Where is this chef's table?"

The chef made the best of it and showed her the way to the kitchen.

"In the kitchen? We're having a romantic dinner for two in the kitchen? Your kitchen?"

MacIntyre, walking beside Shesmu, tried to restrain her incredulity. Was this it? Was this the plan that Henutsenu and her romantic lover Sebek had come up with to get her and Shesmu together? Eat in the kitchen? Scraps? Leftovers?

"It's more about showcasing the ego of the chef, that's why they call it the chef's table," replied Shesmu, leading her through the big swinging doors. "Only I'm not the chef right now, Sebek is."

Shesmu accosted a dark-haired man in a chef's uniform, put an arm around his shoulder, and guided him over to MacIntyre. She heard him whisper, "I'll get you for this, Sebek." She grinned.

"Hi, Cheryl. I'm Nekhetsebek, the interloper chef. Henutsenu has told me all about you."

"Oh, surely not." She grinned again. "Pleased to meet you."

Sebek eyed his boss and said, "Chef's tasting menu? With wines?"

Shesmu nodded. "And watch the pepper."

Sebek laughed and hurried away to get things moving.

Shesmu showed her to a niche with a low table and cushions, enough to seat six. "That's the chef's table. Out of the way, but you can see everything that happens to your food."

They walked over to the table, and Cheryl tried to arrange herself on the cushions. She sat up and took off her sandals after trying to tuck them under her butt. Then she tried tucking her legs under as she had done growing up. As she nearly overbalanced, Shesmu grinned and showed her the way to fold her legs and arrange the cushions. Then he sat as far away from her as he could.

Once she'd arranged her ankles for least pain and greatest visual impact, MacIntyre asked, "What was that remark about pepper?"

Shesmu grimaced. "I'd just as soon forget about it. Somebody put a huge amount of red pepper in Neferaset's dinner the other night. The night before I met you."

"And she still went home with you? Courageous."

Shesmu's eyes got big. "She told you that? Henutsenu? What the hell do I pay her for? It's a plot."

"I don't think Henutsenu likes Neferaset all that much, Shes," said the grinning MacIntyre. "I know I don't."

"Look," he said, "I'd appreciate it if you kept that a secret."

"What, you sleeping with a murderer?"

"No! No. About the pepper."

"Why?"

"Shes and the pepper steak. All over the west coast, I'd be a laughingstock. In every restaurant."

"I wouldn't want that. Your secret is safe with me. Unless you put poison in my food." She looked at Sebek, who was doing something frenetic over by a large steel table. "Was it Sebek's fault?"

"No, he wasn't here yet. Dua was in charge." The sous chef had her back to them and punched something into submission on the table in front of her. "But she didn't see who did it."

"I'd take on the case, but I'm suspended," said MacIntyre.

This banter continued for some time over a glass of excellent, crisp white wine a server brought by. All the while, MacIntyre noticed Dua sending murderous glares in their direction from the various stations as she rushed around. No love lost there, either. None.

"What was that remark about boyfriends?" asked Shesmu out of nowhere.

MacIntyre raised her eyebrows. "Just banter. We'll try the food first, then we can talk about going to bed with each other. Once I see whether you are boyfriend material."

"I'm not."

"Neferaset thinks so. Intermittently."

Shesmu grimaced again. "I love her."

"For now, I'll accept that. But she's tossed you out on your ass so many times it must be pretty sore."

He changed the subject again. "She's not a murderer."

"Sure she is. Help me prove it."

"Help me find the actual murderer." Ah, that was his ploy: pump her for information that could help his lover. Not a chance.

"Easy. She's the actual murderer. Anyway, what's my reward?"

"More dinners?"

"Try again."

"Knowing you're serving Ma'at?"

"I always am. Anyway, I may have doubts about her guilt. She's not acting like a wife who's murdered her husband. She seems…preoccupied."

He nodded, reluctantly. "She's got things going on that I don't understand. And you're harassing her."

"Yeah. Look, Shes, I'm sorry about the other night, when she threw you out. The way she treated you enraged me. You were so vulnerable and sweet and down. I just…reacted." She shook her head. "Don't know what came over me."

Shes smiled, accepting the apology.

MacIntyre said in a rush, "That's a lie. I know what came over me. You. Your face, your presence, your sad, silly self. I wanted to help, but I hurt you instead. I'm sorry."

"It's OK. But, Cheryl, I'm—"

"I understand, in love with her. We'll work on that. Maybe she's not guilty of murder, she's just in over her head in something, but she's sure guilty of being a —"

"Don't say it, please, Cheryl."

She shook her head and pressed her lips tight. Sebek and a server started bringing small dishes of food to the table. They kept coming.

"What's all this?" asked MacIntyre.

"Have you ever eaten a formal Remetjy meal?"

"No. Teach me. All I know about food is that it grows in cans."

"We start with a table full of small plates, each of which has a bit of something special. Here's a special millet cracker with local trout roe, for example. And grilled Kumamoto oysters from Milaya, up north, with a dusting of clove and a few drops of tamarind."

MacIntyre busied herself with a small packet of maize and local salmon wrapped in edible steamed grape leaves. "Delicious!" And it was.

Another glass of wine appeared, different from the first. "Fish course," said Shesmu.

A server cleared some space and deposited a large clay pot. He lifted the lid, and the wonderful smells wafted over the table: sea, spice, herbs, and wine. The server dished out crab claws and meat into small bowls. "A Menmenet specialty, based on an ancient dish from R'aqedyt. Local crabs."

"Reminds me of lobsters I killed growing up in Boston," said MacIntyre.

"So anybody can be a murderer?" asked Shesmu, grinning.

"Yeah," she replied, her mouth absorbing the complicated flavors of the sea. She felt her face contract as the pepper kicked in. "Hot!"

"Don't worry, that's the normal amount of pepper for this dish. Try some mineral water."

"You love hot dishes."

"I do."

"I'm hot."

"No, you're not. Cold as ice."

She refrained from sticking out her tongue at the man. Besides, her tongue was busy with tasting the excellent food. Infuriating man.

Shesmu asked, "What's happening with Pabaky?"

MacIntyre eyed the sous chef; Dua was still sending evil looks in their direction. "We're keeping him for the time being. The hospital treated his arm and released him to us. You should see him: a huge white cast and an even bigger attitude. We're not getting shit from him. He hasn't said why he was following you or why he attacked you."

Shesmu nodded at Sebek, and servers came to clear away all the dishes and bowls. Sebek assembled things on a large iron platter heated to smoking point, meat sizzling as it hit the hot metal. He brought the platter over on a special wooden tray and set it between the medjat and the chef.

"Delta Lamb House of Bastet, with wild mushrooms and onion." The lamb meat glistened and sizzled as Shesmu shot the pieces from the skewers to the platter. He said, "Henutsenu's favorite. Lamb fed on grass from the salt marshes of the delta. What would you prefer, Cheryl?"

Progress; he was calling her Cheryl without grimacing. "One of everything. May I reconsider? About the 'more dinners' reward?" Damn fine food and great company.

A server poured the latest wine, a fruity, peppery Syrah from Russkaya Amerika. MacIntyre knew nothing about wine, but this one got taste buds going that she wasn't aware she had. The atmosphere mellowed even more. MacIntyre told herself to compliment Henutsenu on her favorite dish when she saw her again. As she savored the last piece of lamb, Shesmu signaled again, and glasses of a sweet Muscat wine arrived.

"I discovered this sweet wine in a backwoods First Peoples village near the Russkaya Amerika border. Intense; a little goes a long way. Not a Remetjy custom, it comes from France. Nekhen taught me the ins and outs of it at the Per'ankh, and I like the sweet finish to a strong meal like this one."

Dua had taken a break about the time they had started the lamb, walking stiffly out the back door. She now returned with a sour expression on her face. She saw MacIntyre inspecting her, and her face darkened.

Without warning, Dua's rage flashed like a wildfire in a dry forest. She picked up one of the small garbage cans and ran toward the pair, intending to dump it. Sebek was right there, and Shesmu scrambled up. They took the garbage away from her before anything major hit MacIntyre, who was still trying to untangle her legs. Not the best position for handling an attack. As a medjat, she should be ashamed of herself for getting caught like that.

Sebek pulled on Dua's arm, and she stumbled away, crying. He shrugged. "I'll send her home," he said. "It's the stress."

MacIntyre watched the disappearing sous chef in disbelief. The pair stood looking after her.

"What was that about?"

"Ignore her, she's upset about her boyfriend."

"Well, shit. I'm upset about my boyfriend too, but I don't go around dumping garbage on people."

"I'm not your boyfriend. Let me placate you. The dinner is free, on me."

MacIntyre regarded him with horror, thinking about the bill she might have had to pay.

Shesmu grinned. "Got you."

Horror gave way to impulse. MacIntyre wrapped her arms around him and kissed him on the lips. He froze, then his lips unlocked, his arms circled her, and he made the kiss last, soft lips meeting hers, then tongues. She could taste the sweetness of the wine he'd savored as the fire flowed through her. MacIntyre dimly heard the groans and laughs start from the line.

"Way to go, chef!"

"Where's the *fire* extinguisher, chef?"

"Woo hoo! Make it count, chef!"

Sebek came back, and seeing the clinch, came over and slapped Shesmu on the back. MacIntyre pulled back, releasing him. She licked her lips, tasting him: salt, sweet, sour, all at the same time. She could get used to this kind of food.

"Well, I can see that dinner was a success," said Sebek. "Don't I get a kiss too? I cooked it, not him." MacIntyre obliged, though not with as much enthusiasm, and the line loved that even more. She reminded herself to give Henutsenu a kiss later to balance things out.

CHAPTER TWENTY-TWO
Shesmu Discovers a Deeper Game

ASET'S WARNING ABOUT SNAKES OPPOSED my own complicated feelings toward Hutyt MacIntyre. Was she the enemy, tempting me behind Aset's back to tell her what I know? Or was she what she appeared, a strong-minded medjat attracted to me for reasons only she knew? The complexity came from my own conflicting feelings; Aset's behavior troubled me, and I had responded more to MacIntyre's kiss than I cared to admit to myself. I did not sleep well.

When I woke up in the morning, one thing was obvious: Aset was hiding something, something more important than her marriage or her love for me. If MacIntyre had realized what I was hiding, would she have kissed me like that? No; she would have arrested me as a material witness. Aset confessed to both a major religious crime and a civil offense against Ma'at. I heard her confess and said nothing to the medjat working the case. That medjat was no longer on the case, according to her, but now she was working on me. Could I trust her? Not yet.

I had to talk to Aset. I called her, and she told me to come. My feelings were still complicated as she opened her mansion's door, but then I understood why I was there. Aset stood, lovely and vulnerable, blinking in the light of R'a. All the love I had in my heart flowed out to her as I embraced and kissed her. She looked tired, the shadows on her face telling me she'd slept less than I had, and her kiss was half hearted.

She stepped away from me and glanced out the door. "Is that woman out there?"

"Hutyt MacIntyre? Not that I'm aware," I replied, the guilt from last night's kiss rising in my throat as I smelled Aset's subtle scent of sandalwood and earth. "She said she's off the case."

"Shes, you've got to help me figure out what to do," she said as we walked into the great room overlooking the bay.

"Tell me what's going on."

She sat in her favorite chair and stared out at the view. She swallowed, then said, "I can't."

"You must." I sat on the sofa. "You must see, Aset, that I can't help you if I don't understand what's wrong. And it's way more than just stealing the knife. Way more."

"I didn't *steal* it, I…took it."

"The distinction escapes me, Aset. It will escape the medjau and the Hem-Netjer of Inpu, too."

"Don't, Shes. I can't stand it, the vilification, not from you too." Her eyes would not meet mine.

"Who else is attacking you, Aset? The medjau?"

"I can't tell you."

"Please, Aset."

"I got a phone call last night," she said, then stopped.

I waited.

"It was that trader, Blackmore. He knows, he knows."

"Knows what, Aset?"

"The knife. What it means. Why Nekhen had it." She arose from her chair and stood by the big window.

"Seteh."

Alarmed, her eyes swung around to me. "What do you mean, Shes?"

"Aset. Do you think I don't see what's going on? That I don't know the whole story? Here's what I know. Even the mention of Seteh is enough to send you into a frenzy. Nekhen's family goes back to the time when there were Hemu-Netjer of Seteh in Kemet, in the Empire. The knife is the Knife of Seteh, and it's worth at least a million debenu. If anyone in authority, religious or civil, learns that you took it, you'll be in jail for the rest of your life, whether or not you murdered Nekhen. That's what I mean, Aset."

The tears had come halfway through this aggressive summary of woe. Some women, when they cry, turn into hags. Not Aset. I got up and embraced her, and we held each other. Her tears dampened my shirt collar. But nothing I had said surprised her. It only made her cry.

"Tell me, Aset. Tell me what Blackmore said."

"Oh…Shes. He said, he said don't look for the knife, it wasn't mine anymore. He said…oh, I can't tell you what he said. A terrible man."

"What's going on, Aset? What game are you playing?"

"Don't, Shes. Please."

"You've got to tell me so we can cope with Blackmore."

"It's…too personal."

"Aset. We have been lovers for a year. Personal is what we do. What we are."

"Not that kind of personal, it's, well, it's religious. That's all I can tell you." She sniffled into my collar.

Religious. Just fine. The gods' hands hard at work screwing up our lives. But religious meant she wouldn't tell me. We never talked about gods, only about our love for each other.

"We'll get it back somehow, Aset. I'm not sure how yet, but we will. Then you'll have to get rid of it before anyone finds out about it. You can sell it to the billionaire collector Hernefer."

"No, I can't do that, Shes. It's not mine to sell. It's…a religious thing."

I embraced her. "Aset, I'll get it back. We'll see what happens."

A religious thing. My only religion was Aset. MacIntyre might tempt me, but I loved Aset with my whole heart at that moment, and no god would get in my way.

CHAPTER TWENTY-THREE
MacIntyre Gets Bad News

"Excuse me for a minute, I need to check this message."

MacIntyre tore her gaze away from her lunch friend Henutsenu and tapped on the message from Yaotl. The Aztec crime lord had agreed to use an encrypted text message app to send her any crucial information that might prove useful in her job. Her suspension meant she might do nothing about it, but Yaotl was too important an informant to let go over the temporary error in judgment by her superiors.

Henutsenu said, "From a lover, I hope."

As her mind's eye merged the concepts of Yaotl and "lover," an involuntary laugh broke from her. She made it into a hiccup. "No, sorry. An informant. I'll just be a minute."

Henutsenu smiled her most charming smile and addressed herself to her dessert. The two women were sitting in a courtyard cafe in one of the biggest shopping buildings in Menmenet's business district, off Mentju Boulevard. Henutsenu set up the lunch to talk over what had happened the night before at the Neferti, with Shesmu. Love was on her mind. MacIntyre, while she felt the afterglow of a successful foray, had other things worrying her. A big worry was where her next meal might come from if she didn't get her badge back. Maybe Yaotl could help there.

"Urgent, ask meeting ASAP today if possible. If not, come regardless."

Quite a message.

She checked her afternoon calendar. One benefit of suspension: nothing to do but attend urgent meetings with crime lords. She texted him back with a time, and he texted assent.

MacIntyre turned back to Henutsenu. "Where were we?"

Henutsenu finished the last bite of her chocolate torte and said, "The Kiss."

"The word from the kitchen was that Shesmu was happy, after?"

"I can tell you myself his mood was quite lighthearted after you left."

"Do you think I overdid it?"

"I'd have gone home with him." The Remetjet smiled. "But I understand."

"He's still too fragile for that level of sexual pressure, Henutsenu."

"Chef's not fragile, he's just stupid about love."

"And he's still in love with the Wife."

Henutsenu shook her head. "Last gasp. You can see it in his eyes when you talk to him about it. The doubt creeps in."

"You're an optimist."

"Always, at least with men. Women are harder, more complicated. And smarter."

"What should I do next?"

"Find something that shows him who you are. Something that gets him thinking how great it would be to know you. Something fun that won't damage his ego. Something that seduces him away from that woman."

The image of the Imenhetep Club stick-fighting ring popped into MacIntyre's mind. "I have just the thing. All I have to do is let him win without knowing I've done that. Give him a good battle that lets him think he's better at it than I am." She grinned at Henutsenu's lack of comprehension. "Stick fighting." Henutsenu shuddered but smiled her assent to this tactical advance.

MacIntyre checked the time. "Got to go, Henutsenu. I'm meeting with an informant about something important, and it might get me my badge back. I'll let you know if I make any progress with Shes. You work with him. You can tell me if you see anything I might use."

Henutsenu cheerfully agreed to inform on her boss, another win for MacIntyre's detective skills. If the information keeps flowing, the path of Ma'at grows ever easier to navigate.

Yaotl's house servant took her through the enormous palace and out a back door. Yaotl's private garden was so lush, she wondered whether she'd gone through a portal into a magical Aztec fantasy world. Baskets of money achieved miracles, even in the foggy city of Menmenet.

"Ah, Hutyt MacIntyre, I am so happy you came promptly. Welcome to my garden. We may speak freely here, as it is unlikely your fellow medjau have listening devices in the cacti."

MacIntyre could have told him that nobody in the tech squad had yet sneaked a bug into his palace; she'd checked. But that wasn't something she felt she ought to share with the bastard. He needed more uncertainty in his quiet life.

"What's the urgency, Yaotl?"

"What is your philosophy about death, Hutyt?" The little man glanced at her, smirking.

"Whose death? Is somebody going to kill you, Yaotl?"

"No, Hutyt. Someone will kill *you*."

Well, that was a conversation killer.

"Why would anyone want to kill me?"

"I couldn't say, Hutyt. I simply convey the information to you. I hope it doesn't upset you too much."

"It depends. How likely is it to happen?"

"Quite likely."

"You're talking about a murder contract?"

"Of a sort. You know that my people have a quite sanguinary history."

"Sure, skulls everywhere and cutting out hearts. Is that a threat?"

"No, no, you misunderstand me, Hutyt. My concern is not personal. I am protecting our relationship, which may prove valuable in time. I would not like to see it cut short through inaction on my part."

"So what's going on, Yaotl?"

"There are places in Menmenet, Hutyt, where the people that work for me gather with others of the culture we have created for ourselves. To trade information, to socialize, to get the latest news. You understand?"

MacIntyre had raided one of those clubs. As a rookie patrol officer, she guarded the back door. She looked on avidly as the medjau squad rounded up the flashy Aztec gangsters and their squeezes. A tougher bunch she'd never seen, and the men were pretty rough too. No beating hearts being passed around or anything like that, just a lot of Aztec metoctli in jugs. Nothing came of that raid; they were all out on the street the next day.

"One of my subordinates, whom I will not name, overheard offers being made. Your name is so unusual in Menmenet, Hutyt MacIntyre, that the mention of it stood out from the surrounding noise."

"What was the offer?"

"My man did not hear the specifics, but the reaction was that the money was insufficient to the risk of killing a medjat. Such killings may prove expensive. Medjau do not react well to killings of their own people."

"I can't say I've ever encountered a medja contract killing."

"It is rare here in Menmenet. Rare. But still possible."

"So, nothing came of it."

"Not then. But when my subordinate brought the matter to my attention, I set inquiries afoot. We soon found that, with a significant increase in the contract amount, certain parties engaged to do the deed in a professional capacity. Hence the urgency, you see."

"I appreciate your efforts on my behalf, Yaotl. Details, please."

The little man slipped a piece of paper from his pocket into her hand. "You will find that your colleagues on the organized crime squad are aware of this man. Although he is a professional, his technique is as limited as his intelligence, so it should not be difficult to forestall his efforts."

MacIntyre read the name; nobody she'd heard of. Questions crowded her brain, but only one was likely to find an answer here.

"Why?"

The little man grinned. "It is not personal but religious."

"Religious? How can it be religious?" Unless there were Massachusetts Catholics involved, she could imagine nothing more unlikely than a religion-based murder plot in her non-religious life. Nothing in the Nekhen investigation had turned up any connection to religion, just food. Which was a religion to some, she had to admit.

"I am not aware of the full details, Hutyt. My inquiries turned up only the information that the man associated with a proscribed religious cult, something to do with a Remetjy god named Seteh. Being Aztec, I know little of these things. Something to work with, I should think."

Shit. It had to be: the Wife has hired a contract killer to save her butt. Seteh. MacIntyre remembered the lesson on the god during the prep course for taking the w'abet-en-Ma'at exam. God of the desert, god of isfet or chaos, brother of Wesir. Murdered Wesir to take his throne, then cut him up into pieces. Wesir's sister and wife Aset and her sister Nebethut, the Two Kites, gathered up the pieces and put Wesir back together, the first mummy, to become the king of the underworld. Then Aset slept with the dead Wesir and produced her son Heru, who took back the throne from his bad uncle. An illegal cult. Terrific.

"Oh, and I should warn you, Hutyt, this enterprising gentleman with the contract may not be the only one. It is not an exclusive contract. There are rumors the client has approached several lower-level professionals of one ilk or another, so I would not be complacent about eliminating just this one gentleman. I believe the fee is due only on the successful conclusion of the task."

When they arrived back at the palace door, Yaotl said, "And now, forgive me, Hutyt, but I must leave you, business awaits."

She bowed and thanked him for his information and concern for her wellbeing. She had already formed a plan centered on Shesmu that might even fit into her seduction plans. But she needed to get off the street and get some protection. As she walked through the palace, she saw his weapon of choice mounted on a wall and asked, only half joking, "May I borrow your macuahuitl?"

MacIntyre sat on the couch in Henutsenu's sky-rise apartment on Mentju Boulevard admiring the view of the Djuy-Benty, the two peaks in the middle of Menmenet. She could see the flagpole on the top of the Temple of Ma'at and the big crest of the City Palace just beyond it.

Henutsenu came back from the kitchen holding a glass of white wine, which she handed to MacIntyre with a smile.

"I appreciate this, Henutsenu. I couldn't go back to my apartment, and I had to get off the street, fast."

"Happy to help, Cheryl. You live an exciting life."

"I guess that's the point, to keep living it."

"Right. Sorry."

"I'll make a few phone calls, see what I can do about this. I might have to stay here two or three days, though, if that's all right."

"And nights?"

MacIntyre smiled. "And nights."

"We'll cope."

MacIntyre busied herself with calling every medja she knew, spreading the word there was a contract out on her. Only the more boorish individuals gave her any grief. Mes sympathized. He put her in touch with a friend of his on the organized crime squad. He said he'd organize a take-down on the small-time Aztec hood who'd taken on the contract. He'd let her know when it was safe for her to be on the street again.

MacIntyre tried to relax, sipping her wine and admiring the view as the sun set behind the fog bank over the Djuy-Benty. Henutsenu had gone to work but had given her advice before she left: "Call Shes. This is far too good an opportunity to waste."

So she did. Or, at least, she left a message for him, as he didn't pick up. It was a terrific opportunity. Getting him involved in taking down his ex-lover would finish his love at the same time it would show him what a great job MacIntyre could do.

Shesmu called just as she thought about getting together the dinner Henut-senu had left for her.

"Cheryl?"

"Shes, thanks for returning my call."

"You said it was important."

"Somebody is trying to kill me."

Silence, followed by an uncertain joke. "I can't imagine why."

"No joke, Shes. Somebody put out a murder contract on me. I'm in hiding."

"I'm sorry. Have you…called the medjau?"

The absurdity of the question struck them both at the same moment.

"Shes, I've mobilized the entire Menmenet force," she said with a smile in her voice.

"Um…so, can I help?"

"Well, yes, you can." Now, drive in the wedge, force him to see the Wife as she really was. "Neferaset put out the contract. I'm closing in on tagging her for the murder, so she wants me dead."

"No, that's not possible, Cheryl." There was no smile at all in his voice.

"Believe it, Shes. She's a murderer and will be a serial murderer if we don't stop her."

"No, no, no. I won't listen to this."

"Come on, Shes. The woman—"

"This is just a fantasy of yours."

"I don't do fantasy, Shes. I just kiss frogs and hope for princes. Seteh is the—"

"*What?*"

"I'm not deaf, Shes." She would swear there was panic in his voice. "Let me finish. It's something to do with the god Seteh, according to my informant. Some religious thing. I figure this cult has got Neferaset involved, in deep, and she's murdered her husband for some bizarre religious purpose. Then I got close, too close for comfort, and she put out a contract on me."

"You can't seriously believe this nonsense."

"It's the motive, Shes. She's already got the opportunity. Once we find the knife where she's hidden it, we'll have the means. We'll have everything we need to charge her."

Shesmu's voice turned icy. "Utter nonsense. Cheryl, listen to me. There is no way the Aset I know would have killed anyone for religious reasons. And there's no way she would put a contract out on a medjat, even one like you."

"No need to be rude, Shes."

"Yes, there damn well is! Enough of this idiotic fantasy. Here's rude: get the hell out of our lives!" He hung up.

So much for that idyllic first kiss.

CHAPTER TWENTY-FOUR
Shesmu Gambles for the Knife

"WHAT DO I CARE IF she dies?" said Aset.

I held the phone close to my ear as I walked up the waterfront toward Dju-Keta and home.

"Aset, you don't mean that."

"No, I guess not. But the woman is such a pest!"

"She'll be a bigger pest now. She told me you put out a contract on her."

"What do you mean? What sort of contract?"

"A murder contract. Like what gangsters do to take care of rivals."

A lengthy silence ensued while Aset absorbed this idea. I turned up the street that led to the hill.

"Aset?"

"Yes, sorry. I can't…I don't know what to say. A murder contract? How would I do that?"

"I agree, it's absurd. But that's what she thinks, and she's telling every medja in the city you're responsible."

"It's criminal!" Her voice rose in pitch. "I'll call my sehy! I want it stopped!"

"Has anybody called you about it?"

"No, you're the only one calling me with insulting nonsense, Shes! Look, Shes —are you making this up?"

"No, Aset, I'm not making this up. Things will get rough."

"You've got to help me, Shes! I can't do this alone. We need to get the Knife back." The panic was clear in her voice.

"I'll try, Aset, but that Knife—it's illegal, proscribed. Even possessing it can get us thrown in jail, or worse. It would be better to just forget about it. Let's deal with MacIntyre's delusions and—"

"No! Shes, if you can't do this for me…I'll find somebody else. My sehy, Nebemhep. He could…. Shes, I need the Knife. I *need* it, Shes."

Her voice had gone from panic to anger now. Either I did this for her or she was gone, this time for good. She didn't have to say it. The threat was unmistakable.

"Aset, I'll do what I can. Let me talk with Hernefer. He might have some ideas about how to get the Knife."

"Shes, I'm relying on you. Help me. Get the Knife back!" She hung up, still distressed.

I deferred my call to Hernefer until I got home; I needed absolute privacy for that conversation. As I walked, my heart alternated between renewed love for Aset and doubts about the depth of her love for me. Was she using me? Did I care whether she was using me? Love won as I turned into Meryimen Street and home.

"Hernefer," the billionaire identified himself in his gravelly voice.

I said, "This is Shesmu."

"Shesmu, good to hear from you. I was just thinking of you." I could tell from his voice he had a smirk on his face.

"How so?"

"After we talked, I figured I'd see what I could find out from my network. I had to be careful because I didn't want to alert that thief Blackmore, and it took me awhile to track down the information I needed. The people I usually go to for things like this, I couldn't rely on their keeping it to themselves."

"What did you find out?"

"History. Have you heard the story of Setepenseteh-Akhenr'a R'amesesu of the Middle Empire?"

"I can't keep all those Middle pera'au straight."

"He was the last of his line. You can tell from his nesubit name, Setepenseteh-Akhenr'a, he honored Seteh alongside R'a. In practice, the man put Seteh ahead of R'a."

"I presume this was before the Empire banned Seteh?"

"That's *when* they banned Seteh. This pera'a insisted the rituals of Seteh become the major rituals of his kingship. He wasn't like Akheniten, denying worship of all the other gods. He upset the applecart for the priests of Imen-R'a, though. Specifically, their finances—he redirected most of the tithes to the priests of Seteh."

"The downfall of many a pera'a, as I recall from my school history. Imen-R'a likes his money."

"Indeed. So, one morning, the imperial court awoke to find the mighty pera'a sitting on his throne with a knife in his chest. A ritual execution knife, one the priests used in animal sacrifices. To make an interminable story short, the hemu-netjer of Imen-R'a reasserted themselves, rounded up the usual suspects, and executed them."

"And those suspects were…?"

"Hemu-netjer of Seteh, as the knife had glyphs identifying it as a ritual knife from the Temple of Seteh. The hemu-netjer of Imen-R'a arrested all the Seteh folks and crucified them. They mummified and buried Pera'a R'amesesu, then raised the hem-netjer-tepy of Imen-R'a to the imperial throne. And then they banned Seteh."

"And what happened to the knife?"

"I got most of this from the chief scribe of the archives of Imen-R'a in Men-nefer. I've found our friendship invaluable in my collecting activities. He told me that the chronicles show the Imen-R'a folks entombed the murder knife with R'amesesu. Later, someone started a legend about the blood of Heru being on the knife. The Knife of Seteh thus became a sacred relic."

"But if the Knife went to the Duat with R'amesesu, how did Nekhen get it?"

"This is where it got sticky. My sources in Kemet pointed me to a group of antiquities dealers from Tjehenu, the country next to Kemet. Items from R'amesesu's tomb 'turned up' in the market there about thirty years ago. But not the Knife of Seteh."

"And Blackmore got interested in the tomb."

"Yes, he'd been trading with the Tjehenu dealers. The chief scribe told me that Blackmore approached him with letters of reference from an American university. He said he needed to research R'amesesu for a history project. The scribe checked with the university: the letters were fake, and so was his history PhD, so he kicked Blackmore out of the archives."

"And Nekhen?"

"His family goes back to the hemu-netjer of Seteh. We found that out when you were here. It's possible the family 'extracted' the Knife from the pera'a's tomb, or maybe it never made it into the tomb. Then it passed down through the family for centuries. A symbol of the power of Seteh? Only the family knows." My heart chilled at this comment; the only family left was Aset.

"Hernefer. You told me you have all the known ritual knives except this one. What if the Knife of Seteh was no longer out there?"

"You mean, destroy it? Not a chance."

"No, that's not what I mean. I want to get the Knife back where it belongs, in Nekhen's tomb. Secure, locked down, unavailable. With the ka in the Duat. It's where Nekhen wanted it, but it didn't work out that way."

Hernefer thought about this, then said, "If the details of this become public, we'll all go to jail or worse. Is your plan to do this through the religious courts? Publicly? It won't work."

"No! Secretly. Otherwise my friend Neferaset goes to jail. Or worse."

"Why should I care about your lover?"

Try another tack. "You would know that your collection is complete—no one else would have the Knife of Seteh."

"I'd know that if I had the Knife, too. You're asking me to buy it to give it away. That's money, time, and opportunity cost all wrapped up in one big mistake. I'm not running a charity."

"We can do better than that. Figure out a way to get it away from Blackmore without paying him. I'd buy the thing myself if I had the money, but I don't. You do. Then you can give it back to Nekhen's ka." Ever the optimist, I thought to myself. But Hernefer wasn't buying it.

"My collection is not public. Nobody would go to jail with the Knife in my knife drawer. And Nekhen's ka isn't my problem."

"The tomb is safer," I rejoined. But I could tell Hernefer craved the Knife of Seteh and would do anything to get it. I argued with him some more, but eventually we agreed to disagree while he came up with a plan to get Blackmore's attention and get the Knife. I not-so-subtly made sure he understood that if he dealt with Blackmore without me, I'd go to the authorities. Once we had it, I'd need to deal with his obsession, but I'd worry about that when that time came—if ever.

Hernefer called mid-morning.

"Can you come to my house as soon as you can?"

"What's up?"

"Can't talk right now—can you be here in an hour?"

"Yes, ferry permitting."

"Blackmore will be here at 2. Come before 1." He hung up.

I left word at the restaurant that I wouldn't be in today, then found my warmest jacket for the ferry ride. The fog lay heavy on the bay as the car ferry left its slip. I stayed in the main cabin for once, as there was little to see today, and the temperature outside was arctic. I got a bottle of water from the bar, sat at a window seat, and sipped it, thinking of Aset as I looked at the view of the Tjesut receding. Someone sat down next to me.

"Hi there, Shes."

My head snapped around: it was MacIntyre. She must have followed me onto the ferry without my seeing her. I kicked myself; I needed to watch my back. Missing her little red car meant I just wasn't paying attention.

MacIntyre asked, "Where are we going?"

"*We* aren't going anywhere, Hutyt."

"Cheryl, Shes. Call me Cheryl."

"I'll call you whatever I want."

"Rude. Where are we going?"

While trading this badinage, an idea flickered into being and grew. MacIntyre represented the law, ma'at. The scam at Hernefer's mansion was blatantly illegal. I could use her, use ma'at, to my advantage. I pointed to the top of Iu-Sedeg, fast approaching. "There. I'm saying nothing. If you come along, fine, but keep your mouth closed unless I ask for help. Deal? Otherwise, we'll turn right around and go back to Menmenet."

"Sure, why not? A romantic island adventure!" She smiled. "Sweet. I'm ready." She opened her jacket, and I saw a pistol in a small holster at her side.

"I thought you were in hiding?"

"Henutsenu said you were taking a little trip today. The ferry is perfect for avoiding hit men. So I thought I'd follow you and be safe."

I'd have to have a talk with Henutsenu.

"Could you sit a little further away, please?" I made it into a joke. "I don't want to get hit by stray bullets or anything."

She shifted a little closer to me, her knee touching mine. "That better?"

"No. And I thought you gave up your badge and gun."

"Got one of my own for protection while I'm with you. You're dangerous."

We carried on in this vein until the ferry pulled into the small harbor on the north side of Iu-Sedeg. MacIntyre and I disembarked and drove up to Hernefer's palace, her little red car following mine, but taking the curves a lot better. There was a fresh set of guards this time, more imposing than before. This time, they carried automatic weapons and wore light body armor.

"Wow," said MacIntyre, joining me. "You move in fancy circles, Shes. Even Yaotl doesn't have guys in body armor. I'm underdressed."

"Who the hell is Yaotl? Never mind, I take back the question. Remember what I said, Cheryl?" I tapped my mouth and made closing motions with my hand. She smiled and punched my arm, not lightly.

Hernefer met us in his huge study, greeting me as though he liked me. A tall, thin man stood next to him, giving me a narrow-eyed look. Hernefer introduced him as Idnu Hepuseneb, a medja from the local force. Hepuseneb dressed down in a decrepit business suit, nothing even faintly like a medja. I introduced my medjat in return; she hadn't dressed like one either. She looked like an American banker on vacation.

"Aren't you the homicide semetyt who screwed up the Peteh investigation a year ago?" The idnu frowned.

"Sheesh. One minor mistake...."

"What's a homicide medjat doing in this? And this isn't Menmenet, it's my town." Hepuseneb's statement floated in the air between Hernefer, MacIntyre, and me. I jumped in.

"Hutyt MacIntyre is here as a friend. Backup in case we need it."

"You have any problem with that, Idnu?" asked MacIntyre with a don't-press-me-too-far glint in her eye and a mean-looking smile on her lips.

Hepuseneb sighed. "Not if Lord Hernefer doesn't. He's calling the shots here."

MacIntyre laughed. "Shots. Oooh, good thing I'm armed." She gripped my arm the way a lover would. "Are you armed, lover? I might need protection too."

There's always a trickster in every adventure, and in MacIntyre, I'd found mine.

Hernefer briefed us on the setup for the meet with Blackmore. First came Hepuseneb's disguise; he was going undercover. He took a pair of glasses out of his pocket and put them on, turned meek, and slumped his shoulders a bit.

"Meet Professor Merisekhmet, the foremost scholar of the Middle Empire in Menmenet," said Hernefer. Hepuseneb was the image of a seedy professor. This might work.

It turned out that Hernefer's study was more than just a room, it was a system. Behind a hidden door in a gigantic mural of an ancient hunting scene was a small security office equipped with monitoring equipment. Hernefer pressed his hand on the mural, and the door clicked open.

"This room has most of the valuable pieces in my collection. A security person is in the security room at all times, monitoring things. At night, there are laser sensors all over the room." He ushered his security chief, Hepuseneb, and MacIntyre into the room, then drew back with a hand on my arm and closed the door.

He hissed at me with a scowl, "What is she doing here?"

"She followed me. What's Hepuseneb doing here?"

"Never mind Hepuseneb. I thought Nekhen's wife was your lover. Now it's a medjat. I don't like it, Shesmu."

I had a hard time organizing my thoughts. "That's…she is. Neferaset is my lover."

"So? What about this medjat?"

"No. The medjat is not my lover. She thinks she'd like to be. It's complicated."

"Damn right. Too complicated. Turning into a bad romance novel. Can we dump her in the bay or something? Hepuseneb sounded like he'd be happy to do that."

"I need her here to make her see there's nothing suspicious going on."

Hernefer's eyes bulged a little. "Shesmu…this whole operation is suspicious."

"Not if you handle it right. Taking her into account."

"Well, shit." He contemplated me, still scowling. "I had an idea about legality, so I got the Idnu to come. He doesn't know what's going on, but he'll play his part. We'll just assume that Hutyt MacIntyre is another dupe, right? Let me show you what I've got here."

He waddled over to a table over by some shelves. "This is an ancient offering table I acquired a few years ago. It's got some interesting mechanisms I'll use to do a little magic act. Anything you can do to distract your medjat when Blackmore puts the knife on the table will help, Shesmu. Keep her quiet and don't let her interfere until Hepuseneb arrests Blackmore, all right? She'll be a witness to Blackmore's crimes." The phone buzzed. Hernefer picked it up, grunted, put it down, and said, "He's here."

He opened the door and pushed me into the secret room. Hepuseneb, in his disguise as the seedy Professor Merisekhmet, stepped out to be with Hernefer, and we closed the door. We gathered around the monitors to watch the action.

The study door opened. The shendyt-clad butler announced Blackmore and a friend, Pasen. Blackmore carried a metal suitcase the right size and shape for a clarinet or trumpet. His associate carried nothing except a bad attitude. Muscle.

There was much bowing and many honorifics. Hernefer did his best gracious-but-unscrupulous collector act. Pasen said nothing, folded his arms in front of his chest, and looked alert. Hernefer introduced the professor and invited Blackmore to show his wares.

Professor Merisekhmet and Hernefer listened to Blackmore's sales pitch. Remarkably, he avoided saying the Knife was so illegal it could burn down Hernefer's palace from the heat. Hernefer and Professor Merisekhmet smiled knowing smiles to each other and to Blackmore, and Blackmore smiled back, convinced he was dealing with men of the world. Hernefer asked Blackmore to go ahead, showing him the table.

Blackmore hefted his suitcase over to the table. Pasen walked with him and stood by him. Blackmore fiddled with a padlock and two combination locks on the suitcase, then opened it with a reverence that was half real and half marketing. There was a fine linen bag nestled in foam.

Blackmore lifted out the bag with both hands, opened its drawstrings, and laid the Knife of Seteh on the table with reverence. The critical moment had come. Hernefer, crackling with suppressed excitement, brought over the inspection tools and laid them out. He motioned for Blackmore to take away the suitcase, which was in the way. Blackmore passed it to Pasen, who put it down away from the table. While this was going on, I whispered to MacIntyre, "What do you think, does Hepuseneb sound like he means it? Is he acting OK?" She sized up the "professor" and whispered, "He's perfect." Indirection is the key to every magic act.

As Blackmore turned back toward the table, Hernefer busied himself going over the Knife with his glass. It wasn't long before he straightened up and turned to Blackmore, his face one massive scowl. He gave a growl of disgust.

"You said this knife was Middle Empire, the Knife of Seteh that killed the great Pera'a Setepenseteh-Akhenr'a R'amesesu. What are you trying to pull?"

Blackmore, taken aback, stuttered, "That's, yes, exactly, that's what it is!" His Renkemet wasn't as smooth as before.

Hernefer flicked the putative Knife of Seteh with a dismissive finger. "This knife goes back only a hundred years at most. Look at the handle; look at the metal. Pick it up and feel the weight!"

Blackmore jumped to the table and picked up the knife. Hernefer continued, in a loud voice, "This knife is machine-forged carbon steel, it's even got the company's logo on it. It's ridiculous!" The hard part was over, his having got Blackmore to pick up the knife.

Blackmore's face blanched. He swung around, holding the knife, and yelled at Hernefer in English, "God damn it! This isn't my knife! What the hell have you done with it?" It was funny to watch; but I thought it was time to intervene, as did Hepuseneb, who took out his gun. MacIntyre dropped my hand and started for the door, the security chief right behind her. I stayed put and enjoyed the following scene on a monitor.

"Medjau! Put the knife down—now! Medjau!" shouted Hepuseneb, transforming back into a medja and taking out a gun. MacIntyre had her gun in her hand, striding across the room toward the man with the knife. The security chief was right behind her, also with a gun.

Blackmore, taken from two directions, stood rigid for a full ten seconds. Then he carefully laid the knife on the table. Pasen, still looking blank, had stepped forward toward Blackmore. He froze too. Hepuseneb, with MacIntyre and the security chief to help, put them up against a wall, patted them down, and handcuffed them. By that time, two more local medjau had come into the room to help secure the two prisoners.

I stepped out of the secret room once the two local medjau had taken Blackmore and Pasen away. Hepuseneb assessed the legal situation for Hernefer, ignoring me and MacIntyre. "We'll charge Blackmore with attempted fraud, aggravated by possession of illegal artifacts with intent to sell. If we can trace the knife, we might get him on something more serious."

"I doubt you'll find that knife is valuable. I'm familiar with this kind of ritual knife, and this one doesn't look like much." Hernefer sounded disappointed. "From the way Blackmore talked, he had a knife of terrific historical importance. A con man trying to put one over. I'm sorry we didn't turn up something more important for you, Idnu."

"That's all right, lord, it's what we're here for, to protect you."

Hepuseneb took his leave, bowing to Hernefer and nodding to me. He ignored MacIntyre. We all saw him off with his prisoners. The butler closed the huge front door, and the security chief went about his duties.

Hernefer said, "Would you excuse us for a moment, Hutyt MacIntyre? Shesmu will be right with you."

Before she could object, Hernefer whisked me back upstairs to the study and locked the study doors. He walked over to the altar table and rubbed a palm over the top, showing his appreciation for a fine piece of work. He touched a hidden spot on the side of the table, and a knife appeared on top. The mechanism was smooth enough that there was no noise and no visible motion; the Knife just appeared. Magic.

After examining the Knife with the tools still laid out on the table, Hernefer nodded to himself. He smoothed a finger down the side of the blade. "Beautiful. The Knife of Seteh is part of history. I only wish I could keep it."

Hernefer got a silk bag and slid the Knife into it, folded the top over, and handed it to me using two hands with a ceremonious bow. "It's yours now; return it to its proper place. I've thought about it, and you were right. Keeping the gods on one's side is more important than adding an artifact to a collection. I'm getting too close to the afterlife to offend Wesir, Imen-R'a, or even Ma'at." The fat fraud.

I smiled and pulled the Knife from the bag. "You weren't aware that I've seen pictures of the Knife of Seteh. From the tomb. This," I said, fingering the finely engraved hieroglyphs, "may be an outstanding ritual knife, but it's not the Knife of Seteh. Similar shape, but the handle is wrong, and the glyphs don't contain the name Seteh. Give it up, Hernefer. Still in the table?" I took the false knife back to the table and set it down, then gazed at Hernefer. I waited.

"It's mine," he said, folding his arms.

"It's not," I replied. "The Knife is Nekhen's."

"Nekhen is dead, I have the Knife, and that's all there is to it."

"What about your word?"

"Words are just words."

"What about our agreement?"

"I'm breaking it."

"What about Wesir?"

Hernefer didn't have a simple answer for that one. Words, agreements, and artifacts were part of the mundane world. Wesir was part of the afterlife. We'd see whether Hernefer cared a lot more about this world than the next one. I'd give him that chance.

I argued, "Inpu's judgment for Wesir is final, Hernefer, and the feather of Ma'at won't let through a stolen sacred object worth millions of debenu. You said you were too close—think about it, think about what would restore ma'at to the world. The Knife of Seteh must be in the tomb of the last of the line of priests who cared about it. It's ma'at. Don't let the Knife pollute the mundane world with its evil isfet." Heady stuff, but I saw his face going through changes. Even a billionaire can have religious scruples. Knocks sounded at the study door:

MacIntyre, knowing something was up. I heard her shouting, though I couldn't make out the words.

But Hernefer's face told me I hadn't persuaded him. However much religion he had, it wasn't enough to turn the trick. I shifted my argument from religion to law and used my blonde mace on him as she pounded on the door. "Hernefer, I swear by all the gods that if you don't help me restore the Knife to its rightful place, I will tell MacIntyre everything. We'll all go to jail charged with accessory to murder. Right now, Hernefer. Do the right thing." The knocking turned into pounding. I could hear the butler expostulating with MacIntyre outside the door. I walked over and put my hand on the door handle. "Now, Hernefer!"

"All the gods take you to eternal damnation!" Hernefer reached and touched the side of the table, and then the object on the table was different: the Knife of Seteh, this time the genuine one. I picked it up, bagged it, and said, "Thank you. It's the right thing to do."

He shook his head and grimaced. "Hurts just the same. But I admire you, boy. You know how to play the game."

"Most games," I replied, "not all." I walked over to the door and let in a furious MacIntyre.

"What are you two playing at in here?" she demanded. She had her gun in her hand. The butler came in after her, an apologetic expression on his face.

I lifted the bag. "I needed to buy a present for Neferaset. She's been through so much pain. An antique. I'd get you a present, too, Cheryl, but I don't think we know each other well enough yet. Wouldn't be right."

The ferry ride back to Menmenet was even more chilly than the ride to Iu-Sedeg had been.

CHAPTER TWENTY-FIVE
MacIntyre Makes a Deal

THE DAY AFTER HER ROMANTIC island adventure, Shesmu still pissed MacIntyre off. He had not only tricked her in some way that she still did not understand, he wasn't responding to her as any normal man would after a romantic dinner and first kiss. Rather than obsessing over her own unreasonable romantic expectations, MacIntyre preferred to obsess over her real problem: staying alive. She needed help. She'd heard nothing at all from Djehutymes or any of the other medjau she'd called.

MacIntyre texted Yaotl a brief message: "urgent need to see you re contract negotiations." He ought to understand what she meant by the reference to contracts.

Ping! "Come ahead bring money."

And here she was, still suspended without pay. She checked her meagre savings account with her phone, grimaced, and went in cautious search of an ATM. Her neck was sore from looking over her shoulder all the time; Yaotl's help would take care of that. But help would prove costly this time around.

"Why, Hutyt MacIntyre, I am surprised at you."

"And why is that, Yaotl?"

"You overestimate my influence and knowledge. I am just a humble businessperson, Hutyt."

"I wish you would stop calling me that."

"You have a flighty mind. Ms. MacIntyre?"

"That will do, Yaotl."

"You should learn to handle these sorts of things yourself." Yaotl was severe in his critique of MacIntyre's professionalism.

"It hasn't come up before. They don't teach this at the Medjau Academy, at least not in Menmenet. Are we done with the ritual small talk and protestations of innocence and humility, Yaotl? Because I'm busy trying to stay alive."

The Aztec crime lord pursed his lips in disapproval of her ignorance of the forms of contract negotiation but came to the point.

"It will cost you 1,500 debenu to pay for my time and the time of my associates."

"I can afford 500."

"You can die, too."

"750."

"You can die quickly or slowly. It doesn't matter to me. Not for 750 debenu."

"Damn. Why am I doing this?"

"I assume the question is rhetorical, Hut—Ms. MacIntyre."

"OK. 1,000 debenu. I'm an honest medjat, Yaotl. It's all I have in my savings account."

"I know, I checked. 1,000 debenu it is." She could only call his expression a smirk.

"Do we shake hands on it, or is there a written contract?"

The Aztec smiled. "Money first. Then it comes down to my word and my pleasure in serving you, Ms. MacIntyre. And my interest in keeping you alive." He shook his head but continued smiling. "Aztecs do not shake hands. Dreadful, insanitary practice."

MacIntyre counted out the cash, squared up the bills, and handed them to Yaotl, who put them away in a desk drawer. He said, "Thank you, Ms. MacIntyre. You will not regret this investment in your future."

"What remains of it, Yaotl."

"Indeed. We can help with that, Ms. MacIntyre."

The word from Djehutymes was about as useless as MacIntyre had expected.

"You let him go?" She put a full load of incredulity into her question.

"What could we hold him on, MacIntyre? An earnest wish to make money? He hasn't done anything."

"It's not what he hasn't done, Mes, it's what he will do."

"We warned him. We're keeping close tabs on him."

"How many people, Mes?"

Silence.

"I'm a hutyt-er-semetyt, Mes. I've been working for you for years. How many people? One medja in his spare time, if it doesn't keep him away from his regular caseload. Am I right?"

"Look, MacIntyre, you—"

"Never mind, Mes. I understand. Limited medja resources. No budget for protective activities. Hire your own private protection if you need it. Oh, yeah: any progress to figuring out who hired the bastard?"

"Look, MacIntyre, we—"

"Not to worry, Mes, I've hired my own. Professionals. Tell me when I'm reinstated, OK? I need the money. I need the work. And I love working for you, I do. I hope I stay alive long enough to do more of that."

She hung up. What the hell do we pay taxes for? The city can't even fix the potholes.

"Ms. MacIntyre?"

"Who is this?" MacIntyre sat up on Henutsenu's couch, where she'd been resting her eyes.

"A friend."

"I don't have any friends."

"That's sad. Shall I tell you what you need to know or hang up?"

"Tell."

The voice with the Aztec accent was concise and straightforward. "We discovered the person who set up the contract and negotiated fees with the contract killer. He is a man named Pabaky."

"Now there's a thing. Pabaky."

"Do you wish me to spell it?"

"No, thank you. Got it."

"The man Pabaky is a member of an illicit religious sect that owns and operates a secret temple in Menmenet devoted to the worship of Seteh, one of your gods. One possibility is that the sect wants you dead. Worship of Seteh is illegal. Another possibility is your association with the man Shesmu. Pabaky attacked him one week ago for a reason yet unknown to us, but the medjau arrested Pabaky for the attack. He may harbor ill will because of that attack and the consequent events."

"Yes, I heard about that. Where is this temple?"

"There is an alley on the south side of the Menmenet Cove, Henemibr'a Street. Go down the alley from the waterfront. There are four doors that face onto the alley. The second door on the left."

"How big is this sect? Is there always someone at the temple?"

"Let me check my notes." The voice paused. "We've had a man watching the alley. Only two people entered or left while we watched—Pabaky and a woman. We have no information on the woman. They both appear to live there and are present after midnight but gone during the day and evening. Do you wish us to follow the woman and identify her? It will cost you another 500 debenu. 10,000 to do something about it for you."

A stunning example of cross-promotion of services. "No, I guess not. Is that all?"

The man hung up.

Why waste 500 debenu that she didn't have? Much less 10,000. MacIntyre had a solid idea about this "woman" based on her knowledge of Pabaky. And she could do something about it herself. And about her "association" with the man Shesmu.

CHAPTER TWENTY-SIX
Shesmu Gets the Secret Story

THE PATH UP TO ASET'S door proved much easier to walk with the silk bag in my arms. I'd get a warm welcome. The warmth wouldn't last long when she heard what I had to say.

The light in the portico pushed away the encroaching darkness of the early evening. Aset answered the door, still elegant but showing the signs of sleepless nights. Her eyes flew to the bag in my arms and widened.

"You…you have it? Is that the Knife? The Knife of Seteh?"

"The very one, Aset. Let's go inside."

"Bring it into the library, Shes!" Aset hurried ahead of me. I quickened my pace to keep up.

"Put it on the table!" Aset pointed to an ornate table that stood at the side of the high-ceilinged, vast room full of books. I untied the bag, took out the Knife, and put it on the table.

"Oh, Shes, you did it! The Knife, the Knife!" Aset wrapped her arms around me and we embraced until she let me go. She floated over to the table and picked up the Knife with both hands. She looked at the glyphs on the blade, and, with loving fingers, rubbed them.

"I'm happy you're happy, Aset. There's still a problem, though."

She looked at me, pouting. "Don't be that way, Shes. It's illegal, the Knife, but I don't care now that I have it."

"How do we get it back into the tomb, Aset?"

"What?" She looked at me, mouth ajar, eyes wide. "Tomb?"

"Back into Nekhen's tomb, where he wanted it, Aset."

"No, that's not what I want, it—I can't tell you, Shes, but it's important. Important to me."

"But not to Nekhen. He wanted it in his tomb, forever."

"Yes, Shes, but he didn't understand the power, the history, all of it."

"Explain it to me, Aset, after we figure out how to get it back into the tomb."

Anger flashed over her face. "No. It's not going into the tomb. It's going where it belongs, Shes. With me."

"Are you willing to kill me to do that, Aset? Because I can't let that happen."

"Kill you? I'm not—" Aset looked at the Knife in her hands, then set it back on the table and turned to me. "You think I killed Nekhen, don't you? Don't you?" There was anger in her voice.

"I'm lost, Aset. The Knife has me mystified. Tell me, Aset. Tell me."

She mastered her anger and stood contemplating me for a minute. The decision formed in her eyes. She smiled.

"You can be part of it, Shes. I didn't believe you could be. But you've brought me the Knife. You're so intent on this business with Nekhen, I have to try."

"Try what?"

"To get you to see…what I see."

"What do you see, Aset?"

"Seteh. It's Seteh, Shes. The power of him, the might. You studied him in school, didn't you, Shes?"

"He's a powerful god, Aset. But he's banned. The evil of him got too much for Imen-R'a."

"Those priests, what do they know. Imen is the 'hidden one,' Seteh need not hide. Imen joined with R'a has political power. But Seteh is in the barque of R'a, he fights 'Aapep the evil serpent and wins, every night, every trip R'a takes through the akhet, Shes. His power is of the light, of the day, and of the dark, of the night. He—"

"Aset, stop. I'm not religious. I can't go there with you."

"You must, Shes. Seteh is the god of the future, not Imen-R'a, not Ma'at, not Wesir. Only Seteh can help R'a save the world from the serpent, Shes!" She picked up the Knife. "The Knife knows the power of Seteh. It has the blood of Seteh on it. Those priests, they pretended it was the blood of Heru, that weakling pera'a, but it is the blood of Seteh, Shes. Nekhen told me that."

"Nekhen, Aset. What did Nekhen tell you about Seteh? His family were the priests, the Hemu-Netjer of Seteh."

"Poor Nekhen. He believed none of it. He just didn't understand who Seteh was, how powerful. Nekhen had books, ancient texts he'd inherited from his family." She waved a hand at a section of the library. "I learned about the consequence and power of Seteh from those books. I tried to convince him, explained about the Knife, what it meant, its power. But he just said he must take the Knife from the world along with the last remnants of the sect of Seteh—himself. But he didn't understand, Shes. He wasn't aware."

"Aware of what, Aset?" I'd never heard Aset like this, obsessed with a god. It worried me.

"Aware that others understand Seteh and his power and worship him."

"It's illegal, Aset. You can go to prison if you worship Seteh."

"Oh, Shes." Her voice echoed with sorrow. "Legal means nothing, not for a god like Seteh. Prisons won't hold us. We will grow stronger. More powerful. More numerous. You can join us, Shes. We can be together, worshipping Seteh. Poor Nekhen, he angered them."

"Who, Aset?"

"The sect…I can't tell you. Yes, they killed him. I couldn't, wouldn't, kill him, even though he threatened to take the Knife from the world that needed it. This threat angered them, but I knew the Knife would stay in the world. I made sure…but they wouldn't listen, they wouldn't do what I asked, and they killed him. They called me to the Temple of Seteh that day, and when I got back, I found him."

Her eyes were on me, but she was looking at something far beyond the walls of the library, in a place I couldn't join her.

"Why is the Knife so important to you, Aset? Are you returning it to the sect? What will they do with it? Why did you take it from Nekhen's tomb and put the murder knife in its place?"

Aset smiled. "The Knife is the sacred relic of the Hem-Netjer of Seteh, Shes. With the Knife in my hands, I become the Hemet-Netjer-en-Seteh, the God's Wife of Seteh. I take on the full power of Seteh in the world. Seteh's disciples all over the world must follow me as I lead them out of the darkness into power. Nekhen wouldn't let me have it. It was only fitting that he give it to me when he left for the Duat and that the Knife with his blood on it go with him there. You can be my consort, Shes. If you accept Seteh into your heart, if you have faith in his power. If you can't, just walk out that door and forget about me. Go back to your kitchen and cook. That's what Nekhen did."

A tempting alternative, cooking. But I loved Aset. I had to help her get past all this.

"Tell the medjau, Aset. You can't live with this, with Nekhen's murder—it's shaking your foundations."

"My foundations are rock, Shes. I went to the Temple of Seteh, I explained to the believers about the Knife, that my husband had it. With the Knife, the believers will do as I wish. They said so."

I wondered who the "believers" were, but I knew Aset wouldn't tell me. MacIntyre. MacIntyre could find them if I gave her the space and time to do it.

I pleaded with her. "Aset, they won't follow you. They're murderers, you're not. You're in deadly danger, Aset. You have the Knife. Think, Aset. They killed Nekhen over the Knife. They want that power. You stand in their way. Aset, I don't want to find you with your throat cut, lying on the floor like Nekhen!"

Aset put her hands to her throat, eyes wide. She wasn't blind or stupid, but she was in the grip of powerful forces that didn't need her intellectual capabilities. The Knife of Seteh had at least one power, the power to beguile otherwise reasonable people into a fantasy world. I had to break her out of her dream of power. I had to get the Knife away from her.

"Aset, if the sect learns you have the Knife, they'll try to kill you to get it. It was easy for Blackmore to take the Knife by fooling you. Let me take it and keep it safe for you until you can work out a stronger position with the sect. You can trust me. Let them see you have the Knife, but that it's safe in the hands of a non-believer. Take a photo with your phone to prove you have it. Then we can work out a way to keep you safe while you consolidate the power of God's Wife of Seteh."

Her eyes wavered and looked down at the Knife. She rubbed the glyphs on the blade with a sensuous finger. "I'm not sure, Shes...."

"And Blackmore."

"What?"

"Blackmore, Aset. The antiquities trader. He'll be out on bail soon. He's tricked you once, he'll do it again, or worse. You'll have people trying to kill you from two directions. Please. Give me the Knife. Let them all know you don't have it."

"Oh, Shes...." Her eyes were bottomless wells of darkness.

"If you keep the Knife with you, you'll be dead within hours, Aset. Please."

She smoothed her hand over the Knife blade again. "You'll defend the Knife with your life, Shes? You'll be my consort?"

If I had the Knife of Seteh, I'd better make my own tomb arrangements soon. Aset might not be in danger, but I knew I would be once the murderers figured out that I had the Knife. A month ago, Aset would have cared about me, my safety, my continuing love for her; now she wanted me to fight to the death over an illicit relic of a banned god as consort to an all-powerful priestess.

"Aset, I will do everything in my power to help you."

That help might not be what she wanted or expected. I owed it to the Aset I loved. That Aset had faded away in front of my eyes. I still owed her my help.

But I'd lost her, and I hadn't even known it.

I carried the silk bag that contained the Knife of Seteh home with me. I kept a sharp lookout for cars following me, taking random turns and zig-zags. Nekhen was dead and in his tomb, and I wasn't ready to see the inside of my own, but I felt foolish. No one followed me in the busy traffic as I drove across Menmenet to Dju-Keta and home.

I spent a restless night filled with dreams of knives and religious fanatics. Putting the Knife in its bag under my pillow might have contributed to that. Keeping the thing at my house would not be restful. I knew by dawn I had to find another hiding place. I arose unrefreshed and ate a quick breakfast, then headed out for the Neferti on foot, carrying the bag. The restaurant was the one place other than my house to which I had complete access and control. To hide the Knife there was obvious, too obvious. But I had in mind the perfect hiding place.

Sebek, at work in the kitchen, seethed with resentment.

"Shes, you've got to do something about Dua. She's being a real pain."

"Where is she?"

He pointed to the back prep room, saying, "She spends most of her time in there. She's depressed or something, or she's doing a wildcat work slowdown, or she's just being a jerk. Maybe you can convince her to help on the stations more. I can't." He sounded close to giving up the task. "Shes, I need a sous chef, not a sulking…." He left the phrase unfinished.

I walked into the prep room. Dua sat on a stool doing something to an onion on the prep table with her chef's knife. She looked like she didn't have her heart in it. I said, "Can I talk with you for a minute?" I sat on a stool across from her, putting the bag on the prep table.

Her eyes were red, the look you get after a long cry and not much sleep. The onion wasn't to blame, either. She clamped her mouth tight, way beyond sullen. The Pabaky thing had shaken her into near immobility. She couldn't look me in the eye; her eyes fixed on the bag and stayed there. I didn't like the burning intensity I saw in them. Then she raised them to direct the intensity at me.

"You bastard. What did you do? What did you do to him?"

I assumed she referred to her boyfriend. "I broke his wrist and injured his pride."

"You…" she was incoherent. She looked away, back at the bag. I was too painful.

"He came at me with a huge knife. What do you expect?" I asked.

"A knife," she repeated.

I couldn't help but think of the Knife of Seteh. Dua's eyes still wouldn't find mine and stayed fixed on the bag I'd brought in. I saw the irony.

"Yes, a knife. That thing with the pointy tip and sharp edge." I pointed at hers. It looked brand new, sharp and shiny. "The big kind." She stared down at her knife and started crying again. She pounded on the table with a fist.

"Dua, please, just let me have a minute. You owe me that."

"What do you want?" Her tone wasn't encouraging, her voice raw with emotion. She would not last long in my kitchen; things had gone too far.

"Why was Pabaky following me?"

"How should I know? The medjau have asked all the questions about him I'm going to answer."

"Was it MacIntyre?"

"That blonde bitch? No. Some older son-of-Sebek that smelled like the swamp croc he was."

I rubbed my mouth, then asked, "This had nothing to do with you? What could Pabaky have been thinking? Does he hold a grudge against me? Does he want something from me?"

She put her chef's knife down and laid her hands flat on the table. "Do you imagine Pabaky would just sit still and let you screw me over? Sure he had a grudge, I've got one too. You hired that little bastard in there instead of making me chef. How do you expect that makes me feel? You're just like all the others, take and take and never give."

"You're not ready to run the kitchen, Dua."

"I'm as ready as I'll ever be, but you won't give me a chance, will you, you bastard? Bastard men, asshole chefs. Nekhen was the same. A woman couldn't do the job, never. I hate this!" She slammed her hand down on the table.

I framed my suggestion carefully. "Dua, why don't you take a few days off? Get some perspective, think about things. I'll tell Sebek."

"You can take the job and—"

"Now, come on."

"When Pabaky gets out of jail, we'll get something together."

"Not here." The rejection popped out more strongly than I intended.

She looked at her sliced onion. "No, we'll have to move somewhere else. I hate this city. There's no love in this city. It's a cold city." She picked up the onion and threw it at the wall.

"That's enough! Dua, I've loved working with you, but it's too much. Clean out your locker and leave. I'll have Henutsenu send your check to you."

"Screw you and screw Henutsenu. Take your check and shove it where it hurts." She got up, picked up her knife, weighed it in her hand, and looked at me. Reason prevailed, and she lowered the knife and walked out to the lockers. I picked up the silk bag and took it out to find a temporary resting place. But I had a couple of tasks to do first.

"Did you talk to her?" asked Sebek.

"I did. You have one less employee for lunch today."

"I can't say I'm sorry to see her go. Was it hard?"

I waved a hand. "Don't worry about it. There's some cleanup to do in there. What do you want to do about a sous chef?"

"It's your kitchen, chef."

"Yeah, but you're running it now. Who?"

"Khay. He's ready."

"Done. I'll let Henutsenu know, you let Khay know, and I'll spend the day training him, OK?"

"Sure, glad for the help."

"Is Henutsenu in yet?"

"Yeah, we came together."

On my way through the kitchen, I stopped at the utility shelf and got the roll of duct tape we kept for emergencies. I took the bag into the dining room, made sure no one was around, and crawled under one of the large tables. Two braces along the sides underneath the table left a space big enough to accommodate the Knife. No one would find it there. And the large tables never moved. I taped the bag securely to the underside of the table. Another use for duct tape: hiding illegal ritual knives. I scrambled out from under the table.

Henutsenu came out of the hallway that led to the office. Had she seen me under the table? No sign of it.

"Henutsenu, I'll need a check for Dua."

"Oh, no, chef! She quit?"

"It was a mutual agreement to part."

"Was there much damage?"

Henutsenu had experienced Dua's dark side.

"No. She reconsidered before she used the knife."

She gave me an appreciative smile, thinking I was joking. "I'll get that check. Is she still here?"

"She's left by now. She didn't want to linger. Send the check by messenger. I'll be in the kitchen, training Khay. We'll have to increase his pay. I'll give you the numbers later."

"I'm sorry, chef. It's never easy to lose a good sous chef."

"I wouldn't know. I don't have one. But thanks for the thought." I headed for the kitchen.

CHAPTER TWENTY-SEVEN
MacIntyre Breaks and Enters

MACINTYRE FOUND ENOUGH BLACK ATTIRE in her wardrobe to project the look she wanted: invisibility. Henemibr'a Street was deserted as she slipped into the shadowy alley, pretending to be just another shadow. She huddled in a doorway across from the second door on the left for an hour to wait for any signs of life. Nothing happened.

The morning was chilly but nothing out of the way in foggy Menmenet. She rubbed her hands together for warmth as she waited. She knew Pabaky was in jail, and she guessed Dua would be at the Neferti to open the kitchen. Best to linger a bit to make sure.

At about 9 a.m., she drifted across the deserted alley and listened at the door. Silence. She inspected the lock, took out lock-picking tools, and fiddled. Two minutes did it, and she could slot the deadbolt back with a firm twist of the hook. She stepped inside and put on a pair of latex gloves. MacIntyre didn't want her fingerprints showing up because of this very illegal search. She wasn't after evidence, and she didn't care whether the denizens knew someone had searched their temple. But she didn't want her zeal for ma'at coming back to bite her in the ass.

The space was dank and dark. There were no lights on and almost no morning light coming in through the two small windows. Large, lumpy things loomed out of the dark at her. She used her torch and found the light switch and turned it on.

Jesus!

Five colossal statues of the god Seteh, in various classic Remetjy poses, confronted her. Four of them were human in form, in the four corners of the room. Each of those four ebony bodies had the head of Seteh with its large, square ears and long jackal snout. The fifth, in the center of the space, was a life-size animal version of Seteh with a long body and a long tail split at the end. The lights emphasized the power and wrath of the god Seteh. Her Congregationalist upbringing surfaced, screaming "Devil Devil Devil" at her, and she mercilessly stomped that upbringing to death before it overwhelmed her.

The animal Seteh was behind a table. From its position, MacIntyre guessed it served as an altar for sacrifices or offerings. She wiped a gloved finger across the table; no dust, no obvious residues or substances such as crusted blood. They kept it clean. She looked around the room. The only other thing of interest was a series of swords mounted on racks all along the walls. Later, after she'd explored a bit.

She opened a door at the back of the room. It was a studio apartment with a compact kitchen and an unmade bed. Pots piled up in the sink. A small table piled with papers. She pawed through them: bills sent to Chen Wei Ying Exports, Inc. Water, electricity, garbage, things like that.

MacIntyre opened another door at the back of the apartment to find stairs going down into blackness. No light switch nearby. She eased down the steps. No sense of looming figures, as there was very little light. The torch again found a light switch.

Jesus.

Devil devil devil.

She'd read about this kind of thing. A torture chamber for sexual gratification. Nothing sharp, nothing pointy, just restraints and whips and clothes racks with costumes. Smaller statues of Seteh here and there, grinning with jackal-ferocity. She checked the corners and edges of the room; no sign of blood or body parts, just dust bunnies. No sign of disturbed-soil graves or any of the other trappings of serial killers. Just your average, normal sexual perversion palace. OK. A home gym. MacIntyre's disgust tempered itself with the slightest edge of lust. She suppressed that tiny devil inside her.

MacIntyre went back to the apartment and took it apart, piece by piece. Occult books, sex toys, a cache of money in a decorative jar. Three hundred and something deben in small bills. Not a devil's ransom, too much to be contributions from the devotees. Emergency hospital money in case things went wrong downstairs?

MacIntyre probed through the drawers and shelves, looking for names. Seteh was everywhere, not surprising at the Temple of Seteh. She turned up a tax return form in a file cabinet signed by Dua, confirming her idea about the "woman" cult member associated with Pabaky. Pabaky was not of a class or quality of lover that might attract The Wife. Even if Seteh put his thumb on the scale. No.

Back in the front room, she took each sword off the wall and examined it on the table-altar with her little magnifying glass. Clean as whistles. Polished. Sharp. They weren't swords, they were the Remetjy curved knives used in butchery. Seventeen of them, each hung on its own little rack along the walls. She hypothesized Seteh had a thing for knives. Sharp knives. Heavy knives, chopping knives, not stabbing knives akin to stilettos or daggers. There was a space disturbing the symmetry of the wall of knives. An empty rack. The murder weapon? MacIntyre took one knife down off the wall from a dark corner. With any luck, nobody would miss it. She wanted to show it to an expert.

During her scrutiny of these knives, MacIntyre dropped any remaining suspicions of The Wife. Time for another talk with Dua, Pabaky's girlfriend. Between Dua and Pabaky, she was sure somebody would confess to murder. Knives everywhere provided means and method; all she needed was a motive. Once Mes reinstated her, that is.

MacIntyre carried her prize away from Henemibr'a Street, fully expecting to solve the case. This section of the waterfront was dead quiet most of the time. MacIntyre got back to her little red car with the big knife held down at her side without incident. No one saw her, or at least no one called the medjau about a strange, black-dressed villain lugging a huge knife down the street. As she pulled away from the curb, she saw Dua turning the corner. MacIntyre wasn't in the habit of praying to her goddess. But right then it pleased her to send up a little paean of thanks to Ma'at that Dua hadn't walked in on her.

MacIntyre drove northwest through busy streets filled with normal people going about their business. The knife on the seat next to her was the key to her belief that she would soon close the Celebrity Chef case.

The Temple of Sekhmet-Hut-Her was a nondescript building on Wennefer Street at the base of Dju-Seret. Two statues of the lion-headed goddess were all that distinguished it from the nearby nondescript buildings. MacIntyre was there to see Irsu, the Hem-Netjer of Pathology. He did most of the autopsies of any importance in Menmenet, and MacIntyre had read his report on Nekhen's autopsy when she still had her job. MacIntyre had known Irsu since a messy murder that required extensive medical inference to figure out the identity of the victim. They had achieved a mutual respect over the two years since.

A medjat carrying a large knife into the Temple of Sekhmet-Hut-Her was not a big deal. The temple staff had seen much worse. One phone call from the front desk to Irsu, and she was in. He even came out to walk her back to his lab. Irsu was a lean, square-faced man with a serious, concentrated expression and delicate hands that could handle the fine details of the corpses of murder victims with ease and elegance.

"What might I have the pleasure of doing for you today, Hutyt MacIntyre?" he asked, seating himself at a small desk on one side of the lab.

"I'm working on the Nekhen case, and I have this knife," she replied, laying the knife on the desk. Irsu leaned over and inspected it.

"Do you suspect this knife of being involved in the crime? I believe your team has not yet recovered the actual murder weapon. Is it that you wish to match—"

"No, not quite. This knife turned up in my investigation, and I'd like to see whether it might be the type of knife used. The report didn't have much detail about the murder weapon."

"Yes, I was reluctant to draw too many conclusions without more data. But this," he shook his head. "Doubtful. Let me check the photos."

He turned to the computer next to the desk, logged in, and searched for a minute. A gruesome montage of photos of Nekhen's mangled neck appeared on the screen. Irsu magnified photo after photo, examining each one closely.

"Hm, hm, hm. Yes, but the edge separation and depth…. This knife is very unlikely to make the type of slash wound shown in these photos, Hutyt. This knife," he said, picking up the knife by the handle, "is a chopping knife. It is large, heavy, and thick, and I'd imagine the manufacturer or maker would tell you it is useful for separating or dividing bones and large cuts of meat. This knife would leave a different depth of cut at the beginning and end of the cut. The curve of the blade would need an unlikely pulling action to achieve the shape in the photos. No, this knife is not the kind of knife that produced this wound." He set the knife back on the desk.

"How would the knife that did it be different?"

"It would be smaller, 20-30 centimeters long, with a very sharp, straight edge. That's all I can infer from the wound."

MacIntyre compressed her lips in disappointment. "Oh well, it was a nice try."

"Where did you get this, erm, unusual blade?"

"Can't tell you, especially if it isn't the right knife."

"And," he lifted one end of his mouth in a slight smile, "I understood the medjau have suspended you for pushing too hard on a suspect."

"True."

"I'm sure everything will come out all right, but may I give you some advice?"

"Sure, doc."

"Don't get too far ahead of your facts. Being wrong will not get you your badge back."

She smiled. "Thanks, doc. Being right might not either, but it's better than the alternative. I'll just have to find the actual knife that did the job." She paused, then added, "I'd appreciate your not telling my boss I was here. Since the knife isn't the weapon and all."

"Certainly, Hutyt. Now, I must leave you; I have a body waiting. It's a fascinating case, multiple stab wounds across the—"

"Rather you than me, doc."

CHAPTER TWENTY-EIGHT
Shesmu Copes with a Burglary

ANOTHER NIGHTTIME CALL. 3:30 in the morning. I looked at the screen: Sebek.

"Yeah. Shesmu."

"Sorry to wake you, boss, but there's been a burglary."

That woke me, all right. The Knife. It had to be the Knife.

"Where?"

"The restaurant," he said. "Why the hell else would I call you?"

"Yeah, OK, I'm waking up, sorry. Hold on one second."

I got out of bed, stumbled into the bathroom, and splashed cold water on my face. 3:30 in the morning. Did the minions of Seteh never sleep?

"Sebek? Where are you?"

Irritability came clearly through the wires. "The restaurant. The alarm notified the security company, the medjau are here, the security company called me, and I called you. Got it?"

"Is Henutsenu there?"

"Yes, Henutsenu is here! We came together. We were in bed at my place."

Aha. Right to the source of his crankiness.

"Got it. I will be right there, three minutes. Then you can go home and resume your sex life."

"I appreciate the thought, but I suspect that's done for this day. See you." He hung up.

I pulled on random clothes and drove down the hill to the Neferti and parked in the back. I dashed in through the back door into the arms of a uniformed medja.

"Whoa, whoa, boy. Can't come in here. Crime scene. Get your ass out that door again."

"I'm the owner."

"You look like the dishwasher, my man." The medja was a local, a Ramaytush in appearance. "Got ID?"

I discovered I had not put my wallet in my pants. I then discovered that I had not brought my phone, either. "If you go get Sebek, he's the chef, he'll tell you who I am. He called me."

"Fine. Sebek. Meanwhile, take yourself out that door and wait. I promise I won't let you get cold. Unless you'd prefer cuffs and the floor here?" I shook my head. Deficient sense of humor at 3:45 in the morning. I waited on the loading dock.

The medja, true to his word, brought Sebek before I got cold. To a question from the medja, Sebek grinned and said, "Yep, that's him: Shesmu, the owner of the Neferti." The medja nodded and said, "Pleased to meetcha," and waved us into the restaurant.

The kitchen was full of medjau looking at the mess. Sebek led me around the side of the cook's line and out into the dining room. I glanced at the large table that harbored my secret but said nothing; later.

"Who's in charge?" I asked.

"Him." Sebek pointed to a uniformed medja standing near the hostess station talking to Henutsenu.

She said, "Shesmu, finally. This is Idnu Menna. He's got questions only you can answer."

"How'd they break in?" I asked her. She pointed at the front door. There was damage to the jamb; they pried it open by brute force. That's what must have set off the alarm.

"What's the damage?" I asked.

"I looked around. The safe is locked, nothing missing from it. Everything else in the office is on the floor. Things in the bar are on the floor with bottles smashed. The kitchen—"

"I saw the kitchen."

"Right. A mess. So's the walk-in. Everything off all the shelves, the larger packages ripped open." Henutsenu looked at Sebek. "Anything else?"

"Private dining room trashed, pillows ripped up, serving sideboard a mess."

"What's missing?" asked Idnu Menna, finally getting a word in.

"So far, nothing," said Sebek. "All the valuable equipment is still there."

"Hmm." Idnu Menna looked at me. "Do you have enemies? Could this be retaliation for something? Or a gang extortion warning?"

"No, no enemies who would do something like this. Competitors, but not enemies." Aside from the minions of Seteh, Blackmore, and Pasen, any of whom might do this. And I did not need Idnu Menna looking into that right now.

Henutsenu and Sebek agreed with me and disclaimed any knowledge of a threat to the restaurant.

Menna said, "I learned from our records that you had a recent visit from the medjau, about the Celebrity Chef case. Could this relate to that case?"

"I don't think so. Hutyt MacIntyre asked a lot of questions about my relationship with Nekhen and his wife, but there was nothing in it." I looked at Henutsenu for confirmation, and she nodded. "Why don't you ask MacIntyre about it?"

"She's suspended." The idnu's face took on a mix of disdain and humor. "Bends the rules too much, that one. I heard a gangster put out a contract on her. No, I can't talk to her right now. I'll speak to Djehutymes in Homicide, find out what he has to say."

Menna told us he'd write up a report on the damage for our insurance. I had a choice. I could tell them the whole sordid story of Seteh and his Knife. Or I could sit down, shut up, and let them get on with their useless investigation. A choice that was not a choice.

I was feverish to get down under the big table in the dining room, but I had no opportunity. The medja action died down about 5:30, just before the first employees showed up. I started them on the cleanup. Idnu Menna walked out with me into the dining room to finish things up.

"Anything else?" asked the idnu.

"No, that's all."

The idnu left, taking the rest of the medjau with him. The Ramaytush medja grinned at me as he left.

"Uh, Shes…" said Sebek. Henutsenu gave him a warning glance, and he lapsed into glum silence.

"Tell me," I said with a sinking heart.

"Cheryl…has been staying at Henutsenu's place. If you want to talk to her."

I stared long and hard at Henutsenu, who absorbed my intensity with her usual composure. She said, "Cheryl needed a place to stay because of the gangster thing. She wanted to be off the street."

I shook my head in wonder, then went to see about the kitchen. The kitchen workers had things under control. I said, "Sebek, you can suit up for the day and get things going. Make sure the bar gets fixed up first. I suppose we'll have to close the private dining room until we can get things for it. Henutsenu, you can line up supplies to replace what's not usable any more. OK?"

Sebek trotted off to the kitchen, and Henutsenu left for the office, muttering to herself. I waited until I was sure no one would see me and rolled under the table. The duct tape still secured the silk bag to the underside of the table. I sighed with released tension and detached the bag, stripping off the tape. If Seteh could move this fast, the Knife was not safe here. I had to return it to Nekhen's tomb.

I sat in my car in the Neferti parking lot to think things through. The bag lay on the passenger seat beside me, a silent warning that things weren't getting any better.

One thing was clear: the cult of Seteh knew much more about me than I knew about them. Within hours of hiding the Knife of Seteh in my restaurant, they burgled the place looking for it. I hoped I could just hide the Knife and consult with MacIntyre, but things moved too fast. Enough thinking. I pulled the car out of the parking lot and headed for the Tjesut. If I kept the Knife, I would be dead, disabled, or damned by the time R'a set in the akhet tonight.

I turned down an alley at the base of the hill and parked my car by a fire hydrant. I looked around; nobody in sight. The bag holding the Knife had two long drawstrings. I got out of the car and took my shirt off. I brought the two strings of the bag around my chest and tied them so they held the bag in position against my back. The Knife and bag were flat enough that it would be invisible under my shirt. I put the shirt back on and got into the car. It was uncomfortable, but I could stand it for the short time I'd be wearing this new accessory.

I parked in front of Aset's mansion and again knocked on her door. She answered with an uncertain smile.

"Shes, I didn't expect you, not so soon."

"Things are moving, Aset, and I need you to do something for me. We need to go to the necropolis, to Nekhen's tomb. I need the knife you put in the tomb."

"Why? It's better to keep it there forever."

"I've figured out a way to convince the medjau you aren't responsible for the murder, but I need the actual murder weapon to do it. The less you know, the better."

"But how can we get the knife? The tomb is sealed."

"Did you buy eternal protection insurance on the tomb?"

"Why, no. Nekhen thought it was too expensive."

I smiled. "That's how we get in. You upgrade to that level of protection, and a w'ab priest will install monitoring equipment in the tomb, including sensors in the tomb itself. I learned about this when my mother died and the Hem-Netjer of Inpu took us through the options and upgrade possibilities."

"What do you want me to do?"

"Be your distracting self with the w'ab once he's got the door open to install the equipment. Once you draw his attention away from the open door, I'll slip in and get the knife. It won't take long."

"Oh, I understand. Yes, I can do that. The knife is in a long wooden box with Seteh glyphs all over it. There aren't that many tomb goods in there, so it shouldn't be hard to find." She hesitated. "But are you sure you need to do this?"

"Yes, I'm sure, Aset. Very sure, if you want to quash the charges once and for all. Let's go. I'll drive."

"Is that medjat around? Will she follow us?"

"No, they've taken her off the case and suspended her."

"All right, Shes. Let me get something on."

"Aset?"

"Yes?"

"Put on something sexy."

"Shes...." Aset was scandalized. "That's so inappropriate."

I explained. "I need you to distract someone, and wearing one of those wonderful dresses you have will sure do that. Please, Aset?"

She nodded with an exasperated look at me, then closed the door. I walked back to my car to wait. Aset came out a few minutes later dressed in a shimmery, gold-edged thing that emphasized her best attributes, carrying a coat over her arm. I'd taken that dress off her, once, making love to her. My throat closed, remembering every detail. She'd surely distract a w'ab of Inpu. She distracted me by just walking down the path to my car and getting in. My plan got saved by the Knife digging into my back, reminding me of the true state of affairs. The Knife resting against my back and the Hemet-Netjer-en-Seteh sitting next to me had all my attention as we left for the necropolis.

CHAPTER TWENTY-NINE
MacIntyre Turns the Tables

MacIntyre, bored out of her mind at sitting and staring at the walls in Henutsenu's apartment, needed action. She wrapped a beautiful Remetjy head-scarf she'd discovered in Henutsenu's closet around her blonde hair and put on her sunglasses even though the fog was dense. As she drove, she reflected on the pitfalls of driving a small red convertible sports car. Anonymity not possible. She'd just have to deal.

She strode into the Neferti as lunch service started. The scarf covered her face. Henutsenu was at the hostess station handling a customer and eyed this enigmatic stranger with a slight smile. MacIntyre smiled behind the scarf, anticipating Henutsenu's surprise once she revealed herself. After showing the customer to his seat, Henutsenu returned to cope with this new problem.

"Cheryl! I didn't realize you were coming here today. Is it safe?"

MacIntyre stripped off the scarf and glasses and shook out her hair. "I guess I'm a master of disguise. Shit. Well, it's possible to be too safe."

Henutsenu smiled. "I haven't worn that scarf in years. I can't leave now, it's the lunch rush. Did you want Shesmu? He's not here. You missed him. We had a burglary last night! The medjau were here. Shesmu ran out of here like his house was on fire 3 hours ago."

"A burglary! We need to talk. Can you and Sebek meet with me? After lunch?"

"Yes, all right." Henutsenu cast a glance at her reservations terminal and the line forming behind the blonde American. "No tables, I'm afraid. Lunch in the bar?"

"I'll risk it." MacIntyre squared her shoulders and stepped into the bar to confront her old friend, the bartender. He flinched at the sight of her, but he settled down once she mentioned lunch.

At 2:30, the line of hungry guests vanished, and the restaurant was half empty. Henutsenu turned her station over to one of the wait staff and came into the bar to sit with MacIntyre.

"You said you wanted to talk with me and Sebek?"

"Yes, please. Alibis."

"What about them?"

"I need to check where certain people were at specific times."

"Cheryl, they've suspended you. Did they reinstate you this morning?"

MacIntyre gave her a crooked smile. "No, but I have hopes."

Henutsenu sighed and signaled the bartender. She asked him to call "chef" from the kitchen. Sebek appeared at the door of the bar after a brief wait.

"Cheryl! Glad to see you." He added, "I hope you enjoyed the lunch? Or am I here to take your complaints about the scorched maize-and-pepper pudding?"

"Is that what it was? I thought it was grill smoke," she joked. "No, I need to ask a few questions of you both."

"More grilling," he responded with a smile. "Why don't we grab a table?"

The trio walked over to the little table by the window.

"Not much of a view of the bay," said Henutsenu, shivering. The day looked gray and cold.

"Tell me about this burglary."

They did; there was nothing useful for her in it as the burglars hadn't taken anything. She shrugged and pressed on to her original interest.

"Duaneferet," said MacIntyre.

Sebek looked at her sharply. Henutsenu grinned and said, "You just missed her, too."

Sebek, not smiling, said, "Shes fired her yesterday."

"What?" MacIntyre exclaimed, startled. "Why?"

"She'd gone foolish or something," said Sebek.

Henutsenu said, "Her mood—you interviewed her last week, right? She wasn't chipper about things, you must have noticed."

"Sure did," said MacIntyre with caution. "But now?"

Sebek said, "Worse and worse. The last few days since I've been here, she's been hopeless in the kitchen. I've had to do most things myself. I have to tell you, I got pissed off. Shes came in yesterday morning and I had him talk to her. I don't know what she said to him, but she fired an onion at the wall, and he fired her on the spot."

Henutsenu added, "I cut her last check and sent it to her house by messenger."

"Henemibr'a Street, by any chance?"

"Why, yes, that's right. Do you know it?"

"Oh, yeah. Quite a place. Look, Henutsenu, when did Duaneferet's mood turn sour? Try to remember back. A specific date would help."

"Mysterious. All right." The Remetjet looked at the window and its wall of gray, her face reflective. "Hmm. The day of the murder—that was the day before you first showed up here. Dua, she's usually cheerful and energetic. Two or three days before the murder, she acted irritated. By the time you came in, she was rude all the time, angry. She took it out on you, I'm afraid."

"Sure did." MacIntyre had a tough time imagining the brick with feet she'd interviewed as cheerful. "Did you see her that day? Around 3?"

"Well, I don't get into the kitchen much in the afternoons. Let me think back." Henutsenu thought. "I don't remember seeing her, but the kitchen staff isn't my concern. Chef was out of town, at a cooking demonstration, and she was in charge of the kitchen. I would have noticed if...." Her voice trailed off. She resumed, "I remember now. That was the day she brought her boyfriend in, and he caused all that trouble in the kitchen. I stuck my head in but stayed away. I didn't want to hear any more of the shouting and crazy talk going on. And by dinner, I was dealing with customer complaints and didn't have time. That was a dreadful day here."

MacIntyre turned to Sebek. He raised a palm. "Don't ask me, before my time. I wasn't working here then. Do I need an alibi?"

"Only if you hated Nekhen enough to kill him," replied MacIntyre. "But I don't think you need an alibi for Nekhen's murder, no."

His eyes widened. "Is that what this interrogation is all about? The murder?"

"Yes."

"Oh, Cheryl," said Henutsenu. "You don't mean that Dua...?"

"Yes. Or her boyfriend, Pabaky. Sebek, may I go with you to the kitchen and ask the cooks?"

He nodded, saying nothing, his face grim, an unusual expression for him. Henutsenu patted his arm and hugged MacIntyre.

They walked to the kitchen through the empty dining room.

Sebek looked around. "Break time. Half the team is out back. Khay's here, though. He'll help. Shes promoted him to sous chef when he fired Dua."

Sebek beckoned the new sous chef over.

"What's doing, chef?" asked Khay.

"This is Hutyt MacIntyre," said Sebek.

The sous chef smiled. "We've met. That was a horrible day, Hutyt, but the problems are behind us now."

"I wish that were so, Khay," replied MacIntyre. "I've got a question. You were here the day of Nekhen's murder, right?"

The sous chef shuddered. "Now, that was a *horrible* day. Yes, I was here. We all heard the announcement, Henutsenu told us right during the dinner service. It didn't do our performance that night any good, I can tell you." He shook his head. "Not that it mattered, we were in terrible shape."

"About that. Pabaky, right?"

Startled, Khay nodded. "Why, yes. That's right."

"Here's my question. Was Duaneferet present all afternoon? Was she there at 3 p.m.?"

"It was two weeks ago!"

"Think back. Things were crazy with Pabaky. Do you remember seeing Duaneferet handling things, cooking, or anything like it?"

"That little bastard showed up at lunch with Dua. Let's see, let's see...." Khay's face scrunched up in thought. "She was there for sure by dinner. We were complaining like crazy and then Nekhen's murder...but before that? It was Pabaky, Pabaky, Pabaky. Now I remember. I went looking for Dua. She wasn't around. I thought she'd gone for a walk or something to cool down. She'd gotten pretty hot during lunch."

"By hot, I assume you don't mean from the heat of the ovens."

He smiled. "No, not the ovens. Mad as hell."

Sebek, grinning, said, "I didn't realize the kitchen here was that messed up. But Shes wasn't here, right? Case of the rats playing while the cat's off having a good time?"

Khay rolled his eyes. "I don't have a sense of humor, chef. It was miserable."

Sebek smiled. "I've got to meet this Pabaky. He sounds like a stunner."

"A grease fire on a hot stove, chef," replied Khay.

MacIntyre broke into this dialog to nail down her suspicions. "So you can't say for sure whether she was here, Khay?"

"I can say I couldn't find her."

"And the exact time?"

"I don't know, it was right after lunch." He looked at her disappointed face and said, "But lunch winds down around 2. We take breaks at 2:15. So it must have been around then."

"And you didn't see her again until when?"

"Dinner, or just before. I know she was in the kitchen for the first service."

"And Pabaky?"

"What about him?"

"Was he there the whole time?"

"Shit yes, little bastard," said Khay.

Sebek said, "So Pabaky is in the clear, but Dua—she's your suspect?"

"Suspect for what?" asked Khay, not understanding.

"Nekhen's murder," said MacIntyre. Khay's jaw dropped.

"Back to work, Khay. It's over now," said Sebek in a brisk tone. "Do a reset and get dinner going. I'll be along, OK? We'll work on that new routine Shes set up yesterday."

"Yes, chef." He shook his head with disbelief, then turned to his new domain with resolution.

"I'd better call Shes," said Sebek, taking out his phone.

MacIntyre put a hand on his arm. "I wish you wouldn't. I'd like to do more investigating before this gets around. OK? And don't tell him I was here, either." She didn't need more emotional complications with Shesmu at this point. He'd hate her for going behind his back to his people.

"Sure, Cheryl. Mysterious."

MacIntyre found Henutsenu in the dining room supervising after-lunch clearing. MacIntyre watched while the waiter cleared a large table and removed its soiled tablecloth.

"Did you get what you needed from the kitchen?" Henutsenu asked.

"Yes, I did. Look, can you keep my visit secret? Don't tell Shes I was here, not just yet."

She smiled. "Romantic intrigue? Why is it the man is always the last one to know what's going on?"

"It has something to do with women being a lot smarter than they are."

"True! Will I see you tonight?"

"Unless somebody kills me before I get there. I'll keep my head down and avoid that, knock on wood," replied MacIntyre, rapping her knuckles on the big table.

The next step was to find Duaneferet and put her in jail. MacIntyre sat in her car, considering what to do. She might call Mes. But she'd be telling him unwelcome facts about the god Seteh and her illegal search. She could call Yaotl, but she'd just be digging herself more deeply in debt to a vicious Aztec crime lord. That would come back to bite her in the ass, which was already thoroughly chewed up. An anonymous call to the medjau? Dumped right into the wastebasket labeled "hot tips."

Right now, though, she had to get herself off the street to avoid a hit man killing her where she sat. She tossed the headscarf to the seat beside her as worthless. Back to Henutsenu's, her safe house. She drove off, turning onto Mentju Boulevard for the brief trip to Henutsenu's apartment building.

As she neared the garage entrance, her medjat antennae quivered. Something was wrong. She glanced in the rear-view mirror. White car. It had been parked down the street near the Neferti, now it was behind her. Wouldn't hurt to take evasive action. She sped up past Henutsenu's apartment building instead of turning in and drove north into the business district. The white car turned and closed up the distance. She turned east. The white car closed even more. Not good.

After thinking up ten ways a hit man might take her out, she concluded her odds needed improvement. She would not outrun the white car. No gun, though she had her fighting stick on the back seat. She was on streets in the busiest part of Menmenet in a convertible with the top down. The upside of that was crowds of people looking on who would witness a murder in broad daylight. The downside was the traffic that slowed her down and made her vulnerable. Finding more lonely roads might let her stay ahead of the hit man, but it would encourage him by removing all the witnesses. Yaotl didn't have any trouble eliminating competitors on busy streets. Maybe this guy knew the same hit-man tricks.

Her best bet: stop the car, jump out with her stick, and disable the guy before he could do anything about it. Dangerous, if he had a gun, but she was not the kind to shrink from risk. She started looking for a likely spot. She found a nice, empty bus zone where she could pull in. The white car zipped up next to her and halted, rocking from the abrupt stop. She saw its occupant for the first time: Pabaky, the Seteh worshipper, looking just about as angry as anyone she had ever encountered. She recognized him from the booking photo she'd seen. But her attention centered on the very large knife he held up as he stared at her, grinning like one of the Seteh statues in his nightmare temple.

Tactics flooded MacIntyre's head like a flash flood in a desert arroyo. The popular tourist hotel up ahead, the Hut-'ankh-tepyt: that would do. She knew the rear entrance well. In the second that passed in forming this decision, her lizard brain had noted that Pabaky's white car had space in front of it. She tore out of the bus stop, pulled hard left in front of Pabaky's car, and cut off another car that screeched and honked. She screeched around a corner and down the alley that led to the rear entrance of the hotel. Car horns blared, then shrieked again as her follower attempted the same maneuver and failed. MacIntyre came to a jolting stop in the drop-off zone and killed the engine. She jumped over the door of her little red convertible, reached into the back seat for her fighting stick, and plunged into the rear of the huge hotel.

Two years before, she'd investigated a series of robberies in the hotel as a patrol officer. The number of corridors that could conceal a running thief amazed her. She'd explored and mapped the place, laid in wait, and the next robbery resulted in her nabbing the fleeing robber on the wing. The place was a maze. A hotel executive explained it resulted from twenty hotel renovations over the 100 years since the big earthquake had demolished the old hotel. She would lay odds that Pabaky was not familiar with it and would lose himself as soon as he came after her.

After three turns along different passages, she climbed a set of service stairs and doubled back on the mezzanine level. She found a window that looked out on the sidewalk outside and saw that Pabaky had parked his car behind hers. As she watched, he popped out of the rear door of the hotel with a frustrated look on his face. She'd lost him. Now she had another decision to make. She could fade away and find her way back to Henutsenu's apartment, or she could follow Pabaky and see whether he led her somewhere interesting. Her natural impulse was to take action, not hide. Backup would be nice, but right now she needed different help. She found a dark corner and made a phone call.

"Ms. MacIntyre?" Yaotl's voice had a smile in it.

"Yes. I have a problem."

"You have many problems, Ms. MacIntyre. I assume the most pressing is the individual following you."

"You followed him."

"We did, indeed—and you. It is Pabaky, the man—"

"I know. He's after me with a large knife."

"We followed you and Pabaky to the hotel. My man decided against going in after Pabaky."

"I'll be fine. What I need is to delay Pabaky leaving."

"We can do that. Would you like him permanently delayed?"

Out of curiosity, MacIntyre asked, "How much?"

"We're having a close-out special today. 5,000 debenu."

"I can't afford it."

"I know. A little humor injected into a tense situation often helps. It makes hard decisions easier, especially if the jokes are rotten. What do you wish us to do?"

"I'm going to hire a cab and wait. Delay Pabaky and discourage him from looking for me, then leave. I'll pick him up when he drives away. Then your man can follow me."

"Very well. For 2,500 debenu, my man will drive you."

"No, thanks. That's my retirement, and taxis are cheaper."

"But much less reliable. As you wish. Good luck, Ms. MacIntyre." He hung up.

She walked out the front door. The doorman at her request signaled for the first cab in the taxi line in front of the hotel. He took no notice of the fighting stick; after all, it was a tourist hotel.

"Where to, lady?" asked the taxi driver, a short, heavy man in his fifties with grizzled hair and a sour expression.

"Just cruise around to the back of the hotel. We need to pick up somebody," she replied, handing him a 10-debenu note to get his attention.

"What is this?" He brandished the tenner at her.

"Medjau business."

"Badge?"

She handed him another 10 debenu. "Unofficial medjau business."

"Fine. Shooting starts, you're out of the cab."

She smiled and sat back. The driver worked his way around the busy streets to the back of the hotel. They turned the corner into the alley.

"Stop here. We're waiting on that white car."

Pabaky stood, face scrunched in anger, next to his white car. MacIntyre smiled. He shouted into a cell phone, but she couldn't make out the words. He still carried the knife. She saw a large Aztec man in an ill-fitting suit standing near the hotel door. He approached the angry Pabaky. The man said something, and Pabaky spat in his face and waved the knife. The man took out a large handkerchief, wiped his face, put it away, and hit Pabaky two sudden jabs in the face. He kidney-punched him to the ground and kicked him in the stomach. He kicked the knife away from Pabaky's hand. The Aztec leaned over and said something to the man on the ground, then strolled down the alley and disappeared.

She slid down in the seat behind the driver so she wasn't visible.

"Follow him when he leaves, OK?"

"No guns?"

"Nah, he likes his knife."

"Great. Out of the cab."

The taxi driver seemed to have taken against her.

MacIntyre gave him 5 debenu and said, "Wait."

She watched as Pabaky gathered himself up, found his knife, and got back into his car. The white car started up and headed off down the alley. The taxi followed.

"How good are you?" she asked.

"Good enough to know he'll spot us if we stay too close. Good enough to dump you in a second if there's any more action." The driver kept his attention on the white car, which made three turns and got back onto Mentju Boulevard and headed west. "Not too much traffic, I'll stay back and see what happens."

MacIntyre sat up and leaned over the seat to look at the prey. "He's going somewhere, not looking for me."

"This isn't a wife-husband thing, is it? Because—"

"No, medjau. I think he's trying to kill me."

"Look, lady, I'm just a cab driver."

"Shut up and keep following him."

"And you're no medjat. Medjut don't have blonde hair and blue eyes." His own black eyes gleamed at her narrowly in the rear-view mirror. She put on her sunglasses. She rummaged a little and came up with one of her police cards. Not as good as a badge, but it would do. She showed him the Menmenet Medjau crest on the little card.

"I'm special," she told him. She handed him the card. "Keep it, in case you need something sometime."

"Yeah. Right." The little card fluttered to the floor. But he stayed behind the white car while muttering to himself under his breath. Pabaky drove up Mentju, past the civic buildings, and on up the hill.

"He's heading west," said the taxi driver. "Nothing out there but the necropolis."

"Maybe he wants to visit his dead mother," MacIntyre suggested.

"Maybe he wants to be close to where he'll bury you after he kills you. You got ten minutes, then you're out of the cab," said the driver. MacIntyre considered another tenner but decided her food budget was more important. Now, if it had been Duaneferet, that would be worth it, but Pabaky was only worth 25 debenu at most. Not worth starving over.

They followed the white car around the hill. It drew to the curb outside a sandal shop. Did Pabaky have an urgent need for new sandals?

"Pull in here, so I can watch him," she told the driver, who complied with his customary grace. Pabaky appeared to be talking on his phone, waving his other hand around in frustration. Then he sat, staring off into the distance. Five minutes went by. Another five of them followed. The taxi driver stirred and said, "Out of the cab."

"Another few minutes. Let's see what he does."

"He's doing nothing. Neither am I, and this is my livelihood."

"You've got enough of my debenu to cover the rest of your day."

"Out of the cab."

While this conversation occupied a quarter of her brain, MacIntyre kept her eyes on the white car and its occupant. She saw another car, copper-colored, pull up behind the white car. Its occupant emerged and walked around to the white car. Duaneferet. The figure like a brick and the angry face that could frighten a mob of enraged Aztecs was instantly recognizable. The hell with her food budget —she could live on scraps for a few weeks. She gave the driver another tenner.

"Don't lose them."

"OK, OK." The driver put the note in his wallet to keep the other ones company. MacIntyre was sure he hadn't made that much money for so little work in his life. His lucky day. Unless Pabaky decided on direct action with his humongous knife, of course. But she wouldn't remind the driver about that possibility. Let the poor fellow enjoy life for a while. Taxi driving must be boring. This would liven up his day.

Duaneferet got in, and the white car drew away from the curb. But they weren't going far. The big Temple of Inpu soon loomed up on the left, and the white car swung into the parking lot.

"Go, go!" said MacIntyre, and the driver cheerlessly complied.

CHAPTER THIRTY
Shesmu and MacIntyre Face Seteh

R'A BROKE THROUGH THE FOG and lit up the Temple of Inpu as Aset and I walked over to the entry. I pulled open the door. The sight of the large metal detector made me think twice. I backed away and pulled Aset aside. Improvisation time.

I said, "We need to get Iny down here. We shouldn't go into the temple."

"Why-ever not, Shes? It's frigid out here." Even with her coat, she felt the cold. All I felt was the Knife digging into my back.

"It's a negotiating tactic. Iny out here is away from his own space. It will make it easier for us to get what we want."

Aset looked dubious. I tried again, using religion. "Aset, I don't want to enter the temple. What we're going to do—Inpu is not a forgiving god, I don't want to give him any leverage by going into his temple."

"That makes more sense, I guess," she replied. She put on her coat.

I dug out my wallet and found Iny's card with his phone number. When he answered, I asked him to meet us at the front door, away from prying eyes. He didn't ask what it was about, which I took as a positive development. After a few minutes, Iny came out of the temple with suspicious eyes. When he saw Aset, he stopped and frowned.

"What are you doing, Shesmu?" he asked. "The last time we spoke, I advised you to forget about that tomb. Did you think I didn't mean it? And you," he said, turning to Aset. "You ought to just stay home grieving instead of causing more trouble."

Aset's eyes glinted. She pressed her lips tight to keep the words she wanted to speak inside. She didn't much care for Iny. He was a hard man to like.

I said, "Come on, Iny, just do us one favor. It won't cost you anything but time, and you'll help solve a murder."

"A murder! Now there's a thing." He smiled a sardonic smile, his tone derisive. "Solve a murder. Most days, I'm hard pressed to keep the mummies in line. Just how am I going to solve a murder?"

"By helping us to get the knife."

Iny shook his head. "The knife. The knife in the tomb? We've talked about that. Forget it. You know what that knife is; so do I. I won't have anything to do with it. Solve a murder!"

Aset said nothing and put on a long-suffering widow's expression. She looked Iny in the eye. "I want that knife back. It has no place in my husband's tomb, no place in his journeys in the afterlife, and I made a mistake in putting it there. Now I need it, and I want it back, and I want to protect the rest of the tomb goods. Forever. Against people like you."

I interjected. "We want to upgrade the insurance package on the tomb to eternal life. And we want to do it today."

Iny, surprised, said "Eternal? That's very expensive, you know. And today—not a chance."

"Come on, Iny, use your power of persuasion and round up a w'ab to do the job. You wouldn't want your business selling tomb goods getting around the temple, would you?" A mild threat, but it was the only leverage I had. "The technology upgrade to the tomb will require opening the tomb door, am I right? That's an opportunity. And there would be another fat fee."

"I suppose it is an opportunity, at that," he agreed, now understanding. "Lady Nekhen, are you prepared to spend 10,000 debenu on this? That's for the premium and a special fee for the immediate servicing of the tomb."

Aset's mouth opened and shut. I poked her. She looked at me, annoyed, and said, "Yes, I suppose so. Yes. It's a lot of money, though, for not much. What do you mean, servicing of the tomb?"

"Eternity is a long time, Lady Nekhen. A very long time. Cameras, sensors, monitoring, enforcement; all that costs a lot. The temple invests the money and covers everything from the income. For eternity." His voice expressed his impatience with the widow's inability to grasp the essentials of his business.

Aset gave him a face I'd seen her present to the men in her life who tried to explain the obvious to her. She didn't need explanations, she just didn't want to touch it or deal with Iny at all. I poked her again.

"Eternity," she said. "Yes. I suppose…yes."

Iny cheered up at the prospect of his "special fee." I said, "You set up the tomb upgrade, and we'll work on transferring the money to the temple account. Can you give us the account numbers?" Iny made a call to the accounting department and got the number, then gave us another number for the special fee. He got up to leave to take care of his end of the deal and left without a bow.

Aset said, "Awful little man." She called her bank to arrange the bank transfers, giving me an evil glance as she did so. Her transaction completed, Aset wandered over to a low wall that overlooked the necropolis, with a good view of the ocean. The fog had cleared, and R'a shone in all his glory on the sea, whitecaps and powerful waves hitting the beach far below us.

"This business had better be worth it, Shes. A lot of money."

"You're rich, Aset, and you're going to be powerful. It's nothing to you."

"I suppose you're right. Once I'm acknowledged as the God's Wife of Seteh—"

"And that will be never, bitch!" The voice came from behind. A familiar voice. I turned.

Pabaky. With his biggest knife. And a friend: Duaneferet, who had an even bigger knife. In a moment of incredulity, I struggled with why Dua was taking her revenge on me for her firing here and now. I looked at Aset. Her regal face showed the full disdain of a God's Wife for this petty rebellion.

She said, "You two, you murderous, pitiful servants of Seteh. Go back to your dark little cave and stay there until I come." She waved an imperious hand at them.

Pabaky and Dua? Seteh? The world lurched as I finally understood who had killed Nekhen and why, and everything fell into place. Dua's chef's knife, the murder weapon, was in the tomb. These two had no intention of going back to their cave. I realized how little Aset genuinely cared about her husband, his murder, or me. Pabaky showed his ugly teeth with his most idiotic grin and raised his knife.

Pabaky and Duaneferet came toward us, showing no sign of obeying Aset's orders. I had nothing to defend us except my bare hands this time. There was no way I could get past the two knife wielders to get to my stick in my car. A loud screech from the parking lot got everyone's attention. It was a taxi braking to a halt next to the white car that had brought Pabaky and Dua. The back door popped open, and Hutyt MacIntyre jumped out, fighting stick in hand.

"Medjau! Put down the knives and surrender now!" she shouted at the threatening pair. Dua and Pabaky looked at each other. Pabaky rushed at MacIntyre with his knife up, and Dua rushed at us. Aset screamed. The taxi took off, squealing tires making frantic circles on the tarmac of the parking lot.

Dua's target was Aset, not me. I backed up, then tripped her as she rushed toward Aset. As Dua fell and rolled, I shouted to Aset, "Go get help in the temple! Get Iny!" Aset looked at me with the whites of her eyes showing, but my words broke through, and she ran toward the temple. I ran past MacIntyre and Pabaky, who were circling one another, waving their weapons, to get to my car. I popped the trunk and grabbed my fighting stick. Dua scrambled up and ran after Aset, but I caught her before she closed half the distance. I swung my stick into an arm strike to disable her knife arm, but I wasn't close enough. I missed as she twisted out of the way. She faced me instead of chasing Aset.

I glanced at the other fighters. MacIntyre kept Pabaky out of knife distance with her stick. He had learned more about the effectiveness of sticks from our earlier meeting and didn't rush her, but his slashing knife kept her busy. His right arm was still in a cast, which served as armor against stick attacks from that side.

Dua rushed at me, knife raised and face tight with fierce hate. She was much more comfortable wielding the big knife than Pabaky had been; I'd taught her everything I knew about that in the kitchen. She understood how to hold herself balanced and ready. I dodged away, knocking her attacking arm down with the stick. Dua crouched and moved forward on shuffling feet.

She hissed through clenched teeth, "Get out of my way, chef. That bitch is dead, and there's nothing you're going to do to stop it."

"You'll have to get through me first, Dua. And your boyfriend looks like he's busy for now." Pabaky screamed with the pain of a sharp blow to his side as he let down his guard to slash at MacIntyre. Never a wise move to let down your guard to a werkhet.

Dua hissed some more, this time a short, blasphemous prayer to Seteh cursing me and my ancestors. She moved closer, and I stepped back, holding the stick in a guard position, ready to strike. I watched Dua's feet, and here she came, stepping across while swinging the knife up, trying for my throat. I swung my stick down in a parry, knocking her arm aside, then riposted at her head. She jerked back just out of range before I could connect. I stepped back to regain balance, and Dua rushed with the knife extended, stabbing for my body. Her eyes burned with the fire of a fanatic.

I stepped back to avoid the thrust of Dua's knife. My foot stepped on a small, loose rock, throwing me off balance. Dua raised her knife for a quick kill thrust, but a stick came out of nowhere and slammed into her back, making her stumble forward. As I dodged sideways, I swung my stick and connected with her head, and she collapsed. MacIntyre stepped into my field of vision and kicked the knife out of her hand. Dua was out cold.

I heard screaming and looked over to see Pabaky rolling on the ground, holding his left arm with his right hand. The cast on that arm made him look like a mollusk trying to withdraw into a shell. MacIntyre had broken his other arm. He shouted obscenities.

I regained my balance as MacIntyre approached and steadied me with a helping hand.

"Thanks," I said. "She's—"

"Yeah. The murderer. I'm so looking forward to explaining to my boss how this all happened," she said. She looked toward the temple. "Now, who the hell is this?"

Iny and two uniformed patrol officers of the Temple of Inpu security force ran toward us from the temple. Aset walked behind, again regal, but late to the party.

CHAPTER THIRTY-ONE
Shesmu Robs the Tomb

"Who the hell are you?" demanded Iny.

"Hutyt-er-Semetyu Cheryl MacIntyre, Menmenet Medjau. And you, lord?"

"Lord, my ass. What the hell are you doing in my parking lot?"

She grinned. "Lady Nekhen didn't explain?" She pointed at Aset with her stick. The widow stood still, looking noble and aggrieved.

I introduced the two medjau. "Hutyt MacIntyre, meet Idnu Iny of the Temple of Inpu. Iny, she's the semetyt in charge of the Nekhen case."

"Not since they suspended me," MacIntyre said. "Just to clarify. I'm off duty."

Iny looked at her with a sour expression. "Off duty. Suspended, huh? Give me that." He pointed at the stick.

She flipped the stick and handed it to him, handle first. "I told my taxi driver to call 111, the medjau should be here any minute—if he didn't just drive away like a scared rabbit."

"What the hell is this?" asked Iny, looking the stick over.

"Fighting stick," I said. "Ahamedu. It's a sport."

"A sport. Give me that," demanded Iny, reaching for my stick. I handed it over. Iny's men were examining the two downed minions of Seteh. "What's the deal with these two?"

MacIntyre said, "Murderers. Disciples of Seteh."

Iny frowned. "Seteh is illegal."

MacIntyre nodded. "Congratulations. I'm sure the Temple of Imen-R'a will appreciate your work here in apprehending illegal cultists." Her very blue eyes sent me a sliding look of humor. The implied takedown of Iny had me grinning, but I couldn't go much further than that. I knew a lot more about what was going on than she did, and I wanted it to stay that way.

Approaching sirens heralded the approach of the city employees; MacIntyre's taxi driver had come through for her. While the fuss developed, MacIntyre stepped aside and called her boss, Djehutymes. She kept it simple, just saying she'd apprehended the murderers. She held the phone away from her ear because of his shouting, then explained everything again. Twice. Djehutymes said, "Ten minutes!" He said it with enough force that I heard it from several meters away. MacIntyre informed the temple medjau that the homicide squad was coming as they cuffed the unconscious Dua and got Pabaky on his feet to wait for the paramedics. MacIntyre advised them to keep a tight grip on him despite his arms being useless.

I took Iny and Aset aside. I said, "We need to get down to the tomb. Did you get a w'ab?"

Iny nodded. "Yeah. But I'll need to stay here to deal with this."

That wouldn't do. I said, "We need you at the tomb."

"What for?"

"Moral support. Or maybe immoral, since we're robbing a tomb. We need you to convince the w'ab that everything is on the up and up. And it's important: we need to get the murder weapon to help the semetyt there," I said, pointing at MacIntyre.

"Wait, what?" asked Iny.

"The knife in the tomb, remember? Aset put it in there because she didn't want the medjau to find it and blame everything on her. They didn't find it, but they blamed everything on her anyway. So, now, let's get it out and get it back where it needs to be. To her." I pointed again at MacIntyre. Aset's mouth was opening and closing, and her face was bright red. "Then Lady Nekhen will be free of suspicion once and for all."

Iny said, "Huh. So it's valuable after all." He was shaking his head. "OK, Shesmu, it's your game. I've talked a w'ab into doing the job right now. In fact, here he comes. But there's gonna be a bigger fee. Handling charges." He grinned.

An electric cart came whirring up from the depths of the temple and stopped in front of the little group. A bald w'ab priest sat behind the wheel. He was impatient, his fifty-year-old face full of seams. "Let's get this done, Idnu," he said. "I got things waiting on me, you know? Where is this tomb?"

"Lot C4367," said Iny, looking at a piece of paper he extracted from a pocket.

"Halfway down the hill. Let's go," said the w'ab. Aset joined him on the front seat, and the w'ab's mood brightened as he took in her glamour. Iny and I climbed into the back, and down the hill we went.

* * *

The cart ground to a halt in front of Nekhen's chapel, the stone gleaming white in the rare sun.

"This tomb is new, isn't it?" asked the w'ab, climbing out of the cart.

"Brand new," I replied.

"Why the upgrade?"

"Tomb robbery attempt changed the widow's mind on the insurance premium," I said. Aset nodded, lips tight. Her face was now pale, the red having faded during the ride down the hill.

"You're the widow?" asked the w'ab, looking her over, eyes lingering too long. "You sure you want to do this?"

"I've paid a lot for it, and I want to do it," said Aset, voice modulated to impress the w'ab. It did.

I said, "Why don't you take your coat off, Aset? It's warm in the chapel." She took off her coat to reveal the flirtatious dress, which left little to the imagination. I could tell that she impressed the w'ab no end; he couldn't take his eyes off her now. Iny, too.

After everyone got out of the cart, the w'ab priest shook himself and extracted a tool belt from a chest on the cart and strapped it on over his robe. "I'll just get set up in the chapel, get everything ready, then we open the tomb with the ritual prayers and get it done."

"Thanks, chief," said Iny, slapping him on the back. "I owe you one."

"You owe me three, Iny." The w'ab grinned. He addressed Aset. "Lady Nekhen, is it? Would you care to come with me to make sure you understand everything? I'll be happy to explain things as I go."

Aset whispered, "What do I do, Shes?"

I whispered back, "Charm him, then distract him once the tomb is open. I'll be right by the tomb door, ready to grab the knife."

The stage-play moved into the chapel, the w'ab taking Aset's arm to help her up the steps, and they disappeared through the door. I was about to join them when a large hand gripped my arm and swung me around. I recognized the hard-edged features and thick hands of Pasen, Blackmore's strong-arm man, and I saw Blackmore himself behind him.

"We'd like a word, Shesmu," said Blackmore smoothly. His face was anything but smooth. I looked at Iny, who did not evidence any surprise at their presence. He must have called Blackmore while he was arranging the w'ab.

"I want my knife, you damn thief," said Blackmore.

"Those are strong words from the guy who stole it in the first place," I responded with heat. "And I haven't got it. It's not here."

Pasen grinned and grabbed my other arm, then lifted me off my feet and shook me. I felt the Knife of Seteh shift against my back.

Iny said, "He's not lying, he's after the knife in the tomb that the widow put there when she took the antique knife." He smiled. "Turns out it's the murder weapon that killed her husband. Now she wants to give it to the medjau. Seems they've found the murderers."

Blackmore didn't smile back. "I don't give a shit about murders. I want my knife."

My arms were getting sore from Pasen's grip. He didn't have any trouble keeping me off the ground. He shook me some more. My teeth rattled, but the Knife stayed where it was.

Blackmore pointed a well-manicured finger at my face. "You, Shesmu, are coming with us and getting us the Knife."

I said, "Iny, you're a medja. Are you just going to let this happen?"

"Yep," he said. I had an irrational impulse to laugh but restrained it.

"Look," I said, "You have the upper hand." Two hands, gripping my arms. "We can negotiate something."

"We'll negotiate giving us the Knife, you prick," said Blackmore. "Where is it?"

"In a safe place." I looked again at Iny. "Iny, you don't want that w'ab involved in this. Inpu won't like it."

Iny thought about it. He said to Blackmore, "He's right. I've got a priest in there." He pointed at Nekhen's tomb. "I can't afford for him to know about this. Let's all settle down and work it out."

Blackmore said, "Let him down, Pasen. We'll talk it out."

Pasen's smile disappeared, but he set me back on my feet and let go of my arms. Now, I just had to convince them they'd get the Knife, but I knew I had to get it into the tomb. Nekhen's tomb. I owed it to my friend because of my transgressions against him. He had wanted the Knife with him in the afterlife, a wish I had to respect. I wasn't sure I could do it, and I was even less sure that I could handle Blackmore's reaction to losing the Knife, but desperation motivates hope.

In my most persuasive voice, I said, in English, "Look, Rafe. I'm willing to get you the Knife. Lady Nekhen won't be, but I can deal with that. I took it because of her, but she's—we've broken up. I don't care anymore."

"Aw, that's touching, Shesmu. Where's the damn knife?" said Blackmore in a nasty tone.

"In a safe place," I repeated. I hoped I wasn't lying. In Renkemet, for Iny's benefit, I said, "Let us finish what we're doing here, Rafe. I need to get this done for me. Once I've got the murder knife, I'm home free. It's all over for me, and you can have the Knife of Seteh. You might even sell it back to Lady Nekhen. She's got the money and the need. She's obsessed with the Knife."

Blackmore rubbed his mouth, thinking. Pasen stood, arms crossed, looking at me with a stony expression.

Blackmore decided. "OK, Shesmu. But when the widow comes out of that tomb, you and she are coming with us, and we're having a party until I have the Knife."

I nodded. Aset would love this development. Especially if I got the Knife of Seteh sealed into the tomb. I could feel it pressing against my back.

What I needed was Hutyt MacIntyre. I looked up at the looming Temple of Inpu. But help would not arrive packaged in a can-do blonde whirlwind. Not this time.

I entered the chapel with Blackmore, Iny, and Pasen right behind me. The chapel held us all, but there wasn't much room left once we were all inside. The w'ab stopped his work in the tomb and came out into the chapel.

"Who are all these people?" he asked.

Iny said in a pacifying voice, "Friends of the family. They wanted to be here to support the widow."

The widow herself was looking regal again, her lips pressed together in anger. I walked over to her and whispered in her ear, "It's Blackmore. Iny called him. He's threatening to take the knife. I'm dealing with it. Don't worry."

"You'd better handle it right," she whispered back. "And this w'ab of Inpu is a lecher. Can we hurry this? He makes my skin crawl every time he touches me."

"Just a bit longer. Until I can get the knife."

Aset compressed her lips, then smiled her brilliant Hut-Her smile as she turned back to the w'ab. She took his arm.

"It's so nice to have all these friends here for me, don't you think, lord? And I so appreciate your doing this for me, it will ease my mind about my husband's ka. Could you help me with my offering?" She pulled on his arm, turning him away from the open door of the tomb toward the offering hetep altar. The priest inflated as she walked him over to it, his attention fixed on the stunning vision beside him.

When I was sure his attention had shifted to Aset and her distractions, I slipped inside the open door of the tomb in full view of the others, but they were all in on the scam—or so they thought. Once I was inside, I was out of their sight.

I have to admit now I do not believe in kau or bau or gods or the Duat, at least with my rational heart. But it's another world, in a tomb. The huge sarcophagus, the dusty, aromatic smell, the silence, the waiting eternity beyond the glyphs covering the walls—they create an atmosphere of deep belief in the religious world. You can't escape it. Professional tomb robbers must have hearts of iron to do what they do. The w'ab had set a lantern on a shelf to provide light for his work. The lantern lit the tomb with an eerie glow that magnified the impact of everything else.

The box was easy to find. It was the only container of the right size in the tomb. The w'abu of Inpu had arranged the tomb goods on shelves around the tomb. The box was ebony with inset ivory glyphs extolling the god Seteh; what must the priests of Inpu have thought about that? I guess they pay the w'abu to ignore the eccentricities of tomb residents.

I removed the lid from the box. I took out a blue silk bag covered with Seteh glyphs and looked into it. A 25-centimeter chef's knife—Dua's knife, still stained with Nekhen's blood. It occurred to me that MacIntyre would want forensics to examine it. I had nothing to wrap the knife in, so I took the entire bag and set it on the shelf next to the box. I lifted my shirt and untied the Knife of Seteh, then took the Knife from the bag and set it upright in the box and put the lid next to it, glyphs glistening in the light of the w'ab's lantern, which I turned to illuminate the Knife as much as possible. I took five pictures of it and checked them— beautiful and unmistakably the Knife of Seteh. Those photos would convince Aset that the Knife was in the tomb once the w'ab had locked everything away. I set the lantern back where it had been and shut the Knife of Seteh into its resting place for eternity.

Dua's chef's knife was smaller than the Knife of Seteh. I slid the bag behind me into my waistband and tightened my belt a notch to hold it. I pulled my shirt back down and got out of there.

Only a few seconds had passed, and Aset still had the w'ab's attention over by the hetep. Iny raised his eyebrows, and I nodded once to tell him I'd gotten the murder weapon. He turned and touched the w'ab's shoulder, reminding him of his duty.

"I really must finish the task you've set me, Lady Nekhen," said the w'ab, reluctantly taking his hand away from her waist. He smiled and went back into the tomb. Five minutes later, he came out and shut the tomb door. He activated the fancy electronic seal he'd installed in the door, finalizing it with a short prayer to Inpu. "That should do it," he said. "Good for eternity now, Lady Nekhen. You can rest assured that no one will disturb anything, ever. Now, may I escort you back to the temple? I'd love to show you around, if you have time."

"I'm afraid I must claim Lady Nekhen for now, lord," said Blackmore, clearing his throat. "We have unfinished business."

"I'm sorry, lord, another time? I so very much appreciate your help, lord," said Aset, again touching the w'ab's arm. His face fell, but he accepted the reality of it. He shifted his tool belt and nodded.

"Come on, Idnu," the w'ab said to Iny. "We'll leave these folks to their business and their devotions." Iny decided he didn't want to participate in whatever Blackmore was planning to do with us.

Blackmore blocked the door until he was sure they'd gone. Aset walked toward him and said, "Get out of my way, I'm leaving."

"No, you're not," said Blackmore. "I want my Knife."

"It's not your Knife! It's my Knife, it's Seteh's Knife, it belongs to the god!"

"Screw the god. Pasen?" Pasen gripped Aset's arm.

"Shesmu, make him let me go!"

"Let her go," I said as calmly as I could.

Pasen tightened his grip and said, "Not a chance."

The time had come to explain the new situation to them. Aset wouldn't like it. I drew a deep breath. "The Knife is beyond your reach, Blackmore."

"I'll never relinquish the Knife of Seteh," said Aset. "Now let me go."

Blackmore said, "Ah, now. Never? Let's just see how much pain it will take to change your mind."

"It's not her mind you'll need to change, Rafe," I said. "The Knife is truly beyond reach. It's in there." I pointed at the tomb door, sealed for eternity.

"I know she removed it, Shesmu. We're way beyond that crap."

"Not any more, because I just put it back. I exchanged it for the knife in the tomb, the one that killed Nekhen."

"You're lying!"

I held up my phone. "Photos."

Blackmore looked at the photo of the Knife, face clouding over with anger.

"Shes! You…did you do that?" asked Aset, her eyes huge.

"I did, Aset. It's gone." I showed the photo to her. I addressed Blackmore again. "And you must be aware that the new lock and the monitoring by the Temple of Inpu w'abu and the insurance company will make it impossible to break in. You tried that earlier and failed. With these new protections, you can forget about it. The Knife is on its way to the afterlife."

Pasen released Aset and turned toward me.

I said, "It's over, Rafe. You need to move on to your next con. You don't need the worry of defending yourself against assault charges. Just take your thug and go."

"I'll remember this, Shesmu," said the furious trader. "I'll—"

"Don't make any promises you can't keep, Rafe. Remember that Hernefer has a lot of influence in the antiquities market, and he's willing to use it at my request. You'd need to find a new line of business. If you and your henchman walk out of here, I don't care if you rob the rest of the tombs in the necropolis and sell the lot. Quit while you're ahead."

Blackmore looked like an aggravated bull. After a few seconds of strain while the facts of life worked their way in and dissolved his need to kill us, he said, "Come on, Pasen. There's no sense in hanging around here, we have things to do." Pasen snarled as they left.

The storm clouds had gathered in Aset's face once she'd seen the photo and understood what I'd done. After the two thieves left, the storm broke.

I embraced Aset, holding her tight. I had to; she'd slashed my face with her fingernails before I got her arms under control. Her rage engulfed me. Teeth bared, face flushed, she panted as she struggled to escape my grip. She strove to tear me to shreds with her bare hands. I pushed her back against the wall and held her arms against it. If she'd ever loved me, she was long past such feelings now.

She screamed imprecations and curses; I stopped listening after the fingernails did their damage. I held her against the wall until she went limp as she realized she couldn't do anything to me.

"Are you going to rape me?" she asked. "Take your revenge that way? Why do you hate me so much, Shes?"

I held her close, breathing in the scent I'd loved. Her light perfume filled my senses.

"Let me go, Shes. You're hurting me."

"Are you done, Aset? Can we talk, not fight?"

"Yes," she hissed. "I'm done."

I released her. "Can we talk outside? Walk down to the beach? I can't… Nekhen's ka is too close here."

Aset stumbled out of the chapel. She found her coat on the steps; the w'ab had left it for her. She grabbed it up and half-ran down the little street, struggling into the coat as she fled. I followed, letting her go ahead with her anger and grief. She soon slowed and walked onto the beach past the wind-blown tombs. There were fewer tombs as we approached the beach; it wasn't a desirable neighborhood. The wealthy preferred their tombs dug into the hill rather than resting on the sandy ground at its bottom.

The walk gave me a chance to order my thoughts. Aset knew who had murdered her husband; she'd known since the beginning. Aset had known I had a murderer working for me as my closest assistant. She'd known that the cult of Seteh didn't value human life much. That was OK; she didn't either. She'd immersed herself so much in Seteh worship that she'd lost her own sense of ma'at. I found less and less to admire in my former love.

She walked out onto the sandy beach and stopped, looking at the vast Pacific. Somewhere out there, a storm had generated the powerful waves hitting the beach today. How big would a storm need to be to wash away everything here: the sand, the shore, the roads, the gods…. I caught up with Aset and stood next to her. She'd folded her arms across her chest, and tears streaked her cheeks.

"Aset—"

"Don't say anything, Shes. Just don't. Not yet."

After a few minutes of silent crying, she scrubbed her face with her palms. The smear of her eye makeup didn't improve her appearance. My heart softened a little, even though my face still stung from her attack.

"You stupid, vile son of a bitch," she said, teeth gritted in anger. "The whole time? You planned to deny me the Knife when I trusted you with it? Lied to me the whole time?"

"I had to, Aset. You wouldn't listen—"

"Listen to what, Shes? You stupid…." Aset had no words for my idiocy. She squeezed out her assessment, hissing the words. "You don't understand Lord Seteh. His power, his force in the world."

"I don't, Aset. Nekhen did. Maybe that's why he wanted the Knife of Seteh to go with him into the afterlife. Did he know about the Temple of Seteh?"

"Of course, he was the Hem-Netjer. But to him, those two weren't worthy of being w'abu of Seteh."

"And you told them he had the Knife."

"Yes, I did. They would follow me if they thought I could get it. But Nekhen…" Aset stopped, unable to say that she had unwittingly set her husband up for murder.

"That burglary—you told me you knew who'd done it, who'd stolen the Knife. You suspected it was them, didn't you? But it was Blackmore. Then you gave the Knife to me for safe-keeping so they wouldn't get it." I smiled. "But Dua knew. She saw the bag when I brought it to the Neferti. She and Pabaky tried every way they could to get the Knife and failed. And I put the Knife back into Nekhen's tomb."

"I'd like to kill you, you bastard."

"Aset…."

"I'll have to rebuild, create a new Temple of Seteh. There must be a way…I am the God's Wife of Seteh, with or without the Knife of Seteh. The Knife would have made it easy, but I'll find a way."

"Not in Menmenet, Aset. Here's what's going to happen. Dua and Pabaky won't be able to stop themselves from revealing what they've been doing—what you've been doing. The Temple of Imen-R'a will step in and take them. And you. The priests of Imen-R'a outlawed Seteh worship, Aset. For them, worshipping Seteh is worse than murdering some insignificant chef. Seteh's power counts for nothing here. They'll come after you, and they'll punish the God's Wife of Seteh with the worst they can throw at you. You'll be lucky if they just execute you. You'll have to leave, and you'd better figure out how to do that soon. Very soon."

As the reality of her situation hit her, her anger faded, and the tears started again. After a little while, she said, "You know, Nekhen wanted you to have the restaurant. The Per'ankh. He wanted me to turn over the management to you. It was in his will. But he left the restaurant to me. I own it."

She must have seen the hope flair in my eyes. The Per'ankh was all I'd ever dreamed of as Nekhen's apprentice and sous chef. Being executive chef would make my career—the Per'ankh is among the top-rated restaurants in the world.

She continued, "If I can't live here anymore, I'm going back to Kemet. To Tjaru, in Khentyabet. I'll disappear and find my followers there. They will recognize me as the God's Wife. They will. So, the restaurant? I'm going to sell it, Shes. But not to you. I'm going to make sure you don't get anywhere near that kitchen."

Aset's face showed a cruel triumph, and her eyes were those of a fanatic. Had I just not seen what was there? Or had she changed, distorted into what she'd become by Nekhen's death and by the fantasy of being the God's Wife of Seteh?

This was not a woman I could love. It was not the woman I had loved. I had nothing left to say to her. I turned and walked away, taking my hurt and disappointment with me on the long walk back up to the Temple of Inpu.

CHAPTER THIRTY-TWO
MacIntyre Learns the Truth from Shesmu

MacIntyre sat on a small bench overlooking the necropolis, waiting for Shesmu. With Pabaky and Duaneferet in the hands of the medjau, she was at peace. Even Menmenet had mellowed, the fog dissipating and the sun shining. She sat soaking up the rare Menmenet summer sun and looking at the ocean far down the hill until she drifted off, her day's exercise catching up with her.

"Cheryl."

Her eyes opened, dissipating the happy dream she'd been inhabiting, which she forgot at the sight of Shesmu. She jumped up, hugged him, and kissed him.

"I am so glad this case is over," she said, looking up into his eyes. "Now we can…explore." She paused as her hand encountered a hard object. "What have you got behind your back, a stick? And what happened to your face?"

He smiled and pulled out a blue silk bag from under his shirt and handed it to her. She looked it over; glyphs of Seteh all over it.

"Evidence," he said.

She opened the bag and looked in. She pulled the bag down to inspect the knife it held.

"Do you think this knife is useful?" Shesmu asked.

"What's this mark? A star?"

"Triliteral glyph, phonogram for Dua. Her mark."

"Oh. My. God." Evidence, chain of custody, whatever: Mes would love this. And so did she.

"Exactly."

"And that's why you went to the tomb? With her?" She couldn't bring herself to say Neferaset's name.

"Well…." His eyes looked down, away from hers.

"Shesmu? What are you hiding?" She reached stroked his lips.

He laughed. "I've lifted a huge weight from my ka."

She looked around and saw no one else. "Where is she?"

"She wanted to be alone. On the beach."

"Sad at losing you?"

He grinned. "Not quite."

"Shesmu? What are you hiding?" She made it more insistent.

"Sit down. This will take a while." Shesmu motioned at the bench, and MacIntyre sat. Shesmu sat next to her and explained. He explained Blackmore, Hernefer, and the Great Knife Scam. He explained what had been in the bag he'd showed her at Hernefer's palace, then what he'd done with the Knife of Seteh, and how Seteh had taken over Aset's life. He told her about the drama with Blackmore and Pasen at the tomb and what he'd done with the knives. He confessed what had happened to his face. But he was still smiling for no reason.

"Shesmu. What are you hiding? Is she…did she try to make you fall in love with her again?"

"No. No, I can safely say she did not. She expressed the opposite emotion. I'm lucky these scratches are the only damage she did. I laid out what the Temple of Imen-R'a would do to her. She's fleeing to Kemet to find more Seteh worshippers, and she's selling the Per'ankh to spite me." He looked toward the beach and explained. "It's all I've ever wanted, to be chef of the Per'ankh. She knew that. She knew how to hurt me."

"So why are you smiling?"

"I had an idea, walking up the hill. I need to talk with Hernefer."

"You're planning something. What?"

"Can't tell you, yet. But it's good."

"But you're not in love with her anymore."

"No." His voice was firm.

"Good. I can work with that. Kiss me again."

Shesmu drove MacIntyre back to her American-style apartment south of the city center. As they drove, MacIntyre told him that she'd been staying with Henut-senu for several days to avoid being shot down in the street. She hadn't been back to her apartment, even for a change of clothes.

MacIntyre said, "If we're going to celebrate, I need my party dress. And a shower."

"Are we going to celebrate?"

"Damn right. At the Neferti. I called Sebek while you were trashing your last relationship, he's got the chef's table all squared away for us tonight."

"I've got errands. Can you find your way to the restaurant at dinnertime?"

"Sure. I'll take a cab over when I'm ready. I've got a special taxi driver who loves to drive me."

"Where's your car?"

"Last seen illegally parked outside the Hut-'ankh-tepyt Hotel, presumably now impounded with a huge fine due for towing."

"Sorry to hear that," said Shesmu.

"Cheaper than the funeral costs if I hadn't done what I did, and that murderous twerp Pabaky caught up to me with his knife. But I won't be able to eat for two months now. And as for funeral costs—tombs are expensive! I had no idea. I got a brochure at the Temple of Inpu to read while I waited for you."

"Maybe Yaotl can use his influence to cut you a deal at the towing company."

"You know, that's a great thought."

"And I'm sure that Idnu Iny can get you a professional discount at the necropolis."

"Another great thought, if he can stay out of jail."

"And I'm feeding you tonight, at the Neferti. At least, according to you. Free."

"Way cheaper than my usual dinner."

"And you're staying at my place tonight."

"Am I?"

"You are if the rest of your plan involves serious romance."

"We could start now. In my apartment. Or right here. Then your place, later."

"Errands. Hernefer." But she could see the temptation in his eyes. She pushed her lip out in disappointment.

"You need to work on your priorities. Anyway, at this rate, I'll sublet my apartment, since I'm never there. At least that will bring in some income."

He kissed her and pushed her out of the car, reminding her to take her bag of evidence.

CHAPTER THIRTY-THREE
Shesmu Builds His Empire

"Hernefer."

The gravelly voice spit out the name sharply, but at least the billionaire had picked up. A good sign. I sat in my great room, looking out at the view of the island of Iu-Sedeg and Hernefer's palace at the top of its hill.

"This is Shesmu. I need something from you."

"Bad start. I'm hanging up now."

"Don't. I can make you some money."

A long pause. "Why do you think I need more money? And why do I want your help in getting it?"

"Billionaires always want more money. That's how they become billionaires. Hear me out. You said you admired me the last time we talked."

"Changed my mind once I'd thought about it. But I'll listen."

"How would you like to get into the restaurant business?"

"Hanging up now. The nerve!"

"Thirty to forty percent return on investment, every year, guaranteed."

"I'm listening."

"The Per'ankh is going to be up for sale. I want to buy it, but I need a partner, and I need to not appear in the transaction. You can't appear in it either."

"Why not?"

"Neferaset is selling it. She won't sell if she sees either of us in the deal."

"That's the wife of the murdered chef?"

"Right."

"What the hell are you doing, Shesmu?"

"Things have developed since we last talked, Hernefer."

"What things? You put the Knife of Seteh back into the tomb, right?"

"Right—but it turns out the whole situation was more complicated than I understood."

"You said that before. What happened? Did your blonde medjat friend figure you out and arrest you?"

"No, we're having dinner tonight. That's one welcome development."

"And there are others?"

"It turns out Neferaset thinks she's the God's Wife of Seteh."

Another long pause.

"And what does that make you?" he asked.

"An idiot, according to her, when she learned I sealed the Knife of Seteh into the tomb for all eternity."

"A fair assessment, I suppose."

"Well, yes. From her limited perspective. At any rate, she's leaving Menmenet and selling the Per'ankh to raise money. But she wants me nowhere near it. Pure spite. And I want to be chef."

"And she knows about my role in this melodrama?"

"You bet."

"I could mobilize some resources through my financial team....nominee buyers, offshore funds, that sort of thing. Thirty to forty percent return on investment?"

"Absolutely—the best French restaurant in Menmenet, reservations six months in advance, been around for ten years, no lease, no mortgage, strong balance sheet, huge cash flow. And with me in charge, you get continuity, since Nekhen trained me, and a brilliant future because of my culinary genius."

"Huh. I'll need numbers and due diligence."

"I'm sure Neferaset will put this into the hands of her sehy, a man named Nebemhep. Have your proxies call him. As long as you and I stay anonymous, I doubt there will be any problem with a quick sale at a good price. Nebemhep will be happy to make the sale as easy as possible. Neferaset is in a hurry, and he'll be in a hurry too."

He asked, "How much are you in for?"

I said firmly, "Fifty-one percent. I want control."

"Forty-nine. I *need* control. I'm admiring you again, but I don't trust you, you're a devious, slimeball knife-stealer."

Of course, he was right. Control is overrated. "Done."

CHAPTER THIRTY-FOUR
MacIntyre Gets a Vacation

THE CHEF'S TABLE IN THE Neferti kitchen groaned under the load of small plates Sebek had served up. MacIntyre looked at Shesmu in dismay.

"What is all this stuff?"

"Art. Sebek's art, inspired by finding permanent work. Amazing how a secure revenue stream enthuses people."

"What do you mean, permanent work?"

"I just made him full executive chef of the Neferti, to replace me."

"Wait. Who's going to feed me? What are you doing, Shesmu?"

"You'll find out soon enough. Let's just say I'm empire-building, as we speak."

Sebek brought over another plate. He looked around for a place to put it, and not finding one, said, "You're not eating fast enough, people. Let's go!"

MacIntyre protested, "Sebek, I can't eat this without knowing what it is, and Shes takes too long to explain things. If he explains them at all." Shesmu just sat there smiling the same infuriating smile he'd worn earlier.

Sebek responded, "Just eat, missy medjat. Food doesn't need explanation." He smiled. "A lot of work to be done, Shes. Now that she's on your team, that is."

MacIntyre wasn't a picky eater. She had never considered food as art. Every day was a new adventure in Menmenet. But her interrogation technique needed work; Shes wouldn't tell her anything about what he was planning. She gave herself over to sensory experience for the time being. She even tried the slimier bits to see if they could be edible. Amazingly, they were.

"Good stuff," she said, talking around some unidentifiable shellfish thing.

"Definitely work to be done." Shesmu sipped a sparkling white wine.

"I don't need this to do medja work."

"You're suspended. You may need an income stream, and kitchen work can be very rewarding. Sebek will hire you. Learn the food and you won't be washing dishes. For long."

"I use paper plates at home so I won't have to wash dishes. And I rinse out the cans."

Shesmu closed his eyes. "A lot of work to be done."

"Am I projecting enough mystique to draw you into my web?"

Shesmu opened his eyes. "No."

"A lot of work to be done," she riposted.

"Let's focus on the sex."

"There's a thought." She sampled a dish of something that resembled seaweed wrapped around ground maize and peppers. Hot. "This is good, but it's hot."

"Try this, it's hotter." He pushed a plate over toward her. "It's supposed to be an aphrodisiac, according to the Aztecs."

"I don't think I need any of that." She'd had enough of Aztecs for a while, and Shesmu provided enough aphrodisiac all by himself.

Henutsenu came in through the kitchen door to check on them. MacIntyre rose and hugged her friend. She whispered, "Thank you for everything."

Henutsenu nibbled on her ear and whispered back, "I should thank *you*, I hear. Shes has made me house manager as of tonight, since Sebek doesn't want to work on the business side."

What was the man doing? She could tell that he was going to drive her crazy. Good crazy, though. She hugged Henutsenu again and released her, then sat down and resumed eating.

"How is it all going?" Henutsenu asked. She inspected the remains on the table. "Hum. If this keeps up, I'll need to raise prices in the dining room to compensate." Sebek came with another dish. Henutsenu eyed the dishes. "Is Sebek feeding you all the aphrodisiac dishes he knows? The only thing missing is oysters."

"Sorry," said Sebek. "Last oyster went out to the dining room ten minutes ago."

Henutsenu smiled. "A good thing, I'd say." She looked at MacIntyre. "Do you always dress that way for special dinners, Cheryl?"

"Yes." She wore her party dress, which had gone over well at the last all-girl dance shindig she'd attended. A lot of leg, a lot of frills, and she felt the gold picked up her blue eyes and blonde hair nicely.

The elegant Remetjet shook her head. "It lacks subtlety. Some work to be done there."

"That's what I said," chortled Shesmu. He poured himself another glass of wine after refilling MacIntyre's glass. "It's *hard* work, too, but somebody's got to do it. I'll be happy to help with the dress, later."

MacIntyre tried a plate of crisp, cracker-like objects with little gobs of orange something on them. She ignored her friends' banter and savored the burst of flavor.

"Hi, Mes." MacIntyre poked her head into his office. Djehutymes looked up, frowning.

"MacIntyre. Get in here."

She walked in and sat down.

"Explain to me why I shouldn't fire you. And why are you dressed like that?"

"No chance to go home after the party last night."

"What—no, don't tell me, I don't want to know."

MacIntyre put the silk bag she carried on his desk. She took a nitrile glove out of a pocket and put it on, then carefully removed the object from the bag and placed it in front of him.

Djehutymes inspected the knife and said, "Don't tell me. The murder weapon."

"Yep."

"What's this mark? Wait—Dua? The star glyph?" He smiled. "And bloodstains? Wrapped in a bag covered with Seteh glyphs?"

"Yep."

"Chain of custody?"

"You don't want to know."

"Yes, I do."

"Trust me. You don't. Let's just say if you find any strange fingerprints other than the murderer's or The Wife's, you're going to be interviewing some recalcitrant gods."

"What are you into now, MacIntyre?"

"The Temple of Seteh. Though you don't want to know much about that either."

"I've heard about all I want to hear about Seteh, interrogating those two idiot zealots."

"I figured. You might hear more if you confront The Wife—sorry, Lady Nekhen—with those two, then interrogate her again. Impeding Ma'at at the very least."

"Guess what? The Temple of Imen-R'a dropped by to tell me they're taking over the case. Religious crimes. They're looking for Lady Nekhen, but she seems to have disappeared, according to her sehy. At any rate, it's not our case anymore. Imen-R'a won't want this, since they're only pursuing the religious crimes, not murder." He nudged the knife with a pencil. "I'll entomb it in the evidence room."

MacIntyre groaned, "Well, shit."

"One thing we got from Pabaky before Imen-R'a took him. He and Duaneferet burgled the Neferti but didn't find what they were looking for, some kind of knife. Not this one."

"They like knives. Big knives."

"That's what the semetyu I sent over to their temple said. Full of big knives, they said. And other things."

"Yeah. It's an interesting place." She wouldn't go into that; he wouldn't want to know if he didn't already know.

"So after that pair of idiots found nothing at the restaurant, they waited in their cars nearby. Duaneferet followed Shesmu when he left, and Pabaky followed you."

"Ah, so that's where my plans went south."

"We found that cab driver you told me about." Djehutymes smiled. "Non-reimbursable business expense, MacIntyre. Don't even think about it. Who was the Aztec guy that beat the crap out of Pabaky at the hotel? Or do I not want to know?"

"Just a passer-by. Pabaky annoyed him."

"Oh, and we brought in that small-time hood that was gunning for you. Pabaky was so pissed because the man didn't kill you that he identified him as a hit man in three other murders. You can rest easy now."

"That's great! I'll let my professional protective services go." Yaotl would no doubt send a final bill sometime in the future. She'd found her car in her garage parking space in the morning. This disturbed her because she had the car keys in her pocket and the garage required a security card to get in, also in her pocket. She called Yaotl and discovered that retrieving her car was part of the service, with no charge. She asked about keys and got a laugh before he hung up.

"Who are they?"

She said, "You don't—"

He interrupted, "I don't want to know, right? I'd like to get a look at that passer-by. OK, here's what we're going to do. I'm going to reinstate you." He wrote out a memo. "This will get you your badge and gun from the secure lockup." She reached, but he raised a hand. "Hold on. Now, this calls for a small celebration. So we're going to that bar down the street after work to have a beer, where you'll tell me everything I don't want to know. So I don't have to know it officially. Right?"

"Brilliant plan."

"And then you're going on vacation. Three weeks. Paid. So I don't have to see your face for a while. A long while. Right?"

"Right. Shesmu says Paris is very nice this time of year."

"Send me a postcard. You can while away the hours today, catching up on all the paperwork you didn't do before I suspended you. Right?" He gave her the memo and waved a hand in dismissal.

"Right."

No blood for a while, aside from the meat the French chefs put in front of her and her companion. Suited her just fine.

Glossary

Note that Renkemet forms the plural by adding the suffix "u" or "ut" to a male or female noun, respectively. Nouns form the feminine by ending in "t."

'ahamedu	stick fighting, a sport similar to fencing
'ankhu djet	alive forever; a Remetj blessing
Aset	powerful protective goddess; Greek Isis
ba	the aspect of a person representing the soul or spiritual force; the ba represents the physical presence of the dead among the living and their relationship with others
Bastet	cat goddess; a powerful protective deity
Behedet Mautet	"New Behedet", a town in the northern province of Greater Kemet, in the southern peninsula of Europe; a famous wine-growing region
Bes	protective household god; specifically protects pregnant women and women who don't want to become pregnant until they want to
Boston	the capital of the state of Massachusetts in New England
Caymus	a First People's tribal group with their own regional government to the north of Menmenet; a key wine region
deneb	unit of money, about 3 to the USD
Djehuty	ibis-headed god of wisdom, husband of Ma'at; patron god of scribes, accountants, and diplomats; Greek Thoth/Hermes
Djeser-Djeseru	Holy of Holies: the great mortuary temple of Pera'a Ma'atkar'a Hatshepsut

Dju-Keta	"The Wrinkled Hill," a hill in the northeast corner of Menmenet
Dju-Seret	"The Hill of the Nobles," a hill in the middle-northern sector of Menmenet
Djuy-Benty	"The Two Breasts," a two-peaked hill in the center of Menmenet
Duat	the path leading to the judgment of Inpu and Ma'at in the underworld
haty'a	mayor of a city
hekasepat	head of state
hem-netjer, hemet-netjer	priest, prophet ("god's servant"); priestess ("god's wife")
hemet-netjer-en-Seteh	God's Wife of Seteh; high priestess of the god Seteh
hem-netjer-tepy	high priest, the priest in charge of a temple
Henemibr'a Alley	an alley on the south side of Menmenet Cove ("He Who Is United with the Heart of R'a")
Heru	falcon god of kingship, son of Wesir and Aset; Greek "Horus"
hetep	an altar for making sacrifices or offerings to a god
Hut-'Ankh-Tepyt Hotel	"First Palace," a large tourist hotel in downtown Menmenet
Hut-Her	powerful fertility goddess, Greek "Hathor"
huty-er-semetyu, hutyt-er-semetyu	detective-sergeant (male, female forms)
I'ahmes Creek	"Born of the Moon," a large creek running west to east across the southern part of Menmenet; named for the great Pera'a Nebpehetyr'a I'ahmes, founder of the First Remetjy Empire (Greek "Ahmosis" or "Ahmose")
idnu	Lieutenant, a military or police rank
idnu-er-semetyu	Detective-Lieutenant, a police rank
Imen	the great god of Waset, the Hidden One; Greek "Amun"
Imenhetep	"Imen Is Pleased," a common Remetjy business name (and pera'a name as well)

Imen-R'a	the great syncretic sun god of the Remetjy Empire, its state god
imy-er-medjau	Superintendent of Police, a police rank
Inpu	jackal god of the necropolis; Greek "Anubis"
Iu-Qedju	"Island of Thorns," a small island in Menmenet Bay just north of the city
Iu-Sedeg	"Island of the Concealed," a large island in Menmenet Bay adjacent to the North bay shoreline north of Menmenet
ka	the aspect of a person representing the life force; subject of worship after death
Kemet	an ancient country and empire in North Africa; Greek "Egypt"
Khentyabet	"Foremost of the East," the north-easternmost sepat of Kemet in the Nile Delta, on the road to the northern territories along the Great Green Sea; known for being an ancient center of worship of the god Seteh
Ma'at	goddess of justice and truth, sister of R'a, wife of Djehuty
ma'at	justice, truth, the right way
macuahuitl	an Aztec weapon, a flat wooden club embedded with obsidian blades, sharper than razor blades; used much like a machete as a weapon
Massachusetts	a state in the United States region of New England, one of the original thirteen states of the United States of America; calls itself a "Commonwealth" for historical reasons
medja, medjat, medjau, medjaut	police officer (male, female, plural forms)
Menmenet	"Cattle" or "Earthquake" City, capital of Ta'an-Imenty Republic, city on the top of the peninsula that encloses the southern part of Menmenet Bay
Mennefer	"Beautiful and Enduring," the capital of the Remetjy Empire; Greek "Memphis," in Egypt

Mentju	falcon-headed god of just war and military power; Greek "Montu" or "Ares"; also represented as a powerful bull; name of the main boulevard of Menmenet
Meryimen Street	"Beloved of Imen," a short street that wraps around the crest of Dju-Keta in northeast Menmenet
metoctli	a drink made from the metl, a fleshy leafed Aztec plant
Nebethut	powerful protective goddess, sister of Aset, wife of Seteh; Greek "Nepthys"
New England	a region in the northeastern United States of America
New York	a large city and metropolitan area in the United States state of New York; the original capital of the United States of America
nesubit	king or throne name taken by a pera'a or high official on assuming office
Niut Shepesu	"City of the Nobles," the first capital of the colony of Ta'an-Imenty when it was part of the Remetjy Empire, before Menmenet became the capital of the new Republic; located on a small bay to the south of Menmenet
pera'a	emperor; Greek "pharaoh"
Peteh	a creator god, tutelary deity of the city of Mennefer; Greek "Ptah"
R'a	the great sun god; Greek "Re" or "Ra"
Remetj, Remetjet	a man or woman of Kemet
Remetjy	of or relating to Kemet
Renkemet	the language of Kemet
Russkaya Amerika	the country on the west coast of North America ranging from the Ta'an-Imenty Republic boarder up to the very northern reaches of the continent; became an independent country on the breakup of the old Soviet Union but still has strong ties to the Russian Federation; the capital is Novoarkhangelsk
Sebek	a crocodile god, god of water and marshes, symbol of potency and power
sehy	counselor, attorney

Sekhmet	lion goddess, represents both destructive and protective power
Sekhmet-Hut-Her	syncretic goddess combining aspects of Sekhmet and Hut-Her; goddess of public health; w'abu of Sekhmet-Hut-Her also perform the function of medical examiner
semety, semetyt, semetyu	detective (male, female, plural forms)
senet	a very ancient board game
sepat	state; nation; Greek "nome"
Seteh	god of the desert and chaos; Greek "Seth"
shendyt	a linen wrapping around the waist; a belted linen kilt
Shesmu	underworld god, the "butcher of souls"; also the god of wine and olive oil
Ta'an-Imenty Republic	"Western-Coast," a republic on the west coast of North America; south of Russkaya Amerika, west of the Plains Federation and Washeshu, north of the Aztec Republic; formerly part of the Remetjy Empire; the capital is Menmenet
Tjaru	a town in Kemet, a fortress town that served as the capital of the Khentyabet sepat
Tjehenu	a Remetj country to the west of Kemet in Africa; Greek "Kurinaike" (Cyrenaica)
Tjeny	a small city in the southern part of the Ta'an-Imenty Republic that produces a specialty ham, unusual because Remetjet do not eat pork in general.
Tjesut	"The Heights," neighborhood in the north-central section of Menmenet, location of the Palace of the Republic and many palaces and mansions with magnificent views of Menmenet Bay
w'ab, w'abet, w'abu, w'abut	a working priest (male, female, and plural forms)
Wadjwer	"The Great Green," the Mediterranean Sea
Waset	a major city of Kemet, in the south; Greek "Thebes"
Washington University	a university in St. Louis, a city in the United States on the Mississippi River

Wennefer Street	"Uncovering of Beauty," a street in Menmenet running diagonally over Dju-Seret and down to the bay in north Menmenet
Wesir	the god of the underworld; Greek "Osiris"
werkhet	master status at Remetjy stick-fighting

Pera'a

'Ankh-Kheperu-R'a Neferneferuiten (Life of Manifestations of R'a, Beautiful Is the Perfection of the Iten)

A false pera'a installed on the throne after the death of Pera'a Nefer-kheperu-r'a-w'a-en-r'a Akheniten, her husband. Queen Nefertiti, loath to give up power on the demise of her son Semenkhkar'a, put herself on the throne. The priests of Imen-R'a put a stop to this.

Neb-Kheperu-R'a Tut'ankhimen (Lord of Manifestations of R'a, Living Image of Imen)

Son of the infamous heretic Pera'a Nefer-kheperu-r'a-w'a-en-r'a Akheniten, restored the gods of Kemet to their full power; also known as the Boy Pera'a

Nefer-Kheperu-R'a-W'a-en-R'a Akheniten (Beautiful Are the Manifestations of R'a, Sole one of R'a, Beneficial to the Iten)

An infamous pera'a who nearly destroyed the Old Empire by moving the state religion to the worship of only one god, the Iten (the sun disk). Fortunately the priests of Imen-R'a were able to restore sanity, the gods, and the Empire with Pera'a Neb-Kheperu-R'a Tut'ankhimen, the Boy Pera'a.

Setep-en-Seteh-Akhen-R'a R'amesesu (Chosen of Seteh, Beneficial for R'a, R'a Has Fashioned Him)

Last pera'a of a line of pera'au in the Middle Empire that pressed the worship of Seteh over that of Imen-R'a. Assassinated by an unknown assailant with a ritual knife of Seteh.

Acknowledgements

I'd like to thank the late Dr. Richard Puhr for giving me a lifelong interest in Kemet and the Remetjet. Approved, Dr. Puhr. I'd like to thank Dr. Leonard Lesko for introducing me to real Egyptology and for his truly wondrous dictionary of Late Egyptian. I'd like to thank Dr. Deanna Kiser-Go for her patience and encouragement in helping me to learn hieroglyphic and the rudiments of Middle Egyptian.

I'd like to acknowledge the deep influence of Philip K. Dick and his novel *The Man in the High Castle,* in my opinion the best work of alternate history in existence (at least, in this existence).

Robert B. Parker. Enough said.

As a writer, I need to acknowledge the support and input of Eric Puchner and his writing class at Stanford, who workshopped early drafts of *The Two Kites,* the much-earlier version of *The Jackal of Inpu.* I'd like to thank various writing groups at the Mechanics' Institute in San Francisco for their critiques. Thanks, everybody!

I'd like to acknowledge the support and critical assistance of my family, Mary and Theo. They probably think I'm crazy, and they're probably right.

Please enjoy the first chapter of *The Lion of Bastet,* the sequel to *The Jackal of Inpu.* Check our website at www.poesys.com for availability.

"I don't like cats," said MacIntyre in my ear as we sat down at the small table in the Myu-Myu Club.

"It's just a couple of dances, then we can leave," I replied.

A social obligation. The head of the R'ames Society, Nesimen, was hosting us at a small after-event party. The Society, a nonprofit foundation, promoted talent in the culinary arts. Its annual award ceremony was the social event of the year in the culinary world. Menmenet was the capital and center of food culture in the Ta'an-Imenty Republic, and I was now the best chef in Menmenet. I was owner of the Neferti, my restaurant on the Bay waterfront that served New Remetjy cuisine.

But it was the Per'ankh restaurant that made me the best chef in Menmenet. I had the Best New Chef award certificate in my pocket, my girlfriend at my side, and a glass of an outstanding local white wine in front of me, and all was right with the world. My career was advancing by leaps and bounds since I'd taken over as executive chef of the Per'ankh, the restaurant where I'd apprenticed. It was the best restaurant in Menmenet. French fine dining, not Remetjy cuisine, but you couldn't have everything.

With Nesimen's happy approval, I invited some friends to celebrate with us. Nekhetsebek was my chef at the Neferti, and Henutsenu was the Neferti house manager. Sebek and Henutsenu were an item, which contributed to the roaring success of the Neferti—excellent communication between the front and back of the house.

MacIntyre whispered in my ear again. "It's not really the cats, it's the murders."

"OK, you'll have to expand on that for me," I said, sipping my wine. MacIntyre grinned and drank some of her glass of Hermitage, a big red Syrah from the Rhône. She'd taken a liking to it when we passed some time there on a trip a few months back. She confined her knowledge of wine to telling the difference between red and white. I hadn't introduced her to Anjou so as not to confuse the issue with light rosé, but she was learning fast.

At any social event, Remetjy women compete with one another for the most alluring fashion, and Remetjy fashions tended toward extremes. But MacIntyre was not a Remetjet. She was a transplanted American. As a plainclothes medjat, she dressed halfway between the severe black American business style and the more conservative Remetjy, but tonight she had crossed over and adopted

Remetjy party dress. The dress, what there was of it, was white with faint red and black designs at the edges, the edges shaped and folded to emphasize the attributes of the wearer. On one edge, she wore a gold feather pin, emblem of the goddess Ma'at whom she served as a w'abet, a working priestess. She'd explained to me early in our relationship that she wasn't religious, but you had to be a w'abet to get promoted on the force. That applied especially to promotion to semetyt on the Homicide Squad.

"Djehutymes—you remember my boss, don't you? Djehutymes assigned me to a new case today, a double murder at the Temple of Bastet, the powerful cat goddess. Now I'm seeing black cats everywhere." She sent her eyes toward the two statues of Bastet that adorned the sides of the elevated dance stage in front of us. Two huge, polished-basalt cats. "And meeting the Hem-Netjer-Tepy of Bastet tonight was a surprise, too."

Panekhet, the Hem-Netjer-Tepy of Bastet, was also the Chairman of the Board of the R'ames Society. Nesimen had introduced him to me along with another board member, R'aweben, a financier. I think Nesimen had an idea from his wife about recruiting me for a role with the Society and wanted to show me how influential it was. MacIntyre, being a hutyt-er-semetyu on the Homicide Squad of the Menmenet Medjau, had a cynical attitude toward the power those men represented. She had bowed nicely enough, though. She'd noted to me later that the two bigwigs didn't deign to come to the party with us working-class types.

The other members of our party were at tables to our left. Nesimen was a medium-height, 55-year-old man, a little plump, with a bald head and a cheerful smile on his round face. His wife, Taneferet, the same age, was small and thin with sad eyes and a down-turned mouth.

I called Taneferet "Khenemset Neferet" because she had been my mother's best friend, right up to my mother's early death at 35, when I was 10. Remetjy extended families almost always have an "auntie" like Taneferet to add to the love showered on the children. But a khenemset is a bit stronger than the usual informal auntie; it's more like a godparent in the Christian world. A khenemset's religious responsibilities relate to the goddess Ma'at. Khenemset Neferet had made sure I stayed on the path of Ma'at as I grew up, befriending me and helping my foster parents cope with a willful teenager. We'd lost touch after she married Nesimen and moved south. When Nesimen took the job at the R'ames Society and moved back to Menmenet, we'd gotten back in touch, seeing each other from time to time. It had been Khenemset Neferet who persuaded me to apply for Society membership. Then she talked her husband into putting me up for the chef's award. He needed little persuading, of course. I didn't know Nesimen all that well, as he usually wasn't around when I visited Khenemset Neferet.

The Chief Financial Officer of the Society, Sennedjem, sat with his boyfriend, a man named Filip with some unpronounceable Polish last name. I'd taken against Sennedjem because he'd walked out of the room right in the middle of my acceptance speech earlier in the evening. And the man smirked; that's the only word for it. Both he and his boyfriend looked like eastern Europeans, but only Filip had the name to go with the look. Dark hair and beards, pale white faces, and thin, sneering lips on both of them. Filip looked like a bodybuilder, but Sennedjem looked like he could slither through anything. Fortunately, their table was on the other side of Nesimen's from us. I surveyed them—they'd ordered a bottle of vodka, everyone else had glasses of wine.

I advised MacIntyre, "Ask Henutsenu about Panekhet. She's a Bastet devotee. Maybe she has some insights into the Temple of Bastet hierarchy."

"Already have. Panekhet is a Great Man, according to her, but she doesn't know him personally. I didn't mention the temple murders." MacIntyre looked at the next table over to the right, where Henutsenu entertained Sebek. "And she also said this club was a great place. If you like cats, I suppose," she said. "Wonderful dancing entertainment. Which seems about to start." She took a fortifying swallow of wine.

The musicians were taking their seats in the small band area to the side of the stage, and the lights dimmed. Colored lights came up on the stage to produce a baleful, reddish background. The dancers, all female, appeared one by one from a door to the left of the stage as the musicians played a soft musical prolog. The Bastet statues were back lit, but the statues' eyes picked up reddish glints and glowed. Both music and dancers seemed a little random. The women glided in all directions, without purpose, and the music carried out that theme in sound, the clarinets predominating with low, soft, meandering notes.

I could hardly tell the dancers apart. Each dressed the same, had the same hair, even had the same features, though their skin tones varied from pale to deep black. The costumes they wore were light linen that covered everything but obscured nothing. As far as I could tell, they weren't wearing anything else. Their hair fell to their shoulders in black braids. I looked sideways at Henutsenu, who had the same hair but more richly decorated with gold beads. She smiled, cat-like, at home with the dancers.

The dancers wandered around the stage with their cat-like movements. Clarinets took charge, the tempo increased, and the dance coalesced in the middle of the stage. Their slow gestures coalescing into the same movement, the dancers flowed into a line. The Bastet statues framed them, one on each side of the stage, eyes glinting red, polished-basalt faces reflecting the dancers. The stoney cat faces grinned at me; just special lighting, but effective.

A noise intruded from my left. I realized I'd heard whispers for some time. I looked at Nesimen, whose head turned toward his wife, who looked at the pair beyond her, scandalized.

Sennedjem and Filip argued in loud whispers, the bodybuilder gesticulating. Sennedjem looked up at the ceiling, a smirk on his lips. Neither of them gave any attention to the dance or to the music, just to the vodka. Reaching a crescendo, the music led the dancers into faster and faster movements, their legs and arms waving in unison down the line, bodies undulating, their moves sensuous and suggestive.

Filip leaped up and pushed Sennedjem out of his seat. Sennedjem scrambled, then spun around, grabbed his glass of vodka, and tossed it into his boyfriend's face. The Pole roared and rushed at Sennedjem, carrying him forward toward the dancers. The rest of us sat dumbstruck. I rose, but not fast enough: the two men, struggling and lashing out at each other, crashed over the low edge of the stage into the dancers. The line disintegrated into a mass of arms, legs, and screaming mouths. The music stopped as the musicians froze, gaping.

MacIntyre beat me to it, rushing Filip, and tripped him from behind, then landed on his back with a knee and twisted one arm behind him. As she did this, I had reached Sennedjem, who showed signs of wear with blood on his face. He took his revenge on his incapacitated friend with a vicious kick to the side. I grabbed him around the middle, pinning his arms to his sides, then dragged him back off the stage, out of kicking range.

Nesimen approached with a stormy face, and Sebek was right behind him. Taneferet sat still, the same scandalized look on her face, making little, useless motions with her hands. Henutsenu had disappeared. Then two very large gentlemen charged into the room. They dressed as w'abu of Bastet, the sort of w'abu that dealt with unruly worshippers too drunk to behave themselves. These two would have been more at home at the Temple of Hepu than in the house of Bastet, except they were even larger than the Hepu bull. Henutsenu appeared right behind them, pointing out the problems.

The two w'abu split, one coming toward me and Sennedjem, the other approaching MacIntyre and her charge. Mine laid a hand on Sennedjem's shoulder with a squeeze that had Sennedjem gasping. I let loose and stepped back. The other w'ab stood back a little, admiring the tableaux with MacIntyre and Filip. MacIntyre got up, and Filip rolled over, out of breath and no longer interested in fighting. The w'ab smiled and bowed his head in appreciation to MacIntyre, who was smoothing out her dress. He leaned down and pulled up the Pole with one hand under his shoulder, lifting him off his feet.

Nesimen now approached Sennedjem, the storm breaking. With a pinched expression, he said in forceful tones, "I've warned you before. You're here to represent the society. You can't afford—*we* can't afford embarrassments like this!"

Sennedjem just scowled and said nothing, but at least that smirk had gone. The w'ab walked toward the door, moving Sennedjem along. His partner gripped the struggling Filip's arm and pulled him along. The four men disappeared through the door. The lights came up, and the two statues gazed at nothing with dull eyes. The party was over.

We'd all had our fill of the Myu-Myu Club, so we walked out into the alley behind the Hut-'Ankh-Tepyt hotel, where the Society had held the awards ceremony. Sebek and Henutsenu set off for her flat around the corner on Mentju Boulevard. I was still fizzing from my award and needed to put the melee behind me. MacIntyre said she was up for some one-on-one dancing, as long as there were no cats involved.

"Shesmu," said Nesimen, "I'd like to thank you and Hutyt MacIntyre for your help. I apologize profusely for the conduct of Sennedjem. He's not normally like that."

Khenemset Neferet spoke up from beside him. "He is, Nesimen. He is. You know he is. When are you going to do something about it? His drinking, his scandalous behavior. I've never been so embarrassed." She gave me a flustered look with her sad-looking eyes. It made my heart ache just to see the sadness in her face.

"No need for apologies. These things happen," I replied. "And Cheryl did all the rough work."

"No, that's yet to come," said MacIntyre, grinning. "The paperwork for off-duty incidents—you don't want to know. But, yes, no apologies needed."

Nesimen half smiled, but his mind was on something else. He turned the subject. "Shesmu, I'd like you to consider something."

Time to pay for our entertainment. I noticed Khenemset Neferet perk up; she must have put Nesimen up to whatever he was going to ask of me.

He went on, "I need—*we* need—help to get our message out, to get more members, to make ourselves better known in the culinary world. Our current membership in the restaurant world is aging fast, and we need to attract younger people to revitalize our efforts. Would you consider volunteering as a celebrity spokesperson for the Society?"

Khenemset Neferet smiled now, the sun coming out. I had some reservations, though.

I pointed out the obvious. "If your people all behave like Sennedjem, it's going to be a struggle."

He shook his head with dismay. "They don't. And we keep him out of the papers. Mostly." He smiled. "But with your help, we can neutralize any negatives. Your speech tonight was brilliant! You have a real talent for connecting with people in the industry." A good sales pitch. He'd rehearsed it. I didn't stutter my way through my speech, but it was little more than "thanks for the kudos and the money." But for all of Nesimen's humility about the Society, it was one of the more important institutions in Menmenet's culinary world. My career would only benefit from association with it. I already had two full plates, but one more wouldn't burden me that much.

The hopeful expression on Khenemset Neferet's face gave me no choice. I replied, "Yes, I'd like to help. Perhaps we could get together and review what's required? Tomorrow?" I noticed MacIntyre shivering, even with her coat on. Time to go.

"Yes, of course, sorry. You go on now and have a good time, you and Hutyt MacIntyre. Why don't you come to the Society offices tomorrow and pick up your award check, then drop by my office? I'll be in all day."

"Thanks, I'll do that." I hugged Khenemset Taneferet, bowed to Nesimen, and wrapped a warming arm around MacIntyre as we walked away.

It isn't so tough to take that step off the cliff. It's what comes afterward that's hard. Especially if you're not aware it's a cliff.

Thank You

Thanks for reading *The Jackal of Inpu.*
If you liked the book, please leave a review on the web site through which you bought it.

Sign up to our mailing list for notifications and get a free ebook.

https://www.poesys.com